SOLDIER OF FORTUNE 9

THE BERLIN ALTERNATIVE

SOLDIER OF FORTUNE 9

THE BERLIN ALTERNATIVE

Peter Leslie

First published in Great Britain 1995
22 Books, Invicta House, Sir Thomas Longley Road,
Rochester, Kent

Copyright © 1995 by 22 Books

A CIP catalogue record for this book is available from the
British Library

ISBN 1 898125 43 0

10 9 8 7 6 5 4 3 2 1

Typeset by Hewer Text Composition Services, Edinburgh
Printed in Great Britain by Cox and Wyman Limited, Reading

1

On the far side of the courtyard a very large white cat sat washing itself on the rear shelf of an Aston Martin. The car was one of the earliest two-litre streamlined saloons, with British number-plates – an unusual sight in Paris in 1948. The cat, which had one blue eye and one green, wore a red collar.

Riordan skirted an ancient Citroën, a Berliet delivery van and a Peugeot modestly hiding its headlights behind a radiator grille, and climbed half a dozen steps to a wide mahogany front door. A fan-shaped glass canopy above this shielded him from the rain sweeping across the cobbles.

The mansion, dating back to the remodelling of Paris under Haussmann in the mid-nineteenth century, was built around three sides of the courtyard, which was entered through an archway on the Avenue Kléber, bordering the city's exclusive sixteenth *arrondissement*. A discreet, highly polished brass plate at one side of the doorway announced: 'Solfort Enterprises SA, Advisory Bureau'. A smaller one, just below, was engraved with the words: 'OK Contracts (2nd Floor)'. Above these plaques, an old-fashioned bell-pull jutted from the stonework. Riordan tugged at the ivory knob, and somewhere inside the house a distant bell jangled.

A servant wearing a sleeved waistcoat and striped trousers answered the door. Riordan showed him a visiting card with a few words scribbled on it and was led at once up a shallow, curving stairway to the first floor and ushered into a large room overlooking a walled garden.

Between the two bay windows stood a desk bare except for a telephone and a single sheet of paper. Behind this, in a swivel chair, sat an urbane individual with a pink face and silver hair.

'Colonel Riordan, sir,' the manservant intoned.

'Ah! Splendid. Good to see you,' said the man behind the desk.

Riordan was staring – a tall, craggy figure with curling, iron-grey hair and very bright blue eyes, tough as whipcord. He could have been any age from forty to sixty. 'Just a minute,' he said slowly. 'Wait now. We've met before, haven't we? ... Let's see ... Yes, indeed, I have it! Monsieur Huefer. From Switzerland, right? The spring of '42.'

The man behind the desk smiled. His name in fact was Seamus McPhee O'Kelly, Captain, Royal Navy, Retired. From the Citadel, that strange concrete fortress sunk into the ground just behind the Admiralty Arch in London, he had directed throughout the war the machinations of a top-secret underground organization known as the Combined Operations (Security) Executive. Co(S)E was a cloak-and-dagger formation to whose rascally members operations too sensitive for the regular intelligence services were frequently entrusted.

Bowler-hatted and pensioned off when hostilities ceased, O'Kelly had found civilian life centred around the golf course tedious. His acquired taste for the clandestine refusing to be submerged, he had returned underground, only this time in a private capacity.

For eighteen months now, O'Kelly had been running an agency for the recruitment of hired fighting men or soldiers of fortune – hence the Solfort logo on his otherwise unremarkable business stationery and articles of intent.

A number of clients on his books had in fact been involved in wartime operations for 'Cosy Corner', as CO(S)E was dubbed by those foolhardy enough to volunteer to work for it. Riordan was not one of these. But he was a soldier of fortune, a leader of mercenaries – a term he himself rejected. His military talents had been available, at a price, long before the war.

His previous connection with O'Kelly had concerned the location and destruction of a Nazi experimental rocket base in northern Finland, an operation loaded with such political and diplomatic dynamite that it had been considered too hazardous to entrust it to any overt Allied unit. O'Kelly had secretly hired and briefed, in Occupied Paris and Switzerland, the expert six-man team Riordan had successfully led into the lethal wastes of the Arctic Circle.

'A clumsy device, I'm afraid, and doubtless all too transparent,' he said now. 'My playing the oh-so-Swiss Monsieur Huefer. You probably found him as tiresome as I did. But it was essential – whatever you suspected – that neither you nor your men knew precisely who you were working for. What you didn't know you couldn't tell – and embarrass everybody!'

Riordan grinned, the seamed features lighting up into an almost boyish expression. 'On the subject of role changing,' he said, 'you do know, I suppose, that this house was one of the Gestapo's headquarters and interrogation centres during the Occupation?'

'Exactly why I acquired it,' O'Kelly said. 'Psychological spin-off, what! Dark deeds and all that. I knew that most of the desperadoes whose sins I file at OK Contracts upstairs would be familiar with the site. And at least they'd know their way here – even if it's only by reputation, even if they couldn't bloody read!'

He picked up the sheet of paper from the desk. Behind him, beyond the streaming windows, rain gusted across a sodden lawn and wind threshed the branches of an acacia tree. In front of the shrubbery, a stone urn had been blown from its plinth and the blooms of a scarlet geranium trampled into a gravel path. 'Do sit,' O'Kelly said, waving a hand at a leather armchair in front of the desk. 'I'm just refreshing the memory before we talk.'

Riordan lowered his muscular six-foot frame into the chair.

O'Kelly settled gold-rimmed spectacles on his nose and scanned the full page of single-spaced typing. He was reading a curriculum vitae of the rangy fighting man sitting opposite him.

Barney Joseph Riordan, known as Barry-Joe to his family, Barry to his friends, and simply Riordan to the men he led, was the son of a County Wicklow farmer forced to flee from Ireland in 1916 after a military misunderstanding with the British during the Easter uprising in Dublin. The groundwork in urban guerrilla tactics he had acquired with Sinn Fein proved invaluable after he worked his passage to the Gulf of Mexico on an oil tanker and offered his services to Pancho Villa and Zapata. Much of his subsequent combat experience continued to be with those striving for – or seeking to maintain – independence. He had worked for Haile Selassie during the Ethiopian emperor's courageous attempt to resist Mussolini's Italians, which O'Kelly already knew; he had acted as adviser to the Chinese during the Sino-Japanese conflict in Manchuria in 1931, which he didn't. The Spanish he had learned in Mexico was good enough to enable him to lead one of the International

Brigades against Franco in the Spanish Civil War. After that he had fought for Finland's General Mannerheim when his country was invaded by the Russians. Since the Finnish mission for O'Kelly in 1942 he was known to have been active in Palestine with an experienced assault group during the troubled period marking the end of the British Mandate and the establishment of Israel. But none of O'Kelly's intelligence sources had so far been able to say with certainty which of the warring factions had secretly employed him.

The final paragraph of the report read:

'The subject is a highly skilled leader able to command the respect and loyalty of different categories of warrior. His personal courage and initiative – both tactical and strategic – are unrivalled. So far as is known, he is apolitical: his loyalties lie solely with those for whom he has agreed to work. He will not accept missions customarily described as terrorist, nor will he undertake individual assassination. This is a man to be trusted.'

The last seven words of the evaluation were heavily underscored. O'Kelly let the paper fall to the desk. He removed his spectacles, folded them, and slipped them into the breast pocket of his blazer. 'Yes, well ...' he said.

Riordan smiled. 'Well?'

'I fancy we have business to discuss,' O'Kelly said.

'I'm listening.'

'Fact is, there's a touch of trouble brewing in Berlin. And it needs a firm hand – an unseen and uncommitted hand – to put things right.'

'Mine, for instance?'

'In my opinion, yes. But it depends, of course, on the approval of the client, on those making use of my services. I suggest; they concur — or not, as the case may be.'

'Tell me about it,' Riordan said.

'Frankly' — O'Kelly cleared his throat — 'it may sound at first a trifle, well, banal. It concerns a hostage situation.'

'A hostage situation?' Riordan echoed. He frowned, shaking his head. 'Not really my cup, actually. In Berlin, you said? I should have thought the German police or at any rate the occupying authorities would have been the people best equipped to deal with that. I don't think I could . . .'

'Wait!' O'Kelly interrupted. 'I said it sounded banal at first. Wait until you've heard the rest before you turn down the old thumb.'

Riordan settled back in the armchair and crossed his legs. 'Fire away, Captain, my Captain,' he said, smiling.

O'Kelly planted his elbows on the desk, and steepled his fingers and thumbs. 'First of all,' he said, 'this is not your simple abduction against a sum of money, where the name of the game is to locate the hide-out, raid the place, and hope to hell the hostage survives. The coup has been staged by a well-organized, expert and ruthless gang. Terrorists, in short. And the 'hide-out' is a whole floor of an office block in the centre of the city. Secondly, although money is naturally involved, the hostages are being held against a ransom far more important than mere cash.'

'Hostages?' Riordan raised his eyebrows.

O'Kelly nodded. 'Twelve of them, at least nine of whom are important international figures with an influence on world affairs.'

'Ah.'

'What you might call sensitive material,' O'Kelly said. 'But the trickiest part of all is the actual location of the office block.'

The eyebrows rose again. 'Explain,' Riordan said.

6

'You know as well as I do,' O'Kelly began, 'that the Allies divided Germany into four zones of occupation after the war – ours in the north, the Yanks in the centre, France in the south, nearest their own frontier, and the Russians taking the whole eastern part of the country. Berlin was bang in the middle of the Soviet zone, but since it was the capital it was decided that this one city should remain under four-power control and be divided in turn into four separate zones. The Russians agreed to allow the three other powers unlimited access to Berlin via certain specified road, rail and air routes, for administrative purposes, supplies and so on.'

'And this office block held by the terrorists is in the Russian zone?' Riordan said.

'Exactly. Now the Russians have become extremely obstructive lately about anything concerning access to their zone. This wouldn't matter, to be honest, if the hostages were ordinary civilians. But the majority, politically and diplomatically, are of specific interest to the West.'

'And they won't allow any Western agencies into their zone to make a rescue attempt?'

'Right. The buggers won't even wear the arrival of negotiators to open talks with the terrorists. Yet they sit on their own arses doing sweet FA.'

'I get the picture,' Riordan said. 'What's the price being asked?'

'There are several. Plus getaway money, transport – the whole bazaar. I'll go into it all later, if you agree to take the job on. For the moment, it's enough to say that the release of several miscreants HMG would much rather keep in jail is high on the list.'

'And the hostages they particularly want released?'

O'Kelly permitted himself a wintry smile. 'There's at least one of them – perhaps two – that most civilized countries would be happy to see as hostages for ever! Those the British want out, and quickly, include an Egyptian with a major say in the running of the Suez canal. Lifeline to the Far East and all that; vital at a time when the Arabs are attacking Israel – not very successfully, I admit – and anti-British feeling runs so high in Sinai. Another chap cheering for the red, white and blue is a Middle Eastern princeling with oil concessions up for sale. Eton and Oxford, you know; member of the Athenaeum. His Royal Highness needs to get home pretty damn quick before he's ousted by a left-wing military junta forming up undercover. If they took over, Russian influence in the region would expand considerably, which both the Yanks and HMG would find offensive. There's an Australian diplomat particularly friendly to the present Labour government. And finally . . .'

'Good God!' Riordan exclaimed. 'Four out of twelve: not a bad score!'

'The last man,' O'Kelly said, smiling, 'is probably the most important. African ruler of a newly independent ex-colony. There's been a putsch in his absence, and the PM wants to sit him firmly back on his throne before the rebels strike again. Spheres of influence, as with the princeling. And to that you can add nickel, zinc, a certain amount of copper, and uranium.'

'A black African ruler?' Riordan asked.

O'Kelly nodded. 'Eton and *Cambridge* this one,' he said.

'But what the hell were all these people doing in the Russian zone of Berlin?' Riordan demanded. 'And how come the kidnappers got them all together? Some kind of convention?'

'A trade conference,' O'Kelly told him. 'Ostensible subject: expansion of the world's economies. Real object of the operation: bribery. Substantial kickbacks for those who can offer mining or mineral concessions, very well paid "consultancies" offered to anyone engineering home-country contracts to Soviet industry and exports. That kind of thing.'

'And the conference, of course, was held . . . ?'

'In the block where the hostages are sequestered.'

'Got it,' Riordan said.

'And does it interest you?'

'Oh, I think so. An urban challenge, for a change. I'll probably need six men, including a cat burglar, a safe-breaker and a sniper. Subject, naturally, to sight of plans of the building.'

'No problem,' O'Kelly said. 'They're on file upstairs.'

'At OK Contracts? Stands for O'Kelly?'

'Right. That's where all the business is done. We'll go up there presently. For the moment . . .' O'Kelly pushed back his chair. He opened the bottom drawer of his desk, took out two Waterford crystal tumblers, a large bottle of gin and a small bottle of Angostura bitters, and laid them on the tooled-leather top. 'Service habits die hard,' he said. 'I'm afraid all I can offer you before lunch is a large pinkers.'

'My pleasure,' Riordan said.

His host splashed a few drops of the rose-coloured bitters into each glass, swirled each around, and dumped the excess liquid into the pot of a rubber plant standing by one of the windows. A sudden scatter of raindrops rattled against the glass pane. O'Kelly poured a generous measure of gin into each glass, swirled again, and handed one to Riordan. 'Down the hatch,' he said, raising his own. 'You're on?'

'Definitely.'

'It'll have to be smartish this time. No jailbreaks organized to spirit away a particular merc! When could you start for Berlin?'

'Tomorrow.'

'Splendid. I'll contact the client right away.' O'Kelly picked up the telephone receiver and jiggled the rest up and down. 'Mademoiselle?' he intoned into the trumpet-shaped mouthpiece. 'I want a number in London. Top priority.' He gave the number.

In a surprisingly short time, the phone rang. He lifted the receiver. 'I want to speak to the Foreign Minister . . . yes, Mr Bevin himself,' he said when he had identified himself. And then, a little later: 'O'Kelly, sir, from Paris. I think I've found the right man . . . Yes, sir. Right away.'

Riordan rose to his feet and carried his drink over to a window. The rain was falling more heavily, drumming on the tiles above the bays, flattening branches in the shrubbery. Behind him, he heard O'Kelly's voice reciting a summary of his military career. Things certainly moved fast here: it was only over croissants and coffee that morning that he had been handed the Solfort card by a messenger, with the words 'Please call by as soon as possible' scrawled above the address. It was partly because he was aware of the mansion's wartime history that he had come.

O'Kelly banged the receiver back on to its hook. 'Riordan, you're on!' he enthused. 'We'll breeze up to Contracts and talk money. There's a young woman up there can produce a very fair *pot-au-feu*.'

The luncheon produced among the filing cabinets and teletype machines and modernistic electric typewriters on the upper floor was in fact worthy of a three-star restaurant in the fashionable Left Bank. It was washed down with an admirable Burgundy – Chambolle Musigny from one of the better years of the undistinguished thirties, Riordan noted. But what surprised him more than the unexpected splendours of the meal was an equally astonishing encounter in the anteroom outside the office of O'Kelly's accountant and business manager.

The mercenary leader was on his way through to talk money when a tall, lean young man, perhaps thirty years old, looked up from a table strewn with press cuttings and flipped a lock of dark hair back from his left eye. 'What-ho, squire,' he drawled. 'Everything comes to he who waits, what!'

'Beverley Hills!' Riordan exclaimed. 'What the devil brings you here?'

'I work here, cock,' the other man said. 'Someone has to do the donkey work while you bright lights dance around and dazzle the citizenry with your witty shafts.'

The young man's name really was Beverley Hills – or at least part of it was. He was the younger son of an earl, and the family name was in fact Hills-Loumis-Fezackerlay. He had dropped the last part, he would solemnly say to those who asked why, because it was such a deuced bore, having to have his visiting cards made wider than anyone else's. A one-time winner of the King's Prize at Bisley, Hills was a brilliant marksman, preferring a life of adventure in Europe to the calm of a country estate on the Scottish Borders. He had been a member of Riordan's team – though not perhaps the most responsible – during the assault on the Nazi rocket range in Finland.

'I hope you're not planning to carry Hills off to Berlin,' O'Kelly said genially, coming up behind them. 'He's a wizard at collating the background stuff.'

Riordan shook his head. 'Not this time,' he said, remembering that, the last time he saw him, Hills had made off with a blonde Finnish naturalist Riordan had been hoping to bed himself.

Hills caught the thought almost before it had crystallized in Riordan's mind. He grinned. 'All's fair in love and . . .'

he said lightly. 'One hopes nothing is being held against one, at least in a social sense.'

'If fair means blonde,' Riordan said, equally lightly, 'it was the fact that *something* was being held against *one* that rankled. In the social sense, of course. But that was many girls ago. One hopes – if the formula is not copyright – that being in the background, as it were, brings its own rewards.'

'Nice to have you with us again,' Beverley Hills said. 'Old man.'

It was almost five o'clock when Riordan left O'Kelly's office. Terms had been agreed, a preliminary deposit had been made to a numbered account in a Zurich bank, and three potential members of the mercenary leader's team had been telephoned, two of whom were available. Two more had to be cabled – in London and Vienna – and a third contacted personally in one of the less salubrious districts of north-eastern Paris.

Riordan parked his rented Peugeot in a narrow street near the twenty-four-hour post office in the Rue du Louvre. He went in and asked for a sheaf of blue telegraph forms. When he came out, the rain had stopped and, low down in the west, a rift in the scudding clouds had allowed a flood of late sunlight to gild the narrow façades of the ancient houses bordering the right-hand side of the road.

There was a street-corner café a block north of the post office. Riordan went in, installed himself in a booth at the back, and carefully worded the two telegrams while he sipped a beer. He discarded three forms before he was satisfied with the cryptic message addressed to the contact in Vienna. Having finished his beer, he left money on the table, walked to the toilets and flushed the torn-up remains of the rejected forms. He returned to the post office and dispatched the telegrams.

Although he was an expert and adventurous driver, Riordan did not own a car. He was absent so frequently from his Montmartre apartment that it was not worth the trouble, in overcrowded Paris, of garaging one while he was away. When he was in town for more than a few days, he hired something anonymous from one of the international agencies springing up all over Europe.

The Peugeot he had rented this time was a light-grey 402-B sports saloon with a two-litre engine and spatted rear wheels, distinguished from thousands of others only by a green windscreen sticker which had admitted him to the VIP paddock during an air show at Le Bourget and which he had not yet bothered to peel off.

The sun was lower still in the sky now, not far above the polished roofs and spires of the western skyline. A fugitive ray penetrated the screen below the sticker and silvered the bright metal semicircle beneath the steering wheel which operated the horn. Riordan crossed the street, threading his way between traffic stalled by a parked delivery lorry as he felt in his pocket for the car keys.

The driver of the lorry opened the door of his cab and jumped down on to the road. Riordan stepped on to the pavement and slid the key into the Peugeot's door on the driver's side.

As the lorry's door swung shut, the outside mirror caught the sunbeam and reflected it back across the street. Riordan twisted the key in the lock. He had his thumb on the button which opened the door when the reflected ray, sweeping along the line of parked cars as the lorry's door swung, illuminated the steering wheel, the tops of the leather seats and a loop of wire hanging in the shadows between them.

A loop of wire?

There had been no loop of wire when Riordan parked the car.

The mercenary leader's reactions to danger, sharpened by years of city, jungle and desert warfare, were phenomenally fast. Hurling himself to the rear of the car, he was flat on his face in the street, between the Peugeot and a Renault parked behind it, when the detonation shook the block.

The bomb, Riordan reasoned later, must have been actuated by a trembler coil with a ten or fifteen-second delay rather than a direct contact breaker when the key was twisted in the lock. It was a relatively small charge – perhaps a pound and a half of plastic beneath the seat, with led to a fusing device in the boot and then to the lock mechanism. If Riordan had pressed in the button and opened the door, the explosion would have erupted as he climbed in and settled in his seat.

The livid flash of the bomb burst momentarily dimmed the sunlight as it blew out the glass, mangled the bonnet and punched open the roof of the Peugeot. Less than a second afterwards the street was blanketed with brown smoke. Hundreds of windows were shattered, shop fronts shivered and collapsed, and the stone coping above the entrance to an antique dealer's parted from the wall and smashed down on the pavement.

For a heartbeat there was silence in the street. Then, as eardrums cracked by the blast recovered, shouts, cries, shrill screams and the clatter of running feet. When the smoke thinned, the wrecked Peugeot could be seen slewed halfway across the road with flames streaming from the engine and the tonneau. The driver's door had been ripped away and lay crumpled beneath the tailgate of the delivery lorry. The car in front of it had been overturned and one of its rear tyres was on fire.

Riordan lay in a nest of glass from the Renault's pulverized headlights. His face was blackened, he had lost a little hair, and his left shoe and sock had disappeared. The sole of the bare foot was bleeding, but otherwise he appeared to be unharmed. He pushed himself up on to his hands and knees and rose groggily.

The street was full of people. Some of the drivers caught in the traffic jam had been cut by flying glass. Half a dozen other vehicles had been damaged by the explosion. From the corner café, waiters in long white aprons raced down to surround a bloodied bundle that heaved on the pavement. The lorry driver had caught the full force of the blast as he walked around to unload his cartons and crates.

Shaking his head to free his ears from the ringing caused by the explosion, Riordan became aware of the angry voices around him.

'The third bomb outrage this month!'

'I was in my office. The wall blew in!'

'The bloody Palestinians again. In my opinion . . .'

'I saw it go up. I was sitting at my desk.'

'. . . called an ambulance yet? That poor bastard from the lorry . . .'

'Are you all right?' a woman asked Riordan. 'You should sit down and stay quiet until the ambulance comes. My God, this is like being back in the war again!'

'I'm all right, thank you, Madame,' Riordan protested. 'Really. It probably looks worse than it is . . . No, truly, I promise you . . .'

He limped through the gathering crowd. Nobody seemed to have realized that he has the driver of the devastated Peugeot. And with men to recruit in a hurry, the last thing he could afford to waste time on was a lengthy interview with the police, which would involve a statement laboriously taken down in longhand and then transferred to a typewriter before he was allowed to sign it. He hurried back to the café, went for the second time into the toilets, and squeezed through a narrow window into a backyard filled with dustbins.

Ten minutes later, he had found a taxi and was on his way back to the apartment in Rue Clauzel that he had had since the beginning of the war.

The road to Berlin, he reflected, certainly seemed to be paved with good intentions. But whose intentions were they? And were they really good?

Or was he thinking, perhaps, of the road to hell . . . ?

2

The six men sat around a table covered with a spotless white tablecloth in the grill-room of the Atlantic Hotel in Hamburg. A waitress wearing a black dress and a starched apron was serving coffee.

O'Kelly, pink and bland, looking more like a German businessman than the Germans, presided. Riordan, with four of his chosen team, listened to a briefing on the hostage situation in the Russian zone of Berlin. Also discussed was the worsening diplomatic relations between the Soviets and their wartime allies and why it was considered essential not to exacerbate things by insisting on a confrontation involving the kidnappers and a British or American combat unit. The atmosphere in the heavily furnished room, with its stepped rows of tables, was close, redolent of cigar smoke and the odours of rich meats cooked in wine. Outside the wide windows, rain pitted the leaden surface of the Alster – that long and narrow lake whose elegant waterfront offers such a decorative contrast to the dock areas on either side of the Rhine. It was 24 June 1948, three years and forty-seven days since the British, French, Americans and Russians in Berlin had triumphantly proclaimed the end of hostilities in Europe.

'I have to emphasize this' – O'Kelly's voice was pitched low, beneath the discreet tinkle of cutlery and glass, and the hum of conversation around them – 'and I shall doubtless

17

do so again. And again. The operation you have agreed to undertake must present a profile so low as to be virtually non-existent. Officially, you do not exist. Secrecy must be total. By which I mean that it's just as important to conceal your activities from the four-power authorities and the law-enforcement agencies as it is to hide them from the kidnappers – whoever they are.'

'And the press?' Riordan said.

'Particularly the press. News coming out of Berlin is fairly strictly controlled, of course, in all zones. But the fact that hostages have been taken and concessions demanded against their release is certainly known to the local newspapers. So far, however, the identity of the hostages has been kept secret and the possible political repercussions ignored. A number of eminent visitors have been sequestered. End of story.'

'You said: the kidnappers – whoever they are. Do we not really have some idea about these criminals? Where they come from? What are their motives?' The question came from Pieter Van Eyck, the Dutchman who had been Riordan's choice as number two on several of his more hazardous adventures.

'Apparently not,' O'Kelly replied. 'They have given no indication whatsoever. The only contact they have made has been via teletype to one of the British Control Commission offices. They won't answer phones and they ignore radio signals and loud-hailer messages. Rough guesses, of course, can be made by analysing their demands, but . . .'

'For example?'

O'Kelly sighed. 'I'm afraid I'm not at liberty to reveal that.' He swallowed coffee. 'To come back to the absence of publicity,' he said. 'If the Western press got hold of the full story, of course, they'd make a bloody meal of it. And if they had even a smell of a rumour that some band of mercenaries – sorry, soldiers of fortune – were involved in a rescue attempt, all hell would break loose. Everywhere. So you see why I have to . . .'

'OK, OK,' Riordan cut in. 'Point taken. Shtoom's the word – and we'll take it as emphasized! On the question of secrecy, however' – he touched his face, where a strip of sticking plaster still covered a cut he had received when the Peugeot exploded – 'it seems to me that in certain quarters too much appears to be known already!'

'Tell you the truth, that absolutely foxes me,' O'Kelly admitted. 'Whoever heard of someone trying to eliminate an operative from a mission when he didn't even know totally what the mission was? Tell me, Riordan: could it possibly be unconnected with this mission? Someone with a grudge from a previous encounter? Maybe someone after the person who rented that particular car just before you had it?'

Riordan shrugged. 'Anything's possible. What's probable is something else. Whoever booby-trapped the car worked fast. Nobody but me knew I was going to that post office, and that means I must have been followed. Which in turn means whoever it was *knew* who the driver of the car was. And that implies that the attack was directly aimed at me personally – not at whoever happened to be driving that particular car. Are you with me?'

O'Kelly nodded. 'I can't see how anyone could possibly . . . I mean, I can't think of a reason why . . . Never mind. We'll have to leave it for the moment. But, one way or another, it certainly underlines the need for the most stringent security precautions.'

He glanced around the group. Riordan with his craggy, seen-it-all assurance; Van Eyck, the super marksman, tall, lean, with white-blond hair and almost colourless eyes; Alessandro Aletti, the tough, nut-faced little Italian-American who was a genius with any kind of machinery, especially that powering cars and aeroplanes. The group – for the time being – was completed by two men as different – and yet in some ways as alike – as it was possible to imagine. Both were Londoners, and both from the East End, both had military experience and both were childless widowers. But there the resemblance ended. Brian Crawford, recently demobilized from the British Army on the Rhine, was an ex-regimental sergeant-major with twenty-five years' regular service. A tall, muscular disciplinarian with short, grey hair and a clipped moustache, Crawford – who was always addressed as Sergeant and never as Brian – was a man of very few words, most of which were unprintable. Pensioned off from the BAOR with a gratuity, he had originally joined Riordan on a discreditable foray into the Persian Gulf more out of boredom with civilian life than anything else.

Danny Christal was short, balding, garrulous and disinclined to accept discipline of any kind. Riordan was the only man he had ever called sir. Christal, who had spent the war doing manual work with the Pioneer Corps along with Polish refugees and Jewish expatriates from Central Europe, had made considerable inroads into the north German black market before he was demobbed. Subsequently he had operated a stall in London's Petticoat Lane street market, later – following the laws of supply and demand – specializing in the provision of goods for other stallholders and barkers. Regrettably, these supplies were not always his own property. For Danny Christal was in fact a second-storey man, a cat burglar, by profession. As such he had been an invaluable ally for Riordan in a number of tight corners.

The two men yet to join Riordan's team were equally

experienced, each in his special line. Teddy Nelson-Harmer, a Nigerian with a Cambridge degree in English, was a firearms and explosives expert; Helmut Brod, who was Viennese, proudly described himself as 'Europe's number one locksmith and safe-breaker'.

The Nigerian was due to arrive from London for a separate briefing later that afternoon. Brod had agreed to travel straight to Berlin from Vienna. He would be waiting for them in the hotel O'Kelly had chosen.

'I understand from Colonel Riordan,' O'Kelly told the men assembled at the Atlantic Hotel, 'that you and the missing pair are not known, together, as a team. That is to say that, even if you were seen together on the same plane, nobody would at once say: 'Hey! Here's a combat unit ready for action!' I think, just the same – to pre-empt some clever Dick putting three and three together – that we had better make our way to Berlin separately. Van Eyck, you'll be going as an Anglo-Dutch interpreter instructed to help out at Control Commission meetings. My principals have arranged a passage for you on the plane carrying the British diplomatic bag.'

'Your *principals*?' Danny Christal interrupted. 'Christ, we're working for Ernie Bevin and the bleeding Foreign Office, ain't we? Why not fucking say so?'

'In this kind of work,' Riordan said mildly, 'it's better not to name names. OK?'

His words were drowned by an involuntary bark from Crawford: '*Silence*, that man! The officer ain't finished speaking!'

'You two,' O'Kelly resumed, glancing at the two men in turn, 'will go on the night train, posing as an MP and a recaptured deserter on the way back to a court martial.'

Christal laughed aloud. 'Don't tell me which of us is cast as AWOL!' he said.

'Colonel Riordan,' their host pursued, 'will take the autobahn from Magdeburg. The Russians have already closed the bridge – for "repairs", they say – but there is a ferry every hour. Nelson-Harmer, when he arrives, will be filtered through the American airbase at Frankfurt, and Aletti will go by train too, but on the Ost-Express from the Ruhr, not the overnighter leaving here later this evening. We'll fly you down to Düsseldorf at screech,' he told the Italian, 'and you can enjoy a beer and wurst breakfast before you board.'

Aletti grinned. The son of a Jewish watchmaker in Milan, he had spent much of his childhood with immigrant relatives in New York, returning to Europe with an accent and an English vocabulary as idiosyncratic as any to be heard in the Seventh Avenue garment district. 'Just so long,' he said, 'as the train it should not stop at Dachau or Sachsenhausen.' He shook his head. 'Giuseppe Aletti's first-born in Germany of his own free will! The old man would drop dead he should hear of such a thing.'

'We shall need a certain amount of gear,' Riordan said. 'Weapons, of course. Probably climbing equipment. Specialized footwear and clothing. And a certain amount of forbidden fruit in the nature of locksmith's materials, detonators, forgery essentials and radio supplies. As the Russians have been known to be bloody-minded enough to subject travellers through the eastern zone to searches . . .' He shrugged. 'Well, obviously, every one of us must go in dead clean, don't you think?'

'Oh, absolutely,' O'Kelly agreed. 'Not even a penknife! Let me have your shopping list and I'll see that everything you want is waiting for you when you arrive. Anything up to and including a helicopter, if you think that necessary. Though I don't really advise that in the Soviet zone!'

'Only if we need to fly the coop fast,' Riordan said soberly.

He was about to add something else when he caught sight of a tow-haired busboy parading the tiered grill-room with a card held high on which the words 'Herr O. Chellie' had been scrawled in heavy black ink. O'Kelly saw it at the same time and held up his hand. The youth hurried over and murmured a few words into his ear. O'Kelly dabbed his lips with a startlingly white starched napkin and pushed back his chair. 'Control Commission,' he said briefly. 'Be right back.' He left the dining-room.

It was almost ten minutes before he returned. His familiar pink face now flushed a dark red, he dropped heavily into his chair. 'That's fucking torn it!' he raged. 'The bastard Russians have sealed off every single road and rail link with Berlin, as of midnight tonight.'

Riordan half rose from his chair. 'You mean . . . ?'

'I mean the city's totally cut off from the rest of the bloody world,' O'Kelly said.

3

The inter-Allied crisis which became known as the Berlin
Blockade had its roots in the obstructive tactics adopted by
Russian military negotiators as early as 5 June 1945, less
than a month after the surrender of Nazi Germany, when
the Soviets blocked a proposal to establish the four-power
Kommandatura, the Control Commission which was to
administer the city.

Britain, France and the United States had to wait until
11 July for the first meeting of that body. In the meantime
Russia, in defiance of agreements reached at the Yalta
Conference five months earlier, had annexed the Baltic
states, handed over large tracts of eastern Germany to
Poland and laid steel fingers on Austria, Czechoslovakia
and the Balkans. Berlin, during that period, had been
subjected by undisciplined Russian troops to an orgy
of rape and pillage unequalled in military history, and
stripped of all plant and industrial equipment which could
conceivably be used by the victors.

The shattered shell of the city was nevertheless an invaluable propaganda prize, an emblem of Soviet superiority to
be paraded in front of the satellite states and emergent
nations likely to be coaxed into the Communist fold. The
fact that the German capital had fallen to the Russians
was presented – conveniently ignoring the detail that the
Allied armies had halted on the Elbe for tactical reasons –

as one of the great victories of the war. The only irritant was the four-power agreement giving the Western countries the right to share in the government of Berlin.

If only they could be compelled to withdraw, to evacuate the city, their prestige in Germany, and throughout the world, would suffer a severe blow; they might even abandon their plans to make the western part of Germany into a separate autonomous state. In either case the Russians would have won a bloodless victory of enormous importance.

From 1946 onwards, therefore, Soviet strategic thinking concentrated on a single question: how much aggravation would the Western powers put up with in order to retain their Berlin sectors unmolested?

The aggravation – a continuous and infuriating sequence of legal wrangles, blocked requests and meetings postponed, a deliberate and ceaseless harassment of all those charged with the administration of the city – was focused on the West's one weak legal link. While the Western powers' unquestioned right to a presence in the conquered city was written into the Yalta Agreement, the right to get there – the right of *unrestricted* access – had been purely verbal, and no clause in any agreement ratified it explicitly. The Allies had therefore been obliged to accept three air corridors and a limited number of road, rail and river routes as their only means of crossing the Soviet zone to reach Berlin.

No more than an inconvenience in the movement of troops, this became of vital importance when it was a matter of supplies. Almost two million Berliners depended on the West for food, clothing, heating, medical care and other necessities. Sixteen British and American trains were permitted to cross the Soviet zone every day, together with road and barge transport. The number of trains was later increased to thirty-one. Theoretically this was enough to meet the three sectors' needs. But the necessary supplies were simply not available in the Western zones, a large proportion of which were densely populated industrial areas. The granary of Germany lay principally in the Russian zone, and the occupiers claimed there was nothing to spare: the entire production was required for their own needs.

The deficiency was partly made up by supplies which had to be brought from America and elsewhere, but there was near starvation throughout the country during the savage winter of 1946.

In the following year the campaign of intimidation was stepped up. Bridges across the Elbe were closed for repairs, trains were shunted into sidings for hours, passengers were subjected to identify checks and customs controls. The Russian tactics were designed to create as much tension as possible. Control Commission meetings were sabotaged or postponed. Interminable delays afflicted road and rail traffic into and out of the Western sectors. Berliners in the Soviet zone risked arrest if they carried Western newspapers. Cars from the West were forbidden to enter the Soviet sector without special permits, which were extremely hard to get. Barge captains suddenly discovered that they required new papers to cross the zone, but they were not told what these papers were or where to apply for them.

When the United States offered aid to European countries under the Marshall Plan, Moscow at once forbade all satellites in the Soviet sphere of influence to accept it, effectively creating what Churchill termed an 'iron curtain' separating the continent from the Baltic to the Black Sea. Then, heralding the creation of a separate West German government, the Allies announced the introduction of a new currency which would halt inflation and circulate in their three sectors. It was this which provoked the Russians into a direct confrontation.

The issue of the new currency – the Deutschmark instead of the Reichsmark – was described as 'the final nail in the coffin of four-power government for Berlin' and amounted to an admission by the Allies that the division of Germany was complete. The Russians at once stopped all passenger traffic arriving by road and rail from the Western zones. An American military train was halted at Marienborn because the track ahead of it had been pulled up. Pedestrians and motorists were forbidden to cross into the Soviet zone.

The next step was the severance of all road and barge traffic to and from West Berlin. Supplies of food, coal and fresh milk, all of which were drawn from the Russian sector, were cut off. Then at midnight on 23 June, the grid carrying supplies to West Berlin from the central electricity generators in the Soviet zone was disconnected. Six hours later the Russians announced that the Kommandatura had ceased to exist.

Effectively, the Allied zones of the city were under siege.

It was against this tense background – and the general picture of attempted Communist expansion into the West – that the decision to make use of Riordan's specialized services had been taken. What had not been foreseen was that the situation would degenerate so far as to prevent his team from reaching the buildings from where they were to rescue the pro-Western hostages alive.

4

'The problem,' O'Kelly said, 'is that the Western administration needs damn near fourteen thousand tons of supplies *a day* – and that's just to keep the population fed.'

'But they haven't closed the three air corridors?' Riordan asked.

'No. They can't, physically. Unless they seize the airfields in the Western sectors and shoot or force down our planes using them. Either of which, I am told, would be considered by our masters as an act of war. And nobody believes the Russkis are prepared to risk the possibility of a shooting war at this stage.'

'So the traffic in the corridors will be increased and the Western sectors supplied by air until the situation cools down?'

'That's the thinking so far,' O'Kelly said. 'But the Yanks only have a hundred transport aircraft in Europe, and the RAF perhaps a hundred and fifty. The most they could shift together, top weight, would be seven hundred tons – only half the minimum required.'

'Can't that be stepped up? I mean . . . more planes, extra crews, accelerated arrivals and departures?'

'Up to a point. There's a sketchy plan already in existence, dreamed up over a year ago in case it proved necessary to provision our garrisons in Berlin. They call it an airlift. But it'll take some time to move into top gear.'

'That's OK then,' Riordan said. 'We'll hop a lift on one of the crates making the run. It'll mean we have to go in a bunch instead of separately, but that's a risk worth taking. Weapons and other supplies will be a problem too. Maybe you can fix that through the Berlin garrison?'

'My dear chap!' O'Kelly protested. 'Forgive me, but you've no idea! There's the most colossal flap on. There's not the ghost of a chance of any supernumeraries climbing aboard any plane. Every inch of space has to be accounted for, to be devoted to the operation. The top brass are finding their private transport commandeered. Existing transport planes are being stripped of everything: RDF, radar screens, automatic piloting equipment, seats. It's all being chucked out to make room for the last available pound of freight on every payload. As for the gear' – O'Kelly shook his head – 'I've been specifically warned off involving the local soldiery in any way at all. Any way at all.'

'Then we'll have to collect stuff here, go underground, and make our way through the Soviet zone travelling rough, moving only at night.'

'You don't have the time. The zone's pretty heavily policed. It'd take you days to make it – and the bloody hostage situation could catch fire at any moment.'

'So what do you suggest? You're the boss.'

O'Kelly scratched his head. His pink face creased into a frown. 'Tell you the truth, old boy, I'm fucked if I know. But some way round it has to be found, and pretty damn quick too.'

It was twenty-four hours since O'Kelly had broken the news that Berlin was isolated. The mercenaries were grouped around a table in a booth at the back of a waterfront café. Teddy Nelson-Harmer, the Nigerian, was to join them that evening, although his flight from London had already been cancelled twice. Helmut Brod, it was assumed, would have arrived in Berlin from Vienna, though it was no longer possible to confirm this by telephoning the German capital.

'If we can't board one of the planes using the corridor,' Riordan said, 'how about co-opting us as baggage handlers? They have to have people to chuck out the supplies when the aircraft arrive.'

'No way, I'm afraid,' O'Kelly said. 'It's all too organized. All the crews are enlisted USAF personnel or boys in blue, working shifts.'

It was Danny Christal who came up with an answer. The group had fallen silent after O'Kelly's last thumbs down, then the cheery little cockney drained his stein of beer, set it carefully down on the table, and ventured: 'Beg pardon, sir . . . ?'

O'Kelly looked up. 'Yes, Christal? What is it?'

'Just an idea, sir. Bit of a rumble. From what you say, despite the organization, this airlift lark ain't exactly run to a timetable: take-off 12.05 sharp, touch down 12.26 pip emma, that sort of caper. Not even operated like a bleeding bus service, one every eleven minutes. Just cram in as many flights as you can each hour. Am I right?'

'More or less,' O'Kelly said. 'What of it?'

'Well, sir, if we can't pack in extra crew, why not add an extra plane to the stream? Ferry us blokes in that way? Who's going to notice it if one more joins the traffic jam halfway there? The coves on the receiving end will be too busy taking in whatever comes to count.'

'Ho, very smart!' Sergeant Crawford said scornfully. 'Add an extra fucking plane, just like that! And I suppose you can lay your hands on one any time you want? Take the sodding thing off the shelf like a tin of beans in the bloody grocer's?'

Below his bald skull, Christal's face reddened. 'Well, yes,' he said. 'As it happens, I can.'

Before Crawford could speak again, Riordan cut in. 'Just a moment, Sergeant. Are you serious, Danny? Do you really know where we could lay our hands on a plane? One in a condition to fly?'

'Bet your life,' Christal said.

'What plane? Where is it?'

'Not far from here at all. Near Aumühle, at the eastern end of the Hamburg underground. It's a Yank, a B-25 medium bomber. They call it a Mitchell.'

'Good God! What the hell is it doing there? How did it get there? There's no drome that I know of out there.'

Christal coughed. 'No, there ain't. What happened . . . well, it was soon after the end of the war, see. There was engine trouble and the kite crash-landed. In a clearing in the middle of a forest on the old Bismarck estate. Burst into flames and started a forest fire. My unit was billeted there at the time. Pioneers. Helping to clear the rubble in the city.'

'Yes, but how come . . . ?'

'The crew was killed, but the Yanks never claimed the wreck,' Christal continued. He cleared his throat. 'When it come down to it, the crate wasn't all that badly damaged. Me and my mates fixed it up. You get a lot of expert help in the Pioneers. There was this Pole, for instance. An ex-rigger . . .'

Riordan laughed. 'Don't tell me. You had a black market going, and you hoped you could find a buyer after the war, when supplies would be . . .'

'Well, nobody else wanted the thing,' Christal interrupted defensively. 'We didn't see no harm in putting it right. Somebody could maybe used it – one of the teams moving in cigarettes liberated from the PX by Yankee

31

contacts; fire-water with Scotch labels; chocolate, even. They have to move the stuff somehow.'

'But you haven't found a buyer yet?'

'Not at the right price, no. The fire widened one of those forest rides, but it takes a lot of work keeping it cleared enough for a take-off.'

'You're still in this, Danny, aren't you?' Riordan asked. 'One of the many strings to your smuggler's bow!'

'Not on my jack,' Christal said. 'There's me mates to think of. You wouldn't believe how much . . .'

'Christal,' O'Kelly broke in, 'am I right in thinking that this plane is actually available, ready to fly?'

'Yes, sir.'

'As of today? With space for take-off?'

'Yes, sir.'

'And what you're trying to say, in a roundabout way, is that we could have it, but because of your . . . partners . . . it would have to be paid for? Do I read you right?'

'Well, business is business, ain't it? And, shit, we are *mercenaries*, blokes what get paid for their services, ain't we? After all the work we . . .'

'How much do you want?'

Christal named a sum that made Riordan wince.

'I'll give you exactly half that,' O'Kelly said. 'In dollars. Cash.'

'Done,' said Christal. He held out his hand and O'Kelly shook it.

'There's only one thing,' Riordan said, turning to Aletti. 'Alex, can you fly a Mitchell medium bomber?'

Aletti spread his arms wide. 'Wasn't I part of the team testing the Macchi-Castoldi floatplane it should have won the Schneider Trophy in 1931 if the Spitfire prototype hadn't been faster? I can fly anything.'

O'Kelly pushed back his chair and rose to his feet. 'In that case, I move that we hurry to the nearest U-Bahn station and board the next train for Aumühle.'

Below the station at Aumühle there was a reed-fringed lake, and beyond that the Sachsenwald, a forest stretching several miles to the east and northwards almost as far as the Baltic. The lake, which was known as the Mühlenteich, drained into a weir by an ancient mill. On the shore nearest the railway, a long, low, shuttered building thrust a planking terrace out over the water. A sign projecting from the half-timbered façade carried in cracked and peeling paint the single word 'Fischerhaus'.

'That's where my lot were billeted,' Christal said. 'Built by the bloody Bismarcks in 1760! After Adolf pinched the place from the estate, the lake and the woods were made into a public park, with fishing and boating and all that. But it was reopened after the war, and the occupation types don't seem to know what to do with it – restore it to the family, keep it public, use it for army manoeuvres, or what. At the moment it's like awaiting His Majesty's pleasure. And the BAOR's. Which means it's unused.'

'Except by your smuggling friends?' Riordan put in.

'Well, yes, there's that,' Christal said with a wicked grin. 'We'd never have been able to cope with the demand otherwise.'

'The station's a terminus for the diesels on the Hamburg S-Bahn,' O'Kelly said. 'But I notice the tracks continue eastwards. It's also a link in the state railway system, I suppose?'

'That's right. This is the main line from the city to Berlin. The border of the Soviet zone's only a few miles away. Why do you think we stayed so close to the perishing Fischerhaus?' Christal jerked a thumb over his shoulder at the sign, creaking now in a breeze that ruffled the surface

33

of the lake. 'Makes a very handy store, while it's unused, for . . . certain items in short supply. And me and my mates still have the key.'

'And this is why you've been able to keep a whole aircraft hidden in these woods?' Riordan asked.

'You got it.' Christal gestured towards a clump of bushes at the foot of a tussocky slope. 'There should be a boat waiting among the branches there,' he said.

There was. A flat-bottomed carvel dinghy ferried them to the far side and then up to the head of the lake, with Riordan and Crawford at the oars.

'Pretty efficient,' O'Kelly commented. 'Considering you only made your phone call forty minutes ago!'

'Well, if you're in business . . .' Christal shrugged, then grinned. 'The client is always bleeding right, eh?'

Under his directions, the dinghy ran in beneath a stand of weeping willows, and the men scrambled ashore. They had seen no one since they left the small crowd of passengers straggling away from the station towards a row of neat bungalows on the far side of the tracks.

They walked for a quarter of a mile through the forest, feet hushed by the carpet of pine needles between the dense conifers. There had been no rain that day, and there was blue sky with occasional patches of sunshine between the high clouds, but very little light penetrated the sombre woodland depths. A long way above them, branches sighed in the wind.

'It's straight out of Grimms' fairy-tales,' Riordan said. 'At any moment you expect to see a needy woodcutter or a dwarf with an old crone in a pointed hat!'

'All you see here,' Christal replied, 'except my mates, that is, will be different kinds of deer and an occasional wild boar. Oh, but yes – they do say there could still be wolves in the remote parts!'

They saw no deer, no boar and no wolves. Only the odd furtive rustle, a sudden flapping among the treetops as a heavy bird flew away, broke the menacing forest quiet. Christal's mates were in a hollow beyond a moss-covered stone outcrop. There were two of them, sitting in a camouflaged jeep.

'There's around a dozen in the team,' Christal explained after he had run down the slope to greet his fellow black marketeers. 'But some of us have jobs, some are still enlisted. We run a watch like in a ship: three on, nine off, twenty-four hours a day. Two of the duty watch stay out here with the jalopy, the third back in the old Fischerhaus by a pirated phone. It's his job to alert us if necessary and take orders from clients. We fill the orders quick as we can, and deliver a little nearer the border.'

'Orders like a lorryload of Lucky Strike? Half a dozen crates of Garand assault rifles? A hijacked pharmacy shipment?' Riordan suggested.

'Something like that,' Christal agreed. 'Course, sometimes we have to row in the Yanks for special orders, and that jacks up the price a bit.'

'My God,' O'Kelly said, 'I shouldn't be listening to this!'

The two members of the watch were introduced as MacTavish and Novotny: a wizened Scot wearing Levis courtesy of the Yanks and a lorry-driver's sleeveless, fleece-lined tunic; and a tall, pale man from whose khaki battle-dress the Polish Pioneer Corps shoulder flash and corporal's stripes had been removed.

'Deserters, too, I shouldn't wonder!' O'Kelly muttered to Riordan.

The newcomers crowded into and on to the jeep, hanging on wherever they could. Novotny drove them, skilfully and fast, but without too much bucketing, about a mile and a half deeper into the forest, before halting on the edge of a wide clearing. The jeep coughed into silence. They climbed out and looked around them. The clearing had evidently been enlarged recently: tree stumps littered the scarred forest floor, there were neatly stacked woodpiles on every side, and at one end it looked as though a bulldozer had shored up a bastion of earth to level a depression.

From the clearing, an alley at least two hundred yards wide arrowed away in gentle undulations towards a slight rise in the terrain. 'The ground's not all that soft,' Christal said before anyone could speak. 'And there's another thousand yards, pretty flat, beyond the rise.'

'If that's the runway, what's the total length?' Aletti asked. 'And what height the trees they are at the far end?'

'Taller than this end,' Christal told him. 'You're better taxiing up there, swinging around, and taking off towards the south, using that rise and this slight downslope for extra lift. As for the total length . . .' He glanced at Novotny.

'Four-five,' the Pole replied.

'Christ,' Aletti said. 'And no concrete! So where's the ship?'

The Mitchell was concealed beneath the trees, standing by a log cabin used by the black marketeers as a base, the fuselage and much of the wing surface covered by netting threaded with small branches and leaves.

Christal and his companions removed the netting.

The Mitchell stood revealed – an angular, twin-engined aircraft with a high, cranked wing and double tail group, perched a little precariously on its nose wheel like a scared mosquito about to flee. It was still wearing standard wartime day-bombing camouflage, complete with the white, five-pointed American star, though all the identification letters and squadron numbers had been removed. The plane was clearly a veteran which had been used a great deal – and had been through a lot. There were patches all over the stressed metal skin of the fuselage and most of one wing; blackened scorch marks stained an engine nacelle, one rudder and part of the belly; the bomb aimer's Perspex blister in the nose was cracked and discoloured and one radial cowling was badly buckled.

O'Kelly stared at the machine and sighed. 'Yes, well . . .' he said.

'We couldn't do everything,' Novotny said apologetically. 'Too difficult to get the equipment and the power out here – the spraying plant and all that. Also there's a spot of . . . improvisation . . . here and there. The oleo group was salvaged from a Boston, the nose wheel's off a P-38, and some of the controls are – shall we say? – non-standard.' His voice was pleasantly modulated, the English almost accentless. 'But she flies pretty good,' he added. 'Handles as if she'd never been involved in a serious prang.'

'Yes, but when did she last fly?' O'Kelly asked.

'About two weeks ago. Maybe three.'

'Good God! You mean you've flown the plane from here? From this strip?'

'Sure,' Novotny said. 'Two, three times. At night mostly. It's safer.'

'Safer?' O'Kelly's tone was ever more incredulous.

'Less chance of being spotted as we land or take off. Less chance of being identified by any unit we happen to overfly.'

'But . . . good God, man! – the strip. You aren't exactly overburdened with landing lights or GCA equipment!'

'We only stay up a few minutes,' Novotny said. 'Enough to keep the oil circulating and check the power units and controls. Couple of circuits over the forest.'

'And bumps, no doubt,' O'Kelly said drily, eyeing the improvised take-off path.

'And bumps,' the Pole agreed. 'We're limited, of course, to clear nights when there's at least a three-quarter moon high in the sky.'

'Of course.' O'Kelly's voice remained ironic.

Aletti had been wandering around the plane, resting an experimental hand here, peering between formers there. 'Very expert reassembly,' he pronounced as he returned to the group. 'Especially the spare parts cannibalized from different kinds of ship. The mechanics and controls, they are in tip-top condition.'

'Aye. And why would they not be?' MacTavish spoke for the first time since they left the jeep. His Glasgow accent was very thick. 'With the best bloody rigger 502 ever had coddling them like babbies still at their mother's milk!'

'Don't listen to his boasting,' Novotny said. 'Five-o-two was Coastal Command, operating out of Northern Ireland. They lost more aircraft down in the drink when he was stationed at Aldergrove . . .' He shook his head sadly. 'He wasn't called Rigger Mortis for nothing!'

'Och, awa' wi' ye. Piss off back to sodding Warsaw and make some of them Polish stories come true,' MacTavish said genially. 'As for Five-o-fucking-two, they transferred half the crews to Sunderland flying boats, training from the Short factory on Belfast Lough: they was *supposed* to land in the drink, ye ignorant bugger! Bloody foreigners,' he confided to O'Kelly, 'they're all very well for the rough work, bolting the bits of a Meccano set together' – he nodded towards the Mitchell – 'but when it comes to your actual engineering, keeping your moving parts smoothly at work, you got to have your expert, the man with the craft in his blood. Me father, now, he could work to a thou in metal with his naked eye.'

'Making what?' Novotny enquired. 'The hinges for cell doors?'

'Perhaps,' Aletti said mildly, 'we could engineer a shufti at your actual machinery here? If you gentlemen have terminated your minstrel double act, that is.'

'A pleasure,' Novotny replied. Helped by MacTavish, he climbed up on to the starboard wing and began stripping the cowling from the Wright Cyclone engine. Soon the two of them were deep in conversation with Aletti, peering and prodding, fingering cables and wires and ducts, unscrewing the covers of minor components. When the Italian declared himself satisfied, the three of them moved to the port wing. O'Kelly lit a cigarette. Another twenty minutes passed.

Riordan ducked beneath the belly of the plane and stepped up through an open hatch forward of the old bomb bay. He stood in a narrow cabin lit only by dim red and blue lights glowing on the instrument panel ahead of the pilot's and navigator's seats. Beside the steep step leading to the cockpit, a short tunnel communicated with the bomb aimer's position in the transparent nose.

Aletti had already settled himself in the pilot's seat. He glanced at the controls, scanned the panel, and slid back the side window in the canopy. Staring down at MacTavish, fifteen feet below him on the forest floor, he pointed to the port starter motor and held up one thumb.

The Scot jerked his head at the engine cowling and revolved his index finger. Aletti pressed the 'Energize' switch. The pilot lights dimmed. Riordan heard the stuttering of the booster pump. Gradually a faint whine emerged from the starter motor as the flywheel built up energy. Aletti flicked the switch to 'Mesh'.

The Cyclone engine wheezed, coughed; the airscrew slowly turned, then spun. Aletti stabbed the 'Prime' button and thrust the throttle forward as the engine caught with a bang that shook the whole aircraft from nose to tail. He began experimenting with mixtures and timing and throttle settings. The roar of the exhausts rose and fell.

On the ground below, O'Kelly stood with Christal and Novotny. 'It won't get you into trouble if he warms her up a bit and gets the feel of the thing?' he asked the Pole over the stunning reverberation of the engine.

'What?'

'The noise,' O'Kelly shouted, sweeping an arm around to include the runway and the forest. 'People won't ask questions? Try to find out where it's coming from?'

Novotny shook his head. 'Nearest dwelling's over three miles away. It's impossible to pinpoint a sound source in woodland: the trees absorb most of it and there's nothing hard to make an echo. In any case there's always military traffic from Lübeck passing overhead on the way to Berlin. One of the air corridors starts where the railway crosses the border of the Soviet zone.'

O'Kelly nodded. 'I just wondered,' he said.

Aletti transferred his attention to the second engine. The two of them roared in unison, separately, alternating. Control surfaces, fins, flaps, trim tabs, rose, sank, swivelled. At last the fuel was cut off and the airscrews whistled into silence. Aletti and Riordan dropped through the belly of the Mitchell.

'Well?' O'Kelly called to them.

Riordan looked at Aletti, who nodded and said: 'Passable. Not perfect but good enough for our purpose. Considering.'

'I should fucking well hope so!' MacTavish said.

'You got a deal,' Riordan told Novotny. 'If the captain's in agreement.'

'Swell. When do you want to take delivery?'

'Tonight,' O'Kelly interjected before the mercenary leader could reply.

'Er ... fine,' Novotny said, then coughed. 'The only thing is ... well, if you're pushing off that soon, well, there is this question of ...'

'Relax,' O'Kelly laughed. 'I'm not going with them. 'You can come with me into Hamburg this afternoon. I have certain ... strings. You'll have your money before nightfall.'

The Pole grinned. 'Great,' he said. 'I just wondered.'

5

The moon rose behind the phalanx of pine trees sheltering the Mitchell B-25. By the time it floated above the low cloud bank blanketing the forest tracts in the direction of the Soviet zone's border, the shadows had shortened and lay hard as iron along the bone-white slope of the woodland runway.

Aletti was taking last-minute instructions from Novotny and MacTavish as the other members of the unit crammed into the narrow fuselage with such gear as they had been able to collect in the short time available. Riordan was talking to O'Kelly. The night sky was vibrant with the sound of aircraft.

'It's bloody silly that I could only get hold of hand-guns,' O'Kelly was complaining. 'Nobody in the city at embassy level, that's the trouble. And the piffling little clerks in the Consular Service wouldn't know a semi-automatic or an SMG if it was shoved up their backside. As for explosives . . .' He snorted, shrugging in disgust.

'Relax,' Riordan told him. 'We got the plane: that's the main thing. The trouble with working in secret is that nobody knows anything when you want them to. We can use the handguns for a couple of fast raids when we get there. That should take care of the other weapons; maybe the explosives too. The climbing tackle should be available at some kind of sports shop. There are mountains and ski slopes nearer Berlin than here.'

'Let's hope so,' O'Kelly said.

'Been all over the crate from stem to stern while you and the Pole were junketing in bloody Hamburg,' MacTavish said to Aletti, 'and as far as I can tell she's tickety-boo all over, allowing for her age. Only trouble as I can see might be your port carb: she just might ice up if you run into high cloud. There's a tendency for your needle valve to stick there. If she does, bung the bugger on to fully rich and that should do the trick.'

Aletti nodded. 'Thanks for the tip.'

'One other thing. You want to watch your oil temperature when you're near your ceiling. If she gets too cold, see, it could stiffen up your pitch control.'

'I'll keep an eye on it,' Aletti said. 'But I have every confidence . . .'

'Aye, and so ye should have,' the Scot agreed. 'This is no flaming Anson on a milk run, but I'll stake my life this kite's as airworthy as ever she was in her flying life, or my name's not John Mac-fucking-Tavish.'

Strapped into his makeshift tubular steel and canvas seat, Riordan's number two, the Dutchman Pieter Van Eyck, was cradling an oblong, worn leather case with shiny silver locks. 'What you got in there, then?' Christal asked, leaning over his shoulder from the seat behind. 'Dollars?'

Van Eyck smiled. 'Why are you being so curious? Sandwiches maybe.'

'Don't give me that, Piet. Blimey, you hang on to that bleeding thing like a winning pools ticket or the map to a secret gold mine.'

'More valuable than that,' the Dutchman said. 'To me anyway.' He sprung open the case. Inside, nestling in the shaped grooves of the padded blue-velvet interior, was a dismantled competition rifle. The hand-carved walnut stock was polished to a satin sheen, the pistol-grip and the fore-end of the long, blued barrel were tipped with rosewood, and an elaborate floral pattern had been engraved in the chased-silver plates on either side of the breech. In one corner there was a sniperscope with a rubber eyepiece.

'Cor, what a beauty!' Christal enthused. 'Cost you a packet, I'll bet.'

'A Model 561 Magnum,' Van Eyck said proudly. 'Made by Husqvarna Vapenfabrik in Sweden. With a three-shot magazine taking .358-calibre cartridges fitted with 150-grain bullets. The telescopic sight is a Balvar 5 by Bausch and Lomb.'

'You don't say!' The Englishman's knowledge of firearms was limited to the kind of service revolver or Browning automatic people kept in drawers in the hope of dissuading people like him.

'Don't let him get going on the subject,' Riordan called from the hatchway, 'or you'll be stuck here all night.' He stuffed into an inside pocket a sheaf of papers given to him by O'Kelly. They included Berlin street plans, aerial and ground-level photographs, an architect's blueprint of the interior of the block in which the hostages were held, and municipal maps of the electricity, gas and drainage systems serving the block. 'Take-off in five minutes,' he announced, glancing at his watch.

There was a sudden silence inside the Mitchell. Then Aletti climbed into the pilot's seat with Riordan beside him. 'Good luck!' O'Kelly called through the hatchway. 'Keep in touch. You know how to make contact. And there's always the Berlin fall-back in times of need.' He closed the hatch.

The continuously rising and falling drone of aircraft flying south faded away. A booster pump thudded. There

44

was a whine from a starter motor. Then, abruptly, there was a clattering roar from the first of the Wright Cyclones. Seconds later the other engine burst into life. Down below, the two black marketeers waved, ducking below the wings to pull away the chocks as the plane lumbered out from beneath the trees.

At first the moonlight seemed astonishingly bright. Light flooding through the blister of the empty gun turret showed up the complex of cables and control conduits webbing the soundproofing material which jacketed the stressed metal of the fuselage, the patches where flak had pierced the skin. Bouncing and shuddering, the Mitchell turned into the widened ride, slewing this way and that as Aletti fed bursts of throttle alternately to the port and starboard engines, coaxing the plane towards the slight rise a thousand yards from the far end of the improvised runway. 'How does the ground shape up?' Riordan asked.

Aletti was hunched over the control column, eyes flicking left then right to register obstacles, imperfections in the surface and the distance separating his wingtips from the trees, which seemed to diminish every second.

'Say again?' he called, still staring fixedly through the windshield.

'The ground. Looked at as a runway. How do you find it?'

'Bumpy,' the Italian replied briefly. 'Not as soft as it might be.' He grinned crookedly. 'We're stuck with it anyway!'

Beyond the rise, the final stretch was relatively flat. Aletti swung the Mitchell around into the wind. He pushed the throttles up to thirty inches of boost against the brakes and held the aircraft there while he took a last look at the instruments on the control panel. Booster pumps switched over to emergency . . . pitch locks off . . . superchargers to low gear . . . mixture control OK . . . needles trembling on the red lines to register oil and water temperature . . . hatches secure . . . He flipped off the brakes.

The Mitchell surged down the runway, gradually gathering speed as the clatter of the engines rose to a roar. The wings shivered. An insane vibration shook the cabin as the non-standard undercart was thrashed by the uneven terrain.

Fifty . . . sixty . . . seventy mph came up on the dial while the pedals hardened and the wheel stiffened in Aletti's hands.

In the coloured light diffused from the instrument panel, sweat glowed blue and red and green on the little Italian's brow. At eighty mph he dabbed briefly at the brakes and feathered in a touch of right rudder to counteract the leftward pull of the engines.

The Mitchell was hitting eighty-five when they made the rise. The nose wheel came unstuck and for a heartbeat they were off the ground, then the plane thumped sickeningly down, bounced high, and crashed back to hurtle down the gentle slope towards the distant pines.

The indicator needle moved into three figures. One hundred and five . . . one hundred and seven . . . The plane lurched crazily; the trees were streaming towards them. Aletti's face paled and he gritted his teeth. Then suddenly, smoothly, with the indicator on a hundred and ten, they were airborne, the threshing treetops sliding away beneath the wings like frozen surf.

'Christ!' Aletti breathed thankfully. The Mitchell soared up into the sky.

There had been a great deal of discussion as to how – and where – Riordan and his team were to attach themselves to the stream of transport planes flying supplies, day and night, into Berlin at a rate of one every four or five minutes. The only factor agreed from the start was that the flight must follow the northernmost of the three approach corridors.

This was handled at the beginning by No. 46 Group of the RAF Transport Command, with two squadrons each of eight twin-engined Dakotas flying in a lift of 130,000lb daily in twenty-four sorties. By the time Riordan's Mitchell took off not long before midnight on 26 June, it had been realized that this amount of cargo – originally scheduled as an emergency service for the maintenance of British forces in Berlin – was woefully inadequate for the crisis situation which had developed. Thirty-eight more Dakotas had been drafted in and there were forty four-engined Avro Yorks to come.

Since the RAF base near Lübeck was not yet in a state to handle such heavy traffic, all these aircraft took off either from Wunstorf, or Schleswigland, on the Jutland peninsula. It was the stream from the latter – once a base for the Luftwaffe's first jet night-fighter, the Messerschmitt Me-262 – that the Mitchell was supposed to join.

The flight path followed by the transports lay west of Fuhlsbüttel, the Hamburg civil airport now in the hands of the RAF, climbed, south of the city, on to 67° Magnetic and then set course over a Eureka beacon for a straight-line approach to Gatow airport on the western edge of Berlin. On this final stretch, the Dakotas maintained a height of five and a half thousand feet at an airspeed of no more than 125 knots.

The American airlift took off either from Wiesbaden or Rhein-Main, in the US zone. Both British and American transports flew from Wunstorf.

Clearly, it was imperative that Riordan's 'stowaway' plane joined the northern stream before it set course over the beacon, for it carried no directional equipment, and after that Aletti would have to rely entirely on a visual fix if he was to follow the approach to the capital. The difficulty was that his own initial flight path, if he was to do this, lay dangerously near the approach and departure air lanes leading to and from Fuhlsbüttel.

Soon, as the Mitchell clawed its way higher, the street plan of Hamburg printed itself on the darkness below in curves and rectangles and long, straight lines of brilliance. Beyond the pale ribbon of the Elbe with its flaring dockyards, the waters of the Alster gleamed. Away to the north, Aletti could see the flare paths and twinkling runway lights of Fuhlsbüttel. He had decided to climb higher than the Dakota stream: in moonlight this bright, he reasoned, reflections from the wings or blisters of an aircraft would be easier to spot than a silhouette viewed from below.

At six and a half thousand feet he levelled out, throttled back and began circling in wide sweeps over the dark countryside between the southern limits of Hamburg and the estimated position of the Egesdorf beacon.

The glare of the city faded behind them. Once, several hundred feet lower down, a four-engined plane ablaze with flashing markers and cabin lights slid beneath, flying north on the approach to Fuhlsbüttel. Minutes later three Hawker Tempest single-seaters streaked past, heading for the distant sea. So far there had been no sign of the transport planes the fighters had been drafted to Germany to protect.

Aletti was still sweating, straining his eyes left and right past the Perspex and ahead through the windshield. Apart from manoeuvring the Mitchell, the safety factor was an additional heavy load on his shoulders: other aircraft legitimately in the sky carried identification lights; he could see them, but they couldn't see him. The responsibility of avoiding a collision was entirely his. 'I'm transferring to the bomb aimer's blister,' Riordan said. 'There'll be a wider field of view than we have here.' He left his seat and crawled forward through the tunnel beneath the cockpit.

He plugged in the intercom. 'If the Dakotas are leaving Schleswigland at four-minute intervals,' he said to the pilot, 'and flying at an airspeed of one-two-five, there should be a gap of approximately 10.5 miles between any two planes in the stream, right?'

'Check.'

'So, theoretically, if we happened to intercept the stream midway between two aircraft, the one ahead would be more than five miles away – probably too far for us to see it, even with this bright moon.'

'And so?'

'So, for the sake of argument, suppose we did hit the stream at such a point, and the speed and radius of our circle were such that we continued to do this every single time we came round – well, we could fly all bloody night and never see anything at all.'

'Argument, he says! Here's a guy he's vectored on to a negative wavelength already,' said Aletti. 'A fine thing.'

Riordan grinned. 'I'm just suggesting that, if we tightened our circle for a few turns – and then maybe widened the radius more than it is now – we'd have more of a chance, mathematically, of sighting one of the buggers than we do now.'

'Wilco,' Aletti said.

The Mitchell banked steeply. In the narrow confines of the cabin, the mercenaries choroused their discomfort and discontent. Aletti, as they very well knew, could not hear them: the only intercom in service was that linking the positions of pilot and bomb aimer. It was simply a way of relaxing the tension, of voicing their frustration at the forced inactivity. A modern jet traveller accustomed to high-speed, high-altitude pressurized transport would scarcely recognize a 1940s warplane as an aircraft at all. Oxygen masks were obligatory at anything over eight thousand feet. Conversation without earphones was impossible since the entire machine shook and rattled and shuddered with the appalling racket of the piston engines. Owing to their low power-to-weight ratio, the planes pitched and yawed, or dropped and rose like a lift at the mercy of the slightest turbulence, demanding all a pilot's strength to keep the non-power-assisted control surfaces in the airstream. Under such conditions, the 'passengers' on a long hop – cramped into an unheated, windowless space, unable to see out, denied any form of communication – were subjected to severe strain, particularly if the pilot was obliged to throw the aircraft around in the sky or make any abrupt manoeuvres.

Teddy Nelson-Harmer, the late arrival from London, was wedged into the narrowest part of the fuselage, behind the bomb bay. Although he had worked with Riordan before, he was a stranger to the other members of the team. Perhaps it was the extra sense of isolation that this brought which tempted him to disobey instructions, release his safety belt and make his way forward. He climbed the step into the cockpit and sank into the navigator's seat beside Aletti.

The Nigerian was a big man, perfectly proportioned. His skin was of a polished ebony hue so dark that it was almost blue. His hair was cut very close to his head and the line of his upper lip was echoed by a neat moustache. Like his father and grandfather, he was a graduate of Cambridge; like them he bore in his proud, aristocratic features the unmistakable heritage of many centuries of kings and tribal chieftains. (He had in fact as a student been a victim of reverse racial prejudice, his father, a famous advocate, having threatened to disinherit him if he dared to return to Africa with a white wife.)

Aletti looked at him and grinned. He was in truth an incongruous sight: whereas the other mercs were dressed in the guerrilla's uniform of dark slacks and black roll-neck sweater, Nelson-Harmer had arrived in Hamburg too late to change and faced the Mitchell's gleaming instrument panel still wearing an impeccably cut grey pinstripe suit with a silver tie.

He picked up the headphones Riordan had been wearing. 'A target at last,' the pilot's voice told him. 'The boss picked her up ten minutes ago. Maybe now we can keep on an even keel awhile.' Aletti pointed through the windshield, down and about fifteen degrees to starboard.

Nelson-Harmer leaned forward, shielding his eyes from the moon-white glare with one hand. Immediately below, blast furnaces pumped crimson light above a tangle of railway lines. It took him several minutes to locate their quarry. A fleeting glimpse, pale above a darker blur – a stretch of woodland perhaps – allowed him to concentrate on the right sector of sky. Then he had it. Astonishing, once you had homed in correctly, not to have seen it before: a blunt-nosed, twin-engined plane with a single rudder, gliding easily over the hilly landscape half a mile to the west and several hundred feet below them.

They watched the pale shape, silvery in the wan brilliance of the moon, plane its way above the sinuous curls of a river, past the lights of a small town. A light flashed intermittently from its starboard wing-tip. 'Crazy, ain't it?' Aletti said. 'Alone in all that sky. We can see him; he don't know we're here. We might think he was a loner – but that Dakota's just one of an endless stream of aircraft flying in and out of Berlin day and night.'

'What did you say?' Nelson-Harmer's voice was a deep and lazy drawl.

'I said you'd never know he was part of a continuous stream . . .'

'But you did say a Dakota?'

'What else? Can you think of another reason why we should be up here in this freezing machine, traipsing half-way across hostile Germany? Of course it's a Dakota.'

Nelson-Harmer had not been part of the team's original briefing, nor had he heard the reasoning which resulted in the decision to follow the Schleswigland stream to Berlin. 'The only thing,' he said diffidently, 'is that the plane's not a Dakota; it's an Anson.'

'What?' Aletti's yelp almost cracked the earpiece.

'An Avro Anson. There's a resemblance, I grant you, especially from above, but the configuration . . .'

'Are you sure?'

'Certainly I'm sure. Aircraft identification was my strong point when I was in the University Air Squadron. I got ninety-six per cent when we were up before the selection board. It's an Anson all right.'

'Now he tells me!' Aletti groaned. 'Oh, Jesus God. Captain, art thou listening there below?'

'I heard,' Riordan's voice said in the earphones.

Ten minutes later and thirty miles further north, they were circling again. The Dakota stream was as elusive as ever. 'I *thought* we were too far to the west,' Riordan complained. 'That bloody Anson. Must have been ferrying top brass down to Wunstorf. Or even Bonn if the champagne supplies have lasted.'

The lights of Hamburg were swinging around the Mitchell's greenhouse for the second time when Riordan exclaimed: 'It's no damn use. Following that Anson for more than fifteen minutes has taken us way off course. Without radar, with no means of locating that bloody beacon, we're hopelessly lost. We'll never intersect the northern stream now.'

'What do you want me to do?' Aletti asked.

'Fly east. Then south-east.'

'Yeah, but . . . Jesus! How far east? How many damn degrees south-east?'

'We play it by ear,' Riordan replied brusquely. 'We steer a maverick course and hope to hell we hit Berlin. We should be able to identify Ludwigslust; it's about sixty-five miles due east of here at the confluence of the Elde and the Rognitz. We turn south-east there, about forty degrees.'

'*About* forty degrees, he says!' Aletti exploded. 'High precision already!'

'After that there's not much in the way of sizeable towns; it's all farm land and forest. But if we can locate Pritzwalk, with seven main roads radiating from the town centre, that should lead us on to Neuruppin – at the head of a long, thin lake extending north-west–south-east. Following the line of that should see us on course.'

'Yeah, but if we're not in the corridor . . . ?'

'We might be,' Riordan said; 'we might not be. It's a risk we have to take.'

'And then?'

'Well, if we pass over Oranienburg, we're too far north; if we overfly the Brandenburg lakes, we're too far south for the Gatow approach lanes.'

'A nice, precise flight plan,' Aletti said. 'Very explicit. And if we should be spotted outside the corridor by men with snow on their boots?'

'We'll probably get buzzed by Russian night-fighters,' Riordan said.

'That's all I need,' Aletti said. 'My father he should

spend his declining years visiting the grave of his only son in *Germany*!'

'If you can put the airspeed up to two hundred,' Riordan said, 'we should be approaching Ludwigslust in approximately eighteen to twenty minutes.'

'Not a second too soon,' Aletti said wearily.

The Mitchell droned on above the darkened surface of the earth. Soon the number of lights below diminished. Riordan left the bomb bay and reclaimed his seat next to the pilot. Nelson-Harmer stayed in the cockpit, leaning forward between them. 'We must be over the Soviet zone by now,' he said. 'I wouldn't like to think how many radar sets we're a mysterious blip on.'

'If we're not too far from the corridor, obviously heading for Berlin,' Riordan said, 'it may not matter too much. They have to make allowances for pilot error.' He shrugged. 'Besides, we may still catch sight of a Dakota and latch on to the real thing.'

'Do *they* know they have to make allowances?' Aletti asked.

'If we're too far off course, on the other hand, they'll be asking questions – and we have a radio receiver aboard but we can't transmit, so we won't be able to reply.'

'It seems to me, cock' – white teeth gleamed in the dark face; Nelson-Harmer's English was like something from the pages of Dornford Yates – 'that what we have here is the perfect recipe for hostile action. One hopes our esteemed driver keeps a few aerobatics up the old sleeve.'

'Ludwigslust,' Riordan said tersely. He indicated a group of lights below and a few degrees to port. The converging rivers showed up as silver threads stitching together the pale countryside. Banking, the Mitchell veered south-east. The land tilting towards them now was darker, forested

54

perhaps between swelling hills. Few lights showed ahead, stars dislodged from the northern sky.

They almost missed Pritzwalk, flying ten miles too far to the east. It was Nelson-Harmer who spotted the long, grey ribbons of the macadamized roads arrowing inwards to a barely illuminated town centre off to the right of their flight path.

Aletti changed course again.

Neuruppin was no problem: the lake showed up like polished glass, the surface gleaming in the moonlight. He lined the Mitchell up with the longitudinal axis of the six-mile reach and set the compass.

It was soon after this that Riordan, experimentally twisting knobs, homed in on the angry voice. 'Speaking in Russian,' he said. 'Demanding identification, flight plan, why we're violating their airspace.'

'How do you know it's us he's calling up?' Aletti asked.

'Position. Correct height, airspeed, direction. The fact that we show no lights.'

For a while, as the plane forged ahead, there was no sound from the set but the hiss and crackle of static. The long, bright smear of the lake slid away behind them. Then the harsh voice returned, more menacing than ever.

'He's warning us,' Riordan said. 'Unless we reply at once, action – whatever that means – will be taken.'

'Perfect,' said Aletti. 'You already have a missed rendezvous, mistaken identity, the heroes lost, danger, action, threats. Now they're writing in suspense! The scenario's got everything.'

'How far are we from Berlin?' Nelson-Harmer asked.

'From the centre? Fifteen, eighteen miles. If it wasn't so bloody bright, we'd have seen the glow in the sky already.'

'You want I should still try for Gatow?' Aletti asked. 'We

can't contact the tower, but once we're in visual, I could maybe suss out an approach path and put her down . . . drop her in between two of the Dakota . . .'

He paused. The sudden roar was accompanied by an impact as brutal as a gale-force wind. The plane staggered, seeming almost to halt for a moment in midair. The roar faded to a screech. Through the canopy they saw three Shturmovik single-seater fighters peel off the run which had brought them so close, then plummet away.

'If that's being buzzed, I don't think much of it,' Aletti said.

The fighters re-formed and made a second pass, skimming perilously near the Mitchell, right, then left, before streaking off in different directions.

'That,' Riordan said when the thunder of their passing had dwindled away, 'was just to show us. That they're serious, I mean.'

'Bit of a show-off, wouldn't you say?' Nelson-Harmer observed. 'Line-shooting, if you ask me. We got the point the first time, after all.'

The Spitfire-like fighters shot up the Mitchell a third time, then the flight re-formed once more, throttled back and cruised alongside the old American plane. Inside the canopy, the leader's cockpit was illuminated. They could see his helmeted figure gesticulating, pointing down. 'He's ordering us to follow him in,' Riordan said.

Ahead of them now, incandescent as far as the eye could see, the lights of Berlin blazed into the distance.

'Orders?' Aletti said.

'*Fais semblance*,' Riordan replied.

'How's that again?'

'Make like you're obeying. Start to follow him down.'

'And then?'

'Evasive action. We're way over the Russian sector, and too far north.'

Aletti waggled the Mitchell's wings to signify compliance. They fell in behind the Shturmovik leader, with a fighter flying in close formation on either side. 'I thought Allied ships had free access to the Berlin Control Zone,' the Italian said. 'That's a radius of twenty miles from the Allied Control Commission HQ, and a hell of a lot of that must be over the Soviet sector.'

'Allied ships properly identified as such,' Riordan corrected him. 'In any case we probably penetrated the restricted area surrounding their military airfields at Staaken and Johannisthal. If that's so, and they don't know who the fuck we are – this is a light bomber, remember – they're legally justified in forcing us down.'

'That's nice to know,' Aletti said.

The four planes lost height in widening circles. Very slowly, the lights of Berlin wheeled beneath them. 'They must be making for the field at Schönwalde,' Riordan said.

'Johannisthal's less than five miles from the American field at Tempelhof,' Nelson-Harmer put in. 'Much nearer to our target than Gatow. Do you think, if we made a run for it . . . ?'

'No,' Riordan said tersely. 'The place will be crawling. This is supposed to be a secret operation. It'll be tough enough at Gatow.'

'If we could maybe make the correct corridor,' Aletti began, 'or even the central zone . . .'

'They wouldn't shoot once we were in there,' Riordan said. 'They wouldn't dare. We're already in the wrong, flying without ID, violating their airspace. They wouldn't want to relinquish their moral superiority. I'll bet there are already protests winging their way to each of the Western embassies.'

There was more than once voice in the headphones now. The rasping tones seemed to be jockeying for position, seeking the most telling soapbox. 'A final warning,' Riordan said. 'If we don't continue down like good boys . . .'

'Damned if I take orders from a Russki using a German airfield,' Aletti said suddenly. 'Hang in there – this is where the evasion begins.'

He slammed the throttles forward and hauled the control column savagely back into his belly.

Engines howling, the Mitchell rose up like a startled horse. The nose shot into the sky. The wings shuddered. For an instant the aircraft climbed crazily, then toppled over on to its back in the first half of a loop. Aletti kicked it into a half-roll and it straightened out, screaming back the way it had come after a perfect Immelmann turn.

He banked steeply as the fighters, taken completely by surprise, fell away towards the lights. Ignoring the outraged cries from the mercenaries flung about in the cabin, Aletti roared towards the west.

'By Jove!' Nelson-Harmer exclaimed. 'What a turn-up for the boys! Jolly good show, that man.'

Riordan made no comment. He was studying the street plan pricked out in brightness below. 'About five degrees starboard for Gatow,' he said.

It was less than two minutes later – the illuminations still stretched as far south and west as they could see – that the Nigerian, squatting between the two seats and slightly behind, tapped Aletti on the shoulder. 'Bandits, old man,' he said. 'Four o'clock astern.'

Aletti twisted hastily left, staring over his shoulder. The three fighters, Yakovlev Yak-3s this time, were closing steadily, climbing fast.

Aletti tilted the Mitchell on to one wing-tip and put the nose down.

The lighted streets and squares rushed towards them.

Tracer, luminous and decorative, arced over them from behind and fell away.

'Actually, the Yak's even more like a Spit than a Shturmo,' Nelson-Harmer said. 'If you ask me.'

'What I am asking,' Aletti said, 'is that we should be far enough away not to recognize either.' He kicked the Mitchell into a tight right-hand turn.

The second attack came from below. White streaks of tracer rose lazily towards them, abruptly accelerating with unbelievable velocity to flash past the blister or curve away innocuously beneath it. Momentarily they glimpsed a dark shape with orange flame sparkling from the wings, then the fighter was swept away to be lost in the night.

'Next time they'll be shooting to kill,' Riordan said. 'Christ, we *must* be almost into the Control Zone by now.' He looked over his shoulder. The Yaks, in formation again, were closing. 'Dive!' he snapped.

Aletti flung the plane into a vertical bank and spun into a power dive. Riordan heard the roar of a fighter's engine over the protesting scream of the Wright Cyclones, then the streamlined shadow of a Yak whipped past the blister, hosing tracer and cannon shells harmlessly into the night.

The other Russian pilots had been waiting their turn, holding fire in the blind spot below the Mitchell's tail. Now they too moved in.

'This is their last chance,' Riordan grated. 'Ahead, way ahead after that tower with the red lights, I can see the dark mass of the Grunewald and the moonlight reflected by Havel lake and the Wannsee.'

'Gear!' Aletti yelled, holding the plane in its howling plunge.

Riordan yanked up a lever. There was a sudden roar

from beneath them as hatches opened to allow the oleos to fold outwards with the landing wheels.

At that moment all hell seemed to break loose. The Mitchell lurched heavily, whipped by a stream of tracer and cannon fire lacerating the port wing. Flames leaped from the cowling over the port engine. The blister exploded outwards and a hurricane tore at their clothes and hair. Somewhere beneath their feet, a forceful thumping started.

A red light flashed on the instrument panel. Aletti nodded towards it and gestured in the direction of the noise. 'Undercart's US,' he said. 'Bastards must have shot away one of the oleos. Flapping like a wounded duck.'

'Relax,' Riordan told him. 'They've turned away. We must be in the zone.'

'Relax, he says! With no wheels, an engine on fire and an aeroplane full of holes I should lie back and take it *easy*? Maybe you could do with a cup of coffee and a cigar?'

Riordan smiled. If Alex was being difficult, everything was going to be OK.

Nelson-Harmer returned from the cabin. 'A few more holes in the fuselage,' he announced, 'but nobody's hurt.'

'We were lucky,' Riordan said.

Squeezing his eyes shut against the airstream, Aletti was wrestling with the controls, nursing the crippled plane back on to an even keel, maintaining a shallow dive towards the west. 'Try to put her down at Gatow?' he suggested. 'A belly-flop in the outfield?'

Riordan squinted ahead. Just west of Havel lake, the floodlit airfield was clearly visible now. The pierced steel planking runways had not been laid yet, and most of the surface was grass. A Dakota was touching down near the control tower, a second was waiting to take off on the return flight, and a third — a shadow circling above one of the radio masts — was waiting to land. 'I guess not,' he said.

'Too public, too congested, and without an undercarriage the ground's too hard.'

'You know a softer place? Or you want us to stay in the sky all night?'

'I know a softer place. Lower her gently into the lake. It's more convenient anyway; less of a walk to our RDV.'

Aletti jerked his head towards the port wing. One of the flaps had broken off and whipped away in the slipstream. The cowling detached itself from the engine, flapping over the wing like an enraged bird before it vanished into the void. The engine glowed red, brightening to orange as tongues of fire, licking the pod, began to spread inward. 'You should be so lucky,' Aletti said.

He was sweating, eyes darting from dials and gauges to the flaming wing as the city streamed past below. The thumping from below was growing heavier. Very slowly the chain of lakes and the dark woodland to the east of them drew nearer. The roar of the remaining engine died to a subdued clatter.

'Hit a sheet of water at fifty miles per hour,' Aletti said conversationally, 'you might as well run against a wall of reinforced concrete.'

'Not with a genius at the wheel,' Riordan said.

The Mitchell planed down towards the moonlit surface of the lake. Aletti was punishing the stick, struggling to compensate for the loss of power and lift on the port side. 'Flaps,' he muttered. 'Pitch.' He stroked the column back now as tenderly as a lover to flatten the stricken plane out ten feet above the water that was all at once rushing frighteningly up to meet them.

The airspeed indicator needle sank back past the hundred and twenty mark to a hundred . . . ninety . . . eighty-five . . . eighty. At the last moment, as the Mitchell slowed to its stalling speed, he cut the motor and lifted the nose.

The plane flopped down on to the lake like a bird in a duck shoot.

The impact was harder – and louder – than they imagined: a tearing, splintering crash overlaid with the screech of tortured metal that jarred every bone in their bodies. In the silence that followed, the slap and chuckle of inrushing water, the hiss of the burning engine as it sank beneath the surface, was almost deafening.

'All right, let's go,' Riordan shouted. 'Into the dinghy and head for the east bank, OK?'

He knew they had less than two minutes before the water chased out the air lending the wreck its buoyancy and the plane sank. The belly hatch was already submerged. Dragooned by Pieter Van Eyck, the mercenaries swarmed up into the cockpit. Riordan had no idea how deep the lake was: it might have been shallow, or the bed might have been far enough down to swallow the Mitchell and leave no trace. In any case they had to get away fast, before police or would-be rescuers arrived on the scene.

The rubber dinghy, already packed with such arms and supplies as they had, inflated automatically on contact with the water. Aletti was the last to leave. As he stepped over the padded cockpit rim, he patted the shattered fuselage and murmured: 'She was a good ship, game to the last.'

Three of the Mitchell's formers had snapped when they hit the lake, leaving her sprawled on the surface like a bird with a broken back. She was already low in the water, the port wing drowned and the other canting skywards.

Water was gurgling into the cockpit as they pushed off and paddled towards the east bank, away from the drone of Dakotas and the approaching sirens.

6

The rendezvous was in an abandoned fish loft above one of the boat-houses on the eastern bank of the Havel. When it grew warmer and the sun was higher in the sky, the curving lakeside road, the Havelchaussee, would be bright with parked cars – new Volkswagens, Opels, an occasional Mercedes – and the woodland paths would be crowded with couples and families heading for the boating jetties and narrow, sandy bathing beaches. But this year, even in late June, the skiffs were still up-ended beneath tarpaulin, the pleasure beaches were deserted, and the chairs and tables had yet to be put out on the boardwalk terraces of the waterfront cafés. Perhaps the mounting tension between East and West had communicated itself to Berliners only recently released from the horrors of war.

Riordan and his men had almost a mile to walk before they reached the boat-house. They saw nobody, heard nothing from the footpath but the ripple of water and the stealthy, soft drip of moisture from the depths of the oak and pine and silver-birch forest bordering the lake. By the time they climbed the outside staircase to the loft, bleached and cracked by many winters of neglect, the southern reach of the lake was nevertheless busy with salvage teams examining the wreck of the Mitchell in the dawn light. Between the plane, which the lake had not been deep enough to submerge, and the distant

63

Gatow bank there was a constant put-put of official motor boats.

Helmut Brod, the last of the mercenary team, was there to greet them.

A spare man, not very tall, Brod wore his thin, dark hair parted very low down on the left. He could not have been much more than forty, forty-five at the most, yet already his triangular face wore a slightly wizened look, furtive even. He could have been a bank clerk uncertain about his future. In any case he was completely unremarkable and nobody would notice him anywhere – a supreme advantage for a locksmith working on the wrong side of the law.

'Saw your approach. Very spectac!' he said when the team trooped into the loft. 'Enter an aviator, stage left, with flames.'

Sergeant Crawford made a rare foray into the realm of humour. 'We was savaged by a herd of Yaks,' he said solemnly.

'Good thing you weren't discoed when you peeled off,' Brod said. 'The Con Comm types take a poorish view of zonal penetros, especially if the guilts are, so to speak, non-resid.' His English was fluent, almost accentless, but peppered with his own brand of verbal shorthand. Long before the chic intelligentsia in Paris, Brod was eating in restos, drinking his coffee and brandy in a stube, chatting up the prostos in the Ku'damm and watching his cab fare mount up on the taxim on the way home.

'All right, guys,' Riordan said when Van Eyck had shared out the supplies carried up from the dinghy. 'From now on we're at work: you're earning your money.' He looked around at the six men crowded into the loft. It was just the upper floor of a weathered shack, some of the beams still garnished with rusty hooks, hung with faded skeins of net. There was a table and three chairs, one with a broken leg. Through a dusty window there was a view of reeds along the far shore.

'The hotel we're supposed to be staying at is in the Kreuzberg district,' Riordan said. 'It's not far from the hostages. We don't know each other, of course. Some of us booked in yesterday, some today. Two, Crawford and Christal, not until tomorrow.'

'Not the MP and the prisoner again, I hope?' Christal asked with a sidelong glance at the big sergeant. 'I was fucking demobbed, remember?'

'Not the prisoner and escort, no. You're buddies. You'll be wearing army battledress with the flashes and insignia removed. Deserters, perhaps, on the lookout for a quick buck. In that area you'll be a familiar sight.'

'Just like bleeding Novotny,' Christal said. 'If only we had his luck.'

'The block where the hostages are held will have to be approached very discreetly,' Riordan said. 'Never more than one or two at a time. Just to get the general layout fixed in the mind. It'll be sealed off, surrounded by cops and city councillors and salvage men most likely. I can't tell you how we're going to play it until I've recced the building, preferably from the inside. Helped by Brod here, that's what I'll be doing today. The rest of you wait here until late morning, then make your way separately to this crummy hotel.'

He took O'Kelly's sheaf of papers from his pocket, peeled off five photostats and handed one to everyone except Brod. 'This is a street plan of the area,' he told them, 'with the hotel and the block marked.'

'Maybe we better can locate a place to meet nearer the hostages,' Van Eyck said. 'We cannot be all the time going back to this hotel. Not all of us. If we can find nearby an abandoned building perhaps . . . ?'

'Good thinking, Piet,' Riordan said. 'I'll keep an eye open.'

'Will we be going into action tonight, sir?' Crawford asked.

'Maybe. Depends what I find out,' Riordan said. 'There's a beer hall across the street from the hotel. I'll meet you there by accident between five and six.' He turned to Brod. 'Let's go. It's daylight now, and a long walk to the bus.'

'You certainly catted the pidges, coming in on fire, landing on a *lake*, shooting up the comrades,' Brod said as they joined the footpath and turned north. 'No call-sign, no explano, not even any crew. Worst of all, no supplies to salvage for the starving masses!'

'We didn't mean to,' Riordan said. 'We ran out of road when we mistook an Anson for a Dakota. In any case, it was the Russians who did the shooting.'

They came to a fork in the pathway, one route sloping down to the Havelchaussee and the waterfront, the other twisting away among the trees. 'We take the one on the right,' Brod said. 'It's a quicker way to civilization – which is to say the Heerstrasse at the level of the old Olympic Stadio and the Corbusier building. From there we can take a bus or the S-Bahn straight to the Tiergarten and the Brandenburger Tor.'

He started back as there was a sudden quick rustle in the undergrowth at one side of the path. He halted with a restraining hand on Riordan's arm. The squat shape of a blued-steel automatic pistol had appeared in his free hand.

The rustle was repeated, nearer the path. The lower branches among a clump of bushes moved. A white cat streaked across the path and vanished between the close-packed trunks of a young birch plantation.

Brod laughed nervously, stowing away the gun. 'You never know,' he said.

'One more to put among the pigeons,' Riordan said.

7

Berlin was an injured beauty suffering from post-operative trauma who nevertheless insisted on lipstick and mascara before she would receive visitors. Marshall Aid, the desire of most Berliners to escape from the stigma of Nazism, and the determination, at some time in the future, to regain a respected place in the European economy had combined to produce what was already referred to as 'the economic miracle'. The new currency indeed, according to the Western Allies, was backed 'not by gold but by the German people's industry, their tradition of hard work'.

But there were, of course, inconsistencies, cracks in the enamelled features which became evident on closer inspection.

The Kurfürstendamm, for instance, that renowned two-mile boulevard of restaurants, cafés, theatres, cinemas, nightclubs and fashionable shops, was brilliant with festive lights and chic window displays offering the most prestigious new designs in clothes, jewellery, glassware and electrical appliances.

Yet a single glance would reveal that the elegant nineteenth-century façades, from the second storey up, were still windowless and gaping. Through many of the fire-blackened embrasures it was possible in daylight to see, on the waste land behind the gutted building, one of the immense mountains of bomb-damage rubble which had become a feature of postwar Berlin. These dusty artificial heights, some of them rising a hundred feet above the rebuilt roofs of the city, had been thrown up to clear the choked streets in the immediate postwar period – grim reminders of the wholesale carnage and destruction suffered through Allied air raids and the ruthless Russian advance in April and May 1945. They were less common in the Soviet sector, where reconstruction in the staid Russian style had taken precedence over reindustrialization, although there was one only a block away from the conference centre in which the hostages were held.

This rambling 1930s complex with its mock-heroic sculptured façade – which had miraculously escaped both the bombs and the Soviet artillery – was bordered in front by a severely rectangular public garden and behind by a tangle of narrow streets, some of them still flanked by abandoned and damaged houses. Uncompromisingly functional, except for that sandstone façade, the nine-storey building was situated west of the looping River Spree, in a triangle bounded by Alexanderplatz, Karl-Marx-Allee and the wide Landsberger Strasse. Its floor plan resembled two Es placed back to back, the central arm on each side being joined to the main block only by a covered walkway at fifth-floor level. It was on the top floor of one of these semi-detached blocks that the kidnappers had barricaded themselves and their hostages.

The inner end of the walkway was covered day and night by men with sub-machine-guns, the terrorists had announced, and the staircases and lifts rising from the ground floor were similarly protected. Police had evacuated the entire complex once the abduction was made public.

Brod and his leader arrived separately, the Viennese soon after nine o'clock, Riordan later, after he had checked in at the hotel.

The conference centre was cordoned off by police and an army detachment, and the public garden was littered with floodlights, a troop carrier, three police vans with wire-reinforced windows, and two fire department turntables shining with brass. Half a dozen specialized marksmen with high-velocity rifles stood talking to a uniformed police officer and a Russian colonel holding a loud-hailer.

So far as Riordan could see there were no sightseers. He wandered towards the police vans behind the line of soldiers. Before he had gone fifty yards, a policeman approached and held up a warning hand. 'Where do you think you are going?' he said curtly.

'To the Philharmonia. I want to buy tickets for the concert . . .'

'Take the next block; the road's closed this way.'

'But this is the most direct.'

'I said it's closed.' The policeman took Riordan's arm and spun him around. 'Come on. Get moving.'

'What's going on here anyway?' Riordan decided to test the strength of official discouragement. 'Isn't this where those hostages are being held?'

'No business of yours.'

'But surely one has the right to ask . . . ?'

'Your papers,' the man snapped.

In case his German accent was less than perfect, Riordan had been provided with a Yugoslav passport in the name of Mischa Sujic. He produced the dog-eared document. The official flicked over the pages, glanced from the photograph to Riordan's face, and handed it back. 'Foreign visitors should learn not to meddle with affairs that do not concern them,' he said.

'I was only asking.'

'Keep your questions to yourself. Sometimes it is wiser to

remain silent. Now move on. Get going.' Riordan received a shove in the back, and moved on.

A block away from the cordon, he circled around and approached the conference centre from behind, through the network of dark, bomb-damaged streets. Here too he found that the building had been isolated from the curious. Uniformed police blocked off all five of the cobbled lanes leading to or curving around the centre's island site.

The quarter seemed half deserted anyway. Many of the windows were boarded up, and in more than one case the road was cracked and deformed, pitted with yellow puddles. Between the blackened rafters of one house the sky was visible.

Riordan heard no radio, no voices, male or female. In a weed-covered patch of waste ground strewn with iron bedsteads, bicycle wheels and old motor tyres, a mangy dog sniffed around the rusted and gutted carcass of a pre-war delivery van shored up on bricks. At a crossroads fifty yards away, a tired-looking woman with a string bag full of vegetables limped along the street and went into a corner bar advertising a brand of beer Riordan had never heard of.

He followed her in. The place was poorly lit, heady with the malty reek of Pils. There was sawdust on the floor. Three unshaven men wearing shiny-peaked bargee caps sat playing cards at a table scarred with cigarette burns. He ordered a tankard of dark beer from the surprisingly handsome and well-dressed barman, turning to rest his elbows on the counter and survey the room.

The woman with the bag was already gulping a glass of schnapps. Beneath a mirror decorated in one corner with coloured art-nouveau flowers, Brod sat nursing a long-stemmed glass of white wine. Riordan ignored him.

He drank his beer slowly, made a very slight movement with his head, paid the barman and left.

Brod caught him up as he stood waiting to cross the road at the next corner. A low-slung, racy convertible – the first vehicle he had seen since he entered the quarter – was turning into the side-street. He stared at it appreciatively as it bumped away along the cobbles: a streamlined two-seater with faired-in headlights, a twin-grille radiator cowling and spatted rear wheels. 'Very nice,' Riordan said. 'A BMW 328 – '37 or '8. Wish I could have afforded one when I was younger.'

They crossed the street. 'They seem to have the place pretty well locked up, don't they?' Brod said. 'At least in daylight.'

'What? The conference centre? They certainly do. At night too, judging by those floods. I'd rate the chances of a ground-level entry at precisely nil.'

'And so?'

'So we're left with below ground – or above ground.' Riordan nodded towards the far side of the street. Above the sagging rooflines of the quarter, at one side of the rubble mountain, the gantry of one of the huge telescopic cranes used in the construction of high-rise buildings swung in a slow arc across the bright sky.

'And below?' Brod said.

'We'll have to study the conduit plans and electricity diagrams very carefully.'

'Suppose both those approaches prove imposs?'

'Nothing's impossible,' Riordan said. 'It's just that, as the song says, the impossible takes a little while.'

They passed a small food store with a dingy window display of canned soups, root vegetables, wrapped bread and wursts under a dusty glass bell. Two women wearing headscarves stood talking beside a rack of newspapers on the pavement. Brod took a paper and left a coin in a tin cup.

'Seven guys crawling through a drain, or even splashing through some system of catacombs – that's going to present problems just the same,' he said. 'I mean logistics, supplies, noise, when to come up.'

'I plan to make an entry myself first,' Riordan said. 'Inspect all those points. Investigate the interior layout of the block, possible exits and escape routes, cover. Ideally, I'd want to smuggle myself inside the part where the hostages are held, and if possible contact one of the ones it's important to rescue.'

'Rather you than me,' Brod said.

'Don't be too sure. I may need your help with locks.'

The silence of the old quarter had grown less oppressive. The ring of their footsteps on the pavement was not so noticeable. Children screeched in the distance, sliding down the rubble mountain in soapbox sledges. Beyond the next lane, two hundred yards away, they heard the blaring of horns as traffic circled a roundabout.

'Yeah, but suppose there are no conduits, no catacombs; suppose the crane doesn't reach far enough – if that's what you're thinking. How do we get in to get them out then?' Brod queried.

'In that case,' Riordan said, 'we'd need a man-sized diversion, nothing less than a nearby bomb or a gun battle, to draw the law's attention momentarily away from the block.'

'Maybe that would be the simplest solute of the prob?'

'It would get us in,' Riordan said. 'But even if we managed to . . . settle the matter in secret, there'd still be the problem of getting the product away without anyone knowing.' They started to cross the lane.

'Does even a successful result have to be kept under wraps?' Brod said. 'I should have thought . . .'

'Look out!' Riordan yelled.

Shoving the Viennese violently in the small of the back, he hurled himself into a recessed doorway behind as a car, two wheels on the pavement, exhaust billowing, shot towards them with manic speed.

It was the BMW. Dawdling at the far end of the lane, it had crept forward when they appeared, and then shot fiercely towards them the instant they stepped into the roadway. Missing Riordan's fleeing figure by a hair's breadth, the front bumper struck sparks from the masonry at one side of the doorway before the wheels thumped back on to the cobbles and the car turned into the street. Accelerating away, the convertible was almost at once lost to sight among the cars, buses and army lorries on the roundabout.

Riordan was at the lane's exit, a 9mm Browning automatic in one hand, still shouting when the attacker vanished. The BMW's windows had been raised, the low-slung black canvas top was in place, so it had been impossible to catch even a glimpse of the driver. Riordan turned back into the lane. His push, which had certainly saved Brod's life, had sent the safe-breaker sprawling on the greasy cobblestones. Riordan helped him up. 'No damage, I hope?' he asked.

Brod shook his head, brushing off his trousers with one hand. 'A grazed knee perhaps, lacerated palms, self-esteem badly bruised. But thanks, just the same. Instead of iodine and sticking plaster, it could have been a coffin.' He shook his head again. 'Nice people, those who own the kind of transport you envy.' He stooped to pick up the newspaper, which had flown from his hand. It had opened as it fell, half the pages sinking into a puddle. Brod shook away the sodden portions, glanced at the headlines on the inside page he held, and grinned.

'Something funny?' Riordan asked.

'For you,' Brod said, 'fame at last.' He handed over the paper.

It was a late edition, the ink still smudged on the page. Riordan read: 'GHOST PLANE IN WANNSEE NIGHT LANDING.'

The story beneath the headline was in bold type and boxed in a panel at the top of the page:

'Berliners awakened by the sound of gunfire last night were astonished to see, arriving from the Soviet sector, an aircraft apparently on fire. The machine was thought to have crossed, perhaps inadvertently, one of the military restricted areas in that zone. Rapidly losing height, it passed over the limits of the airfield at Gatow and made a forced landing in the Havel section of the Wannsee.

'Soviet authorities are reported already to have made representations to the Allied Control Commission, alleging airspace violation. Yet none of the occupying powers has any knowledge of the aircraft, a B-25 Mitchell of American design. None of the control towers, at Gatow, Tempelhof or Tegel, had been contacted by any unexpected arrival. Stranger still, salvage crews arriving at the scene within minutes of the crash found no sign of any crew members, alive or dead.

'Most mysterious of all, American authorities liaising with the USAF report that examination of certain numbered components within the wreck show that this aircraft was shot down and totally destroyed, with the loss of all the crew, in northern Germany in March 1945. Officially the machine, whose remains can be seen in the lake today, does not exist.

'We await with interest some explanation for the manifestation of our aerial "ghost".'

'It certainly disturbed the local pigeons, our white cat!' Riordan said. 'Thank God we got the rubber dinghy out of the way. There's nothing whatever to connect the plane or its possible use with the hostage situation here in East Berlin.'

'OK,' Brod said, 'but Christ, what about this damn BMW? I mean, face it, this is attempted murder we're talking about here.'

Riordan's expression was sombre. 'I know,' he said. 'And this is not the first time. My car was booby-trapped within two hours of the original briefing. Somebody wants to stop us doing what we're paid to do. The thing is, who? Who wants to make sure those hostages remain in that block with those terrorists?'

'The rivals in Egypt and West Africa and the Gulf who aim to displace the three most important ones?' Brod said.

'Oh, sure. But I don't think any of them have a long enough arm to reach into eastern Germany. Certainly they'll try to profit from the situation once it's arisen, but I can't see them instigating it. For me, the answer has to be much nearer home. Even so ... well, why would anyone want to squash a possible rescue attempt when nobody seems to be stirring themselves to resolve the situation anyway? Why not just leave them there with their captors?'

'Search me,' Brod said. 'They say the abductos are asking impossible terms. Who are they asking exactly? Not the Russkis, I imagine.'

'The countries their prisoners come from, I guess – each, maybe, to pay what the trade will carry, according to the importance of the hostage.'

'That doesn't make sense. Those countries would have to hold meetings to confer. It could take months. Unless of course they expect the occupying powers to chip in and take over. Not that I think they'd be interested.'

'You have a point there,' Riordan said slowly. 'It's almost as though the kidnappers didn't want their terms to be agreed; as if they'd deliberately made them unacceptable. But why?'

'You tell me,' Brod said.

'We'll put it to the others, back at the hotel,' Riordan said. 'See if they've got any ideas. Meanwhile we have to worry about the leak. There has to be a leak. Shit, how many people knew you and I would be prospecting that part of the old town today? The toughest thing is, this kind of situation makes you begin to suspect your own.'

'None of us could have pulled your car-bomb thing,' Brod said. 'You hadn't contacted any of us: we didn't know there was a job to fuck up.'

'True. None of it makes sense, does it? Unless of course the aim of the operation is to make us suspect each other?'

'Whoever's doing it,' Brod said, 'must be familiar with every detail of our brief.'

Further analysis of the mystery had to be postponed when they arrived at the hotel. There was an ambulance parked on the gravelled turning area below the steps leading to the entrance. Sunlight gleamed on shards of glass scattered among the geraniums below a broken window on the ground floor.

'It's Van Eyck, sir – the Dutchman,' Crawford reported, refraining with an effort from snapping into a salute. 'Sitting in that window, he was, with a glass of beer, when some bugger with a rifle shot him from a car parked across the road.'

8

'I was lucky, damn lucky, that's all,' Van Eyck said. 'I am swilling some beer, see. With peanuts. I throw one peanut up to my mouth, but – careless Piet! – I miss and the peanut drops. It is when I lean suddenly forward to pick it from my lap that the swine out there fires. Paff! I am hit; but only – how do you say? creased? – yes, only creased. KO for ten minutes and a heart attack for the sergeant. One strip of sticking plaster later, and the nurse who has been called helps me up so that I can call for more beer, because mine is spilled.' He grinned. 'Only this time I figure it wise to order also a schnapps, with the beer as chaser.'

'Lucky is right,' Riordan said soberly. 'It could have been curtains. There's someone with a little too much chutzpah working here.' He told the assembled mercenaries about his own narrow escape and that of Brod. 'One thing's for sure,' he said, 'and that is that we're moving out of here. Fast.'

'Where to, squire?' Christal asked.

'I'm not telling a soul,' Riordan said. 'For obvious reasons. Then, if we're rumbled wherever we hole up, we'll know the leak can't have come from inside.'

Van Eyck nodded, wincing as one hand flew up to touch the gauze pad taped above his left ear. 'I am thinking that is a good idea,' he said. 'Two good ideas in fact . . .'

He broke off as Christal nudged him into silence. The cat

burglar nodded towards the staircase which curled down towards the hotel lobby beside the reception desk.

'By Jove!' Teddy Nelson-Harmer said appreciatively.

The young woman slowly descending with one hand on the polished wooden rail was not particularly tall, nor was she especially slim. But she distilled with every suave movement of her body an essence of femininity so compelling, so packed with allure that the eyes of every man in the room locked upon her as inevitably as an iron bar on an electromagnet.

She was wearing a pale-grey skirt with a crisp crimson blouse that was so dark it was almost black. Her silk stockings were dark too, and her full lower lip was of the kind known as bee-stung.

That was the first impression Riordan received. It was to be added to very shortly by others equally intriguing. The girl halted on the bottom stair, poised inquisitively as she gazed at the seven men in the lobby. 'Goodness!' she exclaimed, her voice low and a little husky. 'What a pleasure to see so many guests at the same time! We don't normally have many clients at this time of year.'

Riordan was on his feet. 'Good afternoon, Fräulein. Forgive me, but you are part of the management, perhaps?'

The girl laughed. 'No, no. It is just that I am living here for the moment.'

'In that case' – Nelson-Harmer was at his smoothest – 'perhaps you would permit us to offer you an aperitif?'

'Thank you,' she said. 'I would like that. You are very kind.'

'A delight for us to find so charming a companion,' Van Eyck said.

'Do please sit down,' Riordan urged.

She settled herself in an upholstered chair with a high back and padded arms. Within the loose but well-cut clothes she moved her ample body like a practised whore, yet appeared totally unaware of the effect she provoked. The chair, with its rather severe lines, served both to emphasize the richness of her curves and at the same time lend her an aura of vulnerability.

Nelson-Harmer had gone to fetch the receptionist. The hotel was small, inexpensive, and there was no barman as such. 'And what are you all doing here? Are you together? Are you attending the convention at Prenzlauerberg?'

'Only some of us,' Riordan said quickly, picking up that ball and running with it. 'No, we met here quite by chance. My colleague and I' – he indicated Van Eyck – 'are connected in a small way with the Control Commission. Our Nigerian friend is a lawyer, and these other gentlemen, I understand, have business interests of one kind or another.'

Nelson-Harmer returned carrying a tray laden with glasses and a bottle of *Sekt*. He popped the cork and started to pour.

'And what do you yourself do?' Riordan continued. 'If it is not indiscreet to ask?' He found the gaze of her wide violet eyes, part contemplative, part questioning, curiously unsettling. Her dark hair, cut fairly close, covered her head with springy curls. He felt an insane desire to clench his fingers in it.

Her name, she told them, was Dagmar Harari. Her mother was Hungarian and her father Lebanese. She was a linguist, an interpreter, with a diploma from an international school in Geneva. 'There is a group of us, here in Berlin,' she said. 'A pool, members of a European federation of translators. They can call on us whenever there are conferences, four-power meetings, press occasions, trade fairs, that kind of thing.'

'Sometimes,' Aletti said, 'and I should drop dead if I'm

telling a lie, sometimes we could use your services even among ourselves!'

'It must be a very interesting way to earn a living,' Nelson-Harmer said.

'Oh, it is.' Dagmar smiled, sipping her *Sekt*. 'When it's not infuriating. I'm on call, for instance, for the Prenzlauerberg convention. And the Control Commission meeting next week. If it takes place. But the most interesting work I have at the moment is much nearer here.'

'Oh, really?' Riordan said. 'And what is that?'

'Well, you probably won't have heard, if you have just arrived in Berlin, but there is an international . . . well, an international "incident" really, at another of the city's conference centres. A band of criminals have taken some important foreigners prisoner and are holding them hostage. They want money, of course, and revolutionaries let out of jail, and other things. But nobody can agree to anything, and nothing so far is happening – mainly because none of the terrorists speak German, and nobody official here seems to speak their language. Which is where I come in, because I do.' She took another sip from her glass. 'As their interpreter,' she said, 'I am at the moment the kidnappers' sole link with the outside world.'

There was a sudden silence.

'How very interesting,' Riordan said slowly at last. 'And what is the language the kidnappers speak?'

'Oh, one of the Arabic dialects,' Dagmar said.

'And you translate their demands into German and communicate them . . . to whom exactly?'

'Basically the East German police, but there are always Soviet officers present, so I usually have to translate again.'

'And then you take the replies back to . . . to the conference centre?'

'Well, yes. But there's very little in the way of negotiations to deal with. There seems to be a stalemate there. The criminals have made their demands; the authorities have said no. Many times. Both sides seem content to leave things like that – except for the poor hostages, of course. Most of the work I do concerns demands for food or clothing and suchlike. Arranging even the delivery of radios! It's crazy: like running . . . well running some kind of hotel by remote control.'

'Do you actually go *into* the quarters where the hostages are held?' Riordan asked.

'Oh, no. Nothing as interesting as that. I have to stand at the end of a walkway, and a man comes to talk to me. With another man who has a gun.'

'When you approach the block – crossing that stretch of open ground like some kind of public garden – and when you return with the message, are you escorted?'

'As far as the main building, yes. By an armed policeman usually. But the kidnappers won't allow him to come all the way. He has to remain by the elevators, otherwise they won't keep the rendezvous.'

'So from the fifth-floor lift shaft to the far end of the walkway, you are quite alone?'

'Oh,' Dagmar said, 'so you know the centre? How very . . . unexpected.'

'Just passing by. Taking a look at the scene of the crime, that's all.'

'Normally they discourage anyone, well, unofficial.'

'Yes,' Riordan said, 'they do, don't they?'

On the traffic island in the middle of the roundabout at the far end of the old quarter there was a telephone kiosk. At dusk Riordan closed himself in and dialled a number he had memorized in O'Kelly's office in Paris.

The receiver was picked up on the third ring. A male voice, with a rising inflexion, said simply: 'Yes?'

'The sixth ring,' Riordan said. 'In twenty seconds.'

'Very well. Understood.'

He replaced the instrument, timed twenty seconds by his watch, lifted the phone again and dialled a different number. On the sixth ring, the connection was made and the same male voice said: 'Listening.'

'Riordan. I have a shopping list. We only have handguns.'

'Give me the list.'

The mercenary leader read out a catalogue of arms, ammunition and equipment from a slip of paper which he took from an inner pocket.

The list was repeated, and then: 'That will take two hours. Where do you want delivery?'

Riordan gave an address, followed by coordinates from an official street plan identifying every building in the quarter. 'It's an abandoned house with half the roof missing,' he said, 'next to a vacant lot that's probably an old bomb-site. There's a wreck, an old lorry, shored up on bricks in the lot.'

'We'll find it,' the voice said. 'Two hours.' The line went dead.

Riordan appeared to be coughing as he left the kiosk. His hand went to his mouth. As he crossed the road, he was chewing up and swallowing the paper with the coordinates and the shopping list.

The abandoned house, not far from the tavern where he had encountered Brod, had for several reasons seemed to Riordan a good place to set up a base camp. It was in a street that was largely deserted; it was within a few hundred yards of the hostages; because of the vacant lot, it could be approached – and entered – in more ways than one; and despite the exposed rafters of the roof, it was sheltered and secure enough on the shuttered ground floor. Moreover, through the lot, and a network of alleys and lanes behind it, any comings and goings would remain completely unconnected with the street on which the frontage stood. To all intents and purposes the house was still uninhabited, abandoned.

Riordan had checked all these details as soon as he had finished talking to Dagmar Harari, for it was imperative, after the second attack on him and the failed attempt on Van Eyck, that they leave the hotel at once. Even if they didn't say they were not going to return.

There was little point, after all, planning a secret operation if the base from which you hoped to operate was already blown.

It was after dark when Brod unlocked the rear door of the building — it took him all of fifteen seconds — and the mercs began to arrive. Carefully briefed by Riordan, Nelson-Harmer and Crawford, possible deserters in battle-dress with no insignia, approached cautiously by way of the vacant lot. They slid in through a gap in the board fence at the rear of the weed-covered site, zigzag-ging bent double between hillocks of rubble until they reached the tumbledown wall around the backyard of the house. If anyone saw them shin over this, thinking perhaps squatters were moving in, they weren't saying anything. In Berlin in 1948 it was as well to keep your mouth shut.

In the distance there was a wail of music — accordions perhaps? a group of violins? — and somewhere not too far away a sports commentator on the radio was waxing hysterical over a football match. The moon was not yet up, but the illuminations in the city centre cast a sulphurous glow on the underside of a cloud bank which had blown up from the east.

Aletti sneaked in over a succession of walls, braving the barking of dogs, a clatter of dustbins and an overpowering stench of rotting fruit. Christal had found an alley that led to a closed carpenter's shop three houses away. Making use of an outside storage shed aromatic with sawn pine, he reached a pipe leading to the roof. Once there he headed east and let himself into the hideaway between the blackened rafters above the top floor. Van Eyck, clutching his gun case with its precious contents, was dragged in through a pantry window as he crept along an unlit lane on the far side of the house from the lot.

Fifteen minutes after his arrival there was a loud knock on the back door. The mercenaries were in what had once been the front parlour of the house – a fifteen-foot square of bare boards and peeling walls with a bricked-up entrance door and a narrow fireplace vomiting a cascade of soot. Riordan held up a hand for silence.

Dust swirled in a thin beam of light penetrating the crack between two boards covering the window. On the floor above, something settled and there was a patter of . . . what? Cement dust? Plaster flaking from a wall?

All seven men held their breath. Now they could hear the stealthy drip of water from the rear of the house. The knock was not repeated.

Riordan was holding his Browning automatic in one hand. He crept down a short passageway and eased himself into the ransacked kitchen. By the back door, he paused, listening. Just the water dripping, a little louder now, and a distant rumble of traffic. In the darkness, he felt for the heavy bolt and chain securing the door. He pressed down the latch, and slid the bolt and chain free. There was no sound from the far side of the door.

Standing well away from the opening, he jerked it wide.

A large, shabby suitcase was standing on the step.

There was no sign of whoever had left it there. O'Kelly's backup organization was living up to its director's boasts.

Riordan dragged the suitcase into the kitchen. It was exceedingly heavy. He humped it into the front room.

'Special delivery,' he announced. 'As ordered. At least something goes right.'

The ray of light, filtering through from a distant street-light, gleamed dully on a partly rusted lock and two brass clasps. Christal produced a miniature stainless-steel tool and opened the lock. He sprang back the clasps and threw open the suitcase lid. In the gloom, there was a sudden waft of mildew, overlaid by the metallic odour of machine oil.

Riordan plunged a hand into the case, withdrawing it with a powerful hooded torch. He switched on the flattened beam.

The mercenaries crowded around to approve the rest of the contents. Coils of rope. Climbing tackle. Black wool Balaclava helmets. Commando knives in leather sheaths. Cat burglar's suction cups for the elbows and knees. A dismantled sniper's rifle wrapped in oiled silk. A variety of hand tools. And five stubby machine-pistols with tubed and perforated silencers.

'The basic soldier of fortune kit,' Riordan said. 'No self-respecting merc should be without one.' He started to unpack the gear, handing out items as he spoke.

'Helmets, Balaclava, one for every man . . . ditto knives . . . suction cups for Danny . . . the rifle for Teddy. Piet already has his Husqvarna. That leaves the SMGs for Crawford, Brod, Aletti, Christal and myself.' He breathed a long sigh of relief. 'At last we're in business. I'm taking off now, maybe for a couple of hours, to recce the target. While I'm away, I want you to familiarize yourselves with the artillery. I mean completely, including assembly, dismantling, loading, action – the lot. If you're in doubt about anything, anything at all, check with Piet or Teddy. They're the gunnery guv'nors.'

'Yeah, but . . . what exactly do we have here?' Christal had picked up one of the machine-pistols in its sacking wrap, and was hefting it in his hand. 'This is a Bergmann design, isn't it?' he said, lifting another package. 'An MP-38, as used by the German security forces. But the first one . . . well, it seems shorter for a start. And I'd swear it wasn't so heavy, either.'

'Correct,' Riordan said. 'The heavier one, as you say, is a German MP-38. Its total length is a shade over two feet. There are three of those. The other two are prototypes, a Czech design provisionally known as the VZ-23. Here the length is reduced to seventeen and a half inches, and the weight to less than seven pounds. Both types are chambered for 9mm Parabellums.'

'I say!' Nelson-Harmer's surprise was evident in the tone of his voice. 'Seventeen and a half, did you say? That's quite something, old man. Simply priceless!'

'Done by bringing the barrel back into the gun body and hollowing out the bolt so that when the breech is closed, most of the bolt lies in front of the breech face and surrounds the barrel. They call it the "overhung" bolt design. Another advantage is that the pistol-grip can be located beneath the centre of gravity and used as the magazine housing. This makes changing a clip in the dark much easier: it's never too hard for one hand to find the other.'

'We better can practise while you are gone,' Van Eyck said. 'We may be needing to do this later tonight. And at least we are having plenty of dark here to work in!'

'Take it easy,' Riordan said. He moved noiselessly from the room. Seconds later they heard the latch of the back door click.

*　　*　　*

Riordan lurked in a doorway on the west side of the conference building. The moon had risen. The shadow of the walkway barred the pale tiles between the main block and the wing where the hostages were held. In a few minutes, he knew, Dagmar Harari would be escorted across from the police line for what appeared to be a nightly conference with the kidnappers' spokesman. The difference on this particular night was that, ten minutes earlier, there had been a power cut that had plunged that part of the Soviet sector into darkness. The floodlights bathing the public garden and the conference centre's façade with brilliance had faded and died, leaving the blacked-out building a cardboard cut-out in the wan glow of the moon.

Astonishingly, the meeting would largely consist of demands for food and drink, laundry supplies, cigarettes and other 'necessities', which would be wheeled across on a trolley the following day and deposited in a ground-floor lift for the terrorists to call up when it suited them. The spokesman would reiterate each night the ransom demands and any modifications which had been made, and Dagmar would then communicate the official reply – with concessions, if any – to the previous day's negotiations.

It was a hell of a way to do business, Riordan thought, reflecting on the plight of the wretched hostages – even if they did have enough to eat, drink and smoke. He wondered if the electricity failure would result in a postponement, or even a cancellation, of the rendezvous. If the authorities were adopting the classic attitude to hostage situations – letting the abductors stew for as long as possible – perhaps it might.

He tensed, sensing movement among the police vans and fire engines, shadowy and indistinct on the far side of the public garden. A four-engined transport, probably an Avro

York, swept low above the rooftops, the motors throttled back as the plane headed for the runway at Gatow, several miles to the west. Nearer still, Riordan could hear the drone of American airlift supplies circling the field at Tempelhof, in the US sector. Then, distorted by a loud-hailer but clear as a bell from the far side of the square, the interpreter's voice. Riordan couldn't identify the language, but it was evident from the tone that she was posing a question.

Somewhere above, perhaps halfway along the southern flank of the fifth floor, a metal-framed window slid open. A man called something into the night.

The loud-hailer replied. As far as Riordan could tell, Dagmar was repeating what she had said before.

This time the response was immediate: a burst of words, harsh with the throaty sounds of some Arabic tongue.

Dagmar signed off with a single word, clearly an affirmative.

The window was closed. Almost at once two figures detached themselves from the police line. A distant murmur of voices. The figures moved between the ordered flower-beds of the garden, approaching the conference centre wing. Two powerful torches were switched on, canted upwards to illuminate the upper halves of a man and a woman: Dagmar, curvaceous in a heavy, pale sweater; the man wearing the green uniform tunic and distinctive protective headgear of a Berlin civil policeman.

Riordan withdrew further into the shadowed doorway as they passed the wing, turned in beneath the walkway and headed for the main block. The doors at the principal entrance, he knew, were ray-actuated. The power cut, he assumed, would have put them out of action; Dagmar and her escort would have to use the doorway sheltering him.

Silently he eased open the glass door and slipped inside the building.

The lobby was a wide, open space with lozenges of moonlight flooding through glass walls across a marble floor. Riordan concealed himself behind a fat circular pillar not far from a bank of six lifts.

Dagmar and the policeman approached the door. The German had a key in one hand. Finding the door unlocked – thanks to a ring of keys given to the mercenary leader by Christal – he turned questioningly to the interpreter. Maybe they left it unlocked last time, she suggested. He shrugged. They pushed the door open and walked into the lobby.

Dagmar approached the lifts and pressed a button. An upward-pointing arrow lit up. There was a rush of air as a car descended the shaft.

Riordan stepped out from behind the pillar the moment the doors rumbled apart, a leather-covered cosh gripped tight in his right hand. His arm swung up in a vicious arc, then brought the springy shaft thudding home sideways beneath the policeman's ear, just below the reinforced brim of his helmet. Riordan caught him as he fell.

By the time the girl realized what had happened, swinging around, one hand flying to her mouth to stifle a frightened gasp, the man was unconscious on the floor and Riordan had an arm locked around her neck. 'Don't panic, don't scream,' he whispered. 'Nothing will happen to you; you won't be hurt if you do exactly as I say. Do you understand?'

Above the black-sweatered arm imprisoning her, frightened eyes glanced at his tall, dark figure, the steely gaze behind the slit in the Balaclava. Finally she nodded.

He released her at once. 'I need to take this man's place and accompany you to the fifth floor,' he said in a low voice. 'That's all. After that you're free to pick him up and return to the police line.'

'B-but I don't understand,' she stammered. 'They won't

keep the rendezvous if there's anyone with me. That was made quite clear at . . .'

'There'll be nobody with you,' Riordan interrupted. 'I shall stay by the lift the way he would have done.' He nodded at the policeman.

'But they can *see* the lift from their end of the walkway. Once they realize that you're not . . .'

I'll have my back turned.' Riordan was stripping the uniform tunic from the prone figure, who luckily was bulky. He shrugged it on over his sweater, then jammed the helmet low down over his brow. He had no idea whether or not Dagmar suspected he was the foreigner who had been questioning her at the hotel. He hadn't troubled to disguise his voice. It didn't matter: he had no intention of returning there. 'We must hurry,' he said. 'They know lifts have to be waited for, but not all night.'

He thumbed the button and the doors slid open again. 'Incidentally, how come this works anyway? An emergency generator?'

Dagmar nodded. They walked into the lift. The doors closed. 'So why don't the main doors work?' Riordan asked.

'Because the generator only operates on these shafts. Just to get people down from the upper floors. There are so many power cuts: lots of offices have systems something like this.' She pressed the fifth-floor button. The lift whined upwards.

'What do I do when the meeting's over?' Dagmar asked.

'He'll be out for ten or fifteen minutes, not more. We put his uniform back on. When he comes to, he won't know what happened. Nor will you. He passed out suddenly, and you went up alone. When you returned, he was OK. So the two of you go back to the police line . . . and say nothing. He'll be too embarrassed to report the incident, as long as you don't.'

'Well, I hope you're right,' she said.

Behind the woollen mask, Riordan grinned. 'I usually am,' he said.

The lift bounced to a halt; the doors opened. He stared across a tiled hallway at the arch leading to the covered passage linking the two buildings. It was brightly lit by the moon, since the roof, and the walls from waist height upwards, were glass. Dagmar walked out of the lift and paced briskly along the walkway.

Riordan was aware of two figures, one cradling what looked like a sub-machine-gun, standing some way back from the far end of the passage, but the light was too diffuse for him to make out any details. He couldn't even distinguish physical features or what kind of clothes they wore. He hoped the man with the gun would suffer the same disadvantage.

As the doors of the lift closed, he half turned his back in case the darkness of the Balaclava beneath the helmet brim aroused the armed guard's suspicion. He knew he must remain clearly in view while the girl talked with the second man. It was equally vital that he made no move that could be interpreted as curiosity. There was no reason, though, why a policeman on a boring assignment shouldn't display a touch of impatience while he waited.

Potted palms stood on either side of the walkway arch. Further along, the glass wall of the hallway was bordered by a line of display stands with photographs and leaflets, remnants of the last conference held in the building. Keeping his face turned away from the opposite façade, Riordan strolled slowly the few yards to the nearest stand, peering down as if he was trying to decipher something in the moonlight.

Head bent and shoulders a little sagging, he returned to

the lifts. A metal-framed bench with four imitation-leather seats was set against an inner wall just beyond. He sank into one of these, leaning forward with his hands interlaced and his elbows resting on splayed knees.

From beyond the arch, he could faintly hear voices, the girl's husky contralto alternating with the glottal exhalations of Arabic. By the time her footsteps approached along the walkway five minutes later, Riordan's hawklike eyes had committed to memory every window and sill and niche and crevice of the opposite façade, every visible pipe, together with brick patterns and masonry details and the layout, as far as he could judge it, of the fifth floor of the main block.

He could see in the pale light that Dagmar's features were strained and anxious as he rose to call the lift. 'Something wrong?' he asked.

'I don't know why I should tell you, whoever you are,' she said. 'But yes, they've suddenly started to get tough. If their ransom demands are not met by this time tomorrow, they threaten to kill one of the hostages . . . and another the day after, and one every twenty-four hours after that until they get what they want.' She shivered. 'People like that! Now I know what it means when they say something makes your blood run cold.'

'Terrorists don't always carry out their threats,' Riordan said. 'Like the taking of hostages itself, it's just another form of blackmail.'

On the ground floor, the policeman was still lying by the pillar. They propped him up while Riordan buttoned the tunic back on him. He left the helmet by the pillar. 'Poor guy,' he said. 'He had some kind of attack and hit his head on the stonework . . .'

When the girl heard the German groan two minutes later and went to help him to his feet, Riordan had already vanished into the shadows of the building's interior.

9

Fifty feet above the ground, Riordan had been spread-eagled against a white-tiled wall when power was restored and the floodlights blazed into life again. Since so much of the night had passed already, he had been in two minds about an immediate attempt to penetrate the kidnappers' stronghold, but Dagmar's report of the death threat against the hostages had decided him: time was running out; information on the enemy's base was vital.

A careful study of the blueprints and municipal plans furnished by O'Kelly had revealed that there was, strangely, no ground-level entrance to the conference centre: the only way in was along the fifth-floor walkway. He assumed that the lower storeys were reserved for archives, storage units, perhaps library or research sections, in any case departments which required no day-to-day access. The water supply, however, together with the electricity and drainage conduits, was channelled to the block underground, all three services being housed in a narrow concrete tunnel which could be reached via an inspection hatch in the boiler room in the main block's basement.

Riordan was in the boiler room before Dagmar and her dazed police escort left the building.

Huge cylindrical oil tanks winking with brass gauges and dials flanked the installation that in winter fed steam heat to the floors above. Even in springtime, the air was heavy with the acrid smell of the stored fuel, and moonlight flooding through the glass bricks of a skylight set in the paved surround above lit a baseboard on one wall alive with the tick and whirr of clocks and time switches controlling some distant plant in the deserted building.

The inspection hatch was immediately below this board. It was closed by a cast-iron plate about two feet square which had to be lifted out of brackets flush with the opening. Riordan seized the D-grips on either side of the cover and heaved. The plate refused to move. He strained with all his strength, flexing his knees to get below the grips so that he could maximize the effort by thrusting upwards. Nothing.

Sweat was trickling between Riordan's shoulder-blades. Panting, he switched on the hooded torch. Clearly it was a long time since any examination had been made: the lower flange of the inspection plate appeared to have rusted solid with one of the brackets. He thumped the lower part of the iron grips with the heel of his hands; he struck the panel with doubled fists; finally he turned away and back-kicked it with all his force.

The lip of the rusted bracket broke away and the plate shifted with a hollow clang that reverberated around the basement like a thunder-sheet in a production of *Macbeth*. Cursing beneath his breath, Riordan lifted it away and stood it against the wall. He paused, listening. Together with the booming echoes of his earlier attempts to free the inspection cover, this final racket seemed to him to have been loud enough to call in the entire security force surrounding the conference centre.

Apart from the ticking of the minuterie, the cellar was silent. Dust motes eddied in a moonbeam slanting through the skylight. Riordan leaned in through the hatch and unscrewed the hood from his torch.

He saw a vaulted concrete tunnel, blinding white after the gloom of the basement, some four feet high. The curved walls of the tunnel were festooned with cables and ducts and bunches of electrical wiring, and lead piping on the floor ran alongside a heavy earthenware conduit that presumably connected the outflow from the wing with the main drainage system.

Leaning further in, Riordan swivelled his torch to the left. The bright beam lanced ahead, illuminating the fat brown conduit, copper pipes, furred cobwebs shifting in a current of air. Somewhere in the distance something scurried away.

The tunnel ran straight for perhaps fifty feet, then veered left again to curl out of sight. Riordan eased his lean length in through the opening and crouched down over the drainage pipe. Theoretically there was plenty of room for a man to move, even a big, muscular one. But since there was no flat floor and it was necessary for feet and knees to accommodate themselves to the hard, cold surfaces of the various ducts running on either side of the central drain, progress was both awkward and slow.

Before he reached the turn in the low passage, the muscles in Riordan's ankles and calves were aching, his knees were bruised, and his back ached from the contorted position he was forced to adopt. Sharp clamps positioning what he assumed were telephone cables twice lacerated his right hand.

Once the corner was turned, he stopped to regain his breath. And listen. Somewhere ahead water dripped. He could hear liquid chuckling in a distant underground channel. And then pipes abruptly sang, a high, thin, barely discernible humming provoked by an equally faint vibration that shook the fabric of the tunnel.

A chill breath stirred the hairs on the nape of Riordan's neck. He was aware suddenly of the hundreds of tons of cold earth weighing on the fragile structure of this man-made passage, of the incomparably complex skein of cables and drains and conduits webbing the underground strata below the city streets, layer upon layer, generation after generation, among the skeletal remains and pottery shards strewing the damp subsoil.

The vibration increased in intensity, the humming changed key and grew lower and louder. It approached a distant climax, then faded away and died as rapidly as it had begun.

Perhaps one of the U-Bahn tunnels lay not far away. It was too late for passenger services, but a maintenance engineer's train could be passing. Either that or a convoy of heavy lorries traversing the neighbourhood.

Riordan's small world fell silent again except for the persistent drip of water somewhere ahead. Evidence of subterranean life was no surprise to Riordan. What did seem odd was that there had been no sign of life nearer at hand. With a dozen hostages and an unknown number of terrorists lodged in the building he was approaching, he would have expected at least an occasional rush of water along the main drain flooring the tunnel. The fifth floor, after all, housed toilets, shower rooms and a kitchen.

He shrugged. The tunnel stretched for another hundred feet. Brushing aside a curtain of cobwebs, he continued his uncomfortable journey.

A loud click from an electrical junction box halted him again a few yards from the end. It was followed by a steady ticking sound, and then silence once more. A lift, maybe, passing from one floor to another?

Moving very cautiously, he approached the inspection plate barring the tunnel's exit. According to the plans he had studied, this arched panel, cast-iron like the first one, could be removed from the outside or the inside. The torch showed him that the plans had been followed. Two grips projected from the cold metal surface. Laying down the torch, he grasped both, heaving upward and outward with his back braced against the curved wall.

The plate lifted free of its retaining brackets, tilting away. Moonlight flooded the passage.

Momentarily dazzled, Riordan allowed his hold to slacken for a split second. The heavy panel tore from his grasp, fell outwards, and plummeted to the ground outside with a metallic clangour that resembled a thunderclap.

Riordan froze, biting his lip. For what seemed to him like minutes, he waited for the angry, questioning voices, the windows thrown open, the clatter of feet on a stairway. He heard nothing but the distant roar and rumble of the city.

Through the open hatch, he stared at white tiles, grimed here and there with soot. Since all the services were supplied to the conference wing from the main building – they were visible from where he crouched, curving up to vanish through the tunnel's roof – the offset block had no need of a basement or boiler room: the inspection hatch opened at sub-basement level on to an air-shaft in the centre of the block.

When it was clear, against all odds, that the noise of the falling hatch had raised no hue and cry, Riordan climbed through the opening and stood gratefully stretching his limbs in the pale, cold light. In the rectangle of dark sky overhead, the moon was visible, low above the rooftop.

Riordan sighed. The passage through the tunnel had been tiresome, but the really tough part lay ahead. The aim of the operation was somehow to get inside that part of the fifth floor where the hostages were held. Once he had made contact with them, for however short a time, the rescue would automatically become much simpler; without the knowledge and help of the victims, the difficulties would be multiplied.

But reaching the fifth floor in the first place was the problem. The fire-escapes were on the far side of the building, within view of the police cordoning the block. There was a door on the far side of the air-shaft which could be forced to gain entry. But this would lead only to the lift shafts and the emergency staircase, both of which were guarded by armed men on the fifth-floor landing, and possibly at lower levels as well. Riordan had rejected such an approach the first time he studied the plans. The only way to escape the terrorists' surveillance, he had decided, was to reach the fifth floor on the *outside* of the wing, and then break in through a window that was already beyond the entrance watched by the guards.

Theoretically, there was a way to do this. Not far from the open hatch, a thick pipe climbed the wall of the air-shaft. It was joined by feeder pipes on each storey, and presumably itself fed into the drainage tube flooring the tunnel, for it disappeared into the wall just above the level of the hatch.

Practically, however, there was a difficulty, because although the pipe could be climbed as far as the fifth floor, the window to which it gave access was on the wrong side of the landing: the only way to reach a window beyond this was along a narrow sandstone ledge circling the air-shaft. Fifty feet above ground level, at night, and lacking appreciable handholds, this was a fearsome challenge. But Riordan had already decided that it was the only thing to do. Slipping the torch inside his waistband a few inches from the Browning automatic, he approached the pipe.

The climb was not too difficult for an agile man in good shape. Ridged junctions interrupted the smooth column every ten feet; the outflows joining it at each floor provided footholds; suction pads borrowed from Christal and strapped to each knee were sufficient to steady him even if they wouldn't support his entire weight.

Riordan wedged a foot into the bend of the pipe where it penetrated the wall, reached up both hands and drew himself up level with the bend. He straightened his legs, stretched as high as he could, grasped the pipe, and hauled himself up again, thrusting fiercely with his feet as the soft soles of the combat boots curled around it.

He locked his hands around the first junction, raised both knees as high as he could, clamped the suction pads in position, and straightened once more. In this way, frog-like, in alternating hoists and muscle-wrenching thrusts, he raised himself from storey to storey.

Halfway up he rested, panting. His calves and shoulders ached. Sweat ran down his back. A muscular flutter trembled the backs of his thighs.

When he reached the fifth floor he stopped again, supporting his weight with one foot on an outflow pipe. His head was level with a small window of frosted glass, presumably of a shower room or toilet.

Immediately below the outflow, the sandstone ledge stretched away to his left.

Until the corner of the air-shaft, it ran along a blank wall, but after that there was a row of windows, larger and wider than the one above him. And these would be beyond the landing, which, according to the architect's plan, was level with the corner of the shaft.

The ledge was three inches wide, the corner perhaps nine feet away. With one hand still curled around the pipe, Riordan warily slid his right foot out along the ledge, then transferred his other foot to it. He let go of the pipe and stood on his toes, facing the wall with his arms spread.

Gingerly, inch by inch, he began moving away from the pipe.

A three-inch strip of stone – in theory – should be wide enough for a man to move along. But when the ledge forms part of a sheer wall, the bulk of the body becomes critical, for if its centre of gravity shifts too far away from the median line of the ledge it will overbalance and fall. To succeed, the climber must either face the wall and move on the balls of his feet with his heels projecting into space, or rest on his heels with his back to the wall, in which case he is excruciatingly conscious of his exposed position and risks suffering from vertigo. In either case the centre of gravity will be further out than the limit of the ledge, so the body must be flattened against the wall as much as possible and prevented from toppling outwards by the tension and thrust of braced muscles in the legs and feet.

In the absence of handholds, Riordan was only able to balance on the ledge at all because he was both lean and muscular. With his arms flung wide and every available square inch of his frame pressed to the glazed tiles of the shaft, he advanced his right foot a few inches, shifted his weight, brought up his left, slid the first away again – thrusting desperately upwards and inwards with his calf muscles all the time. His cheek pressed against the wall and his eyes were fixed unswervingly on the corner of the shaft. He knew that if he looked down and saw the fifty feet of space below his heels he was likely to fall. Even to turn his head and face the tiles might displace his weight enough to unbalance him. He was a hardened fighter, a man not afraid to advance against hostile gunfire, but exposed on this ledge he felt as though the trembling of the blood through his veins was sufficient to shake him from his perch and hurl him into oblivion.

As he had climbed the pipe, wisps of cloud sailing across the face of the moon had provoked the illusion that the building was toppling towards him; he had to thrust away a recurring impression that the pipe was about to pull free of the wall and crash to the ground with him still clinging to it. Now, alone above the drop, it was the sounds around him that became exceptionally important. They were invested with special significance: loud enough to drown the world, they became his isolated universe. The slither of his soles along the stone . . . a tiny rasp as the wool of his Balaclava caught on an imperfection in a tile . . . the hoarse, quick bellows of his breathing (for the deep breath he needed so badly could push him away from the wall). Somewhere over the rooftops a church clock chimed three quarters. It was only half an hour since he had left Dagmar.

There was another vertical pipe in the corner. Without it, Riordan would have been lost. Because to step across ninety degrees of yawning space and flatten himself against an adjoining wall with no leverage, no thrust and nothing to cling on to would have been physically impossible. He clung to the smooth, cold tube, gasping with relief.

There were windows on the next leg of the journey. And the nearest, which should open into the suite where the hostages were held, was only four feet away.

Seizing the pipe, he steeled himself to step across. It was at that moment that power was restored and the floodlights in front of the centre blazed back to life.

The air-shaft was drenched abruptly with a brilliance reflected down from above, but mainly arriving directly through uncurtained and unshuttered windows paired in empty rooms on the lower floors.

Thinking himself perhaps indistinct or at worst one

suspect shape among many in the subdued and treach-
erous radiance of the moon, Riordan now found himself
dazzlingly illuminated, an image sharp and iron-hard in the
pitiless glare reflected from the floods, as unmistakable to
an examining eye as a butterfly pinned to a board in a
display case. If one of the kidnappers, passing through
a room on the far side of the shaft, happened to glance
through a window ... He put the thought from his mind,
stepped across the gap, and then, relinquishing his hold on
the pipe, set out on the last few perilous feet of his climb.

Somehow they were the worst of all. Vulnerable now
and defenceless in that harsh light, he was bathed in an
icy sweat. A breeze sprang up from nowhere and plucked
at his clothes. He was more than ever conscious of the
chasm beneath him, of the knife-edge separating his life
from his death. His calf and his thigh muscles were on
fire. In the murmur of voices suddenly audible from the
police line beyond the block, he fancied he could detect
suspicion, even certainty ...

But at last the hellish traverse was over. He stood in front
of a window and rested his shaking arms on the sill. There
was a jeweller's diamond-tipped cutter in his pocket, but
the glass didn't need to be cut: the window, unlocked and
unlatched, moved easily, silently up under the pressure of
his hands. As he lowered his stretched arms to grasp the sill
again, a fragment of the sandstone ledge crumbled beneath
his weight and broke away.

Riordan fell.

His legs dropped away into the void; his flailing arms
struck the sill with an impact that shocked the remaining
breath from his body ... and miraculously one of them
hooked over it and held. For a giddy moment he hung
suspended over the shaft with all his weight tearing at
that arm. Then he managed to strain up with the other

hand and find a purchase, relieving the effort. At the third attempt, he was able to will his muscles to haul him back up to a position from which he could collapse across the sill and ease himself into the room beyond.

It was a small room, dark after the brilliance outside. When the thudding of his heart had subsided, he moved cautiously forward with outstretched arms. He could make out filing cabinets along one wall, and a metal desk with a knee-hole chair on a swivel. He re-hooded his torch and switched it on again.

Yes ... a small, bare office, anonymous, with no visible papers, books or directories. The filing cabinets were empty. Probably one of several rooms placed at the disposal of delegates when conferences were held. He was surprised not to see the door nevertheless outlined with cracks of light from the corridor outside, for the office must be near the entrance.

Riordan extinguished the torch. The Browning, its slide already pulled back, was in his hand. Creeping forward again, he depressed the handle of the door. It swung silently inwards.

Darkness. Silence. A thread of light beneath a door at the far end of a corridor. Riordan stole towards it, dropped to one knee, and peered through a keyhole. As he expected, he was looking at an entrance lobby. But there was no sign of the guards: the wide space, with its featureless reception desk and chrome-framed chairs, was deserted. He supposed the guards remained outside all night, surveying the stairhead and the lifts.

Riordan had been aware of lights coming on at various points in the building when power was restored. It was normal that an empty lobby should remain illuminated all night when anyone wishing to leave had to pass through it. What was less normal, in the circumstances, was the fact that there was so far no sign of light further in. With twelve unwilling captives at the mercy of an unknown number of armed kidnappers, he would have expected to find lights blazing all over the fifth floor.

He had formed no plan of action once he was within the block; contact with the victims would have to be played by ear. Once he had located them. Any communication would, of course, be easier in the dark, but locating a likely contact was going to be tough.

Riordan was now at the far end of the corridor, crouched by a door which, according to the plans, led to the main conference hall in which the hostages were undoubtedly being held. No light showed through the keyhole.

He frowned. Come to think of it, it was odd that there was no sound as well as no light. With that number of people involved, he would have expected, even in the middle of the night, to be aware of a human presence. He listened, every nerve on the alert, for a cough, a snore, the restless shifting of a body, any movement a bored guard might make. There was nothing. Apart from the night noise of the city filtering through, the building was silent as the dead.

As the *dead*? Surely they wouldn't have gone that far . . . ? He shook his head. They're not crazy. There would be no point. Very slowly, he twisted the handle and eased open the door.

Yet again he received a surprise. There was nothing to see or hear, OK. But what of his nose? With a fair number of people cooped up already for several days in a limited space, there should surely be the smells of occupation? Stale cigarette or cigar smoke . . . sweat . . . the intangible smell of fear. Food was delivered to the block every day. Where were the odours, savoury or displeasing, of recent cooking?

Riordan rose abruptly to his feet. He opened the door wide and swept his hand over a bank of switches on the wall inside. The big room blazed with light. It was unoccupied. He saw a rostrum, a display screen, a long polished table and rows of chairs – but no people. No ashtrays overflowing, no cups, plates or glasses, no newspapers crumpled and no radio. Not a blanket rug or pillow to be seen.

He strode through and jerked open a door beside the stage. Another dark passageway. He found a light switch, illuminated a line of doors, the open entrances to shower rooms, lavatories and a kitchen. All of them were empty. There were no towels, nor any other signs of occupation in the toilets or showers. In the kitchen, piles of unused dishes were stacked in cupboards above immaculate stainless-steel sinks. There was no food in the refrigerator.

Riordan returned to the lobby. He unlocked and opened the main entrance doors. No guards stood at the stairhead opposite the lifts.

A lot of minor mysteries were now explained: the lack of reaction when the inspection plate fell with such a clatter; the total absence of sights and sounds and smells; of surveillance on the part of the guards; of evidence that the place was being used to hold captives.

It was no wonder that there had been no movement in the pipes and ducts leading to or from the block while he was in the tunnel. For as far as the fifth floor was concerned, there were no hostages, no kidnappers, no signs of recent occupation whatsoever.

The place was deserted.

10

'The entire set-up is an elaborate fake,' Riordan told his team. 'As phoney as a three-pound note. But who exactly is this false scenario designed to fool?'

'You got some choice there!' Van Eyck said.

'Exactly. The security forces cordoning off the place? The Western occupying powers? The Soviet authorities? Or all of those? Or maybe just the press and the folks who read newspapers? Tick the box which gives, in your opinion, the correct answer.'

'There has to be some point to it,' Van Eyck said. 'We perhaps can take it that there *has* been a kidnapping, that there *are* hostages . . . somewhere?'

'I would think so. Otherwise why the fuck would we be here?'

'And that those hostages are the people we have been told they are?'

'Same answer. The fake took some setting up – all that security presence, the requests for food and stuff, the meetings with the interpreter girl. Why would the terrorists bother if the captives were not important?'

'Unless a second lot of hostages, even more important, should be involved,' Aletti suggested.

'Come off it, Alex,' Riordan said. 'In that case the news that your second lot was missing would surely have leaked out somehow. And wouldn't the first batch be trumpeting, Hey! The papers got it wrong; we're not missing at all!'

'Unless they *are* still missing too. All of them.'

'Well, yes, there is that,' Riordan said dubiously. 'But let's not over-complicate things. I reckon we can take it that the twelve guys quoted were in fact taken at the end of the trade conference, that they have in some way been spirited away from the centre, and that they are still sequestered somewhere.'

'Permission to speak, sir?' the usually taciturn Crawford said.

'Go ahead, Sergeant.'

'Being as how we're in the Soviet zone, and the squads surrounding the target are Russkis as well – and not a single sodding Western observer has been let in – could it be on the cards that those security types are in on the deal? That they know bloody well there's no fucking hostages on the fifth floor of that block?'

'It's a point we have to consider,' Riordan said. 'It'd make the set-up more elaborate still. But at least it would explain how the kidnappers managed to get their prisoners out of there.'

'You don't mean . . . the Comrades are in cahoots with the terrorists?' Christal sounded incredulous.

'Not necessarily in cahoots, no. Turning something like a blind eye,' Riordan said. 'We've been told, after all, that it suits them to have at least three of the hostages out of the way for the moment.'

For a while the seven mercenaries fell silent. They were propped against the walls or sprawled on the floor of the front parlour in the abandoned house in the old quarter. Light from a grey dawn filtered through the cracks in the boarded-up windows. A patter of rain could be heard on the cobbles outside.

Nelson-Harmer's deep, mellifluous chuckle broke the silence in the empty room.

'Something funny?' Riordan asked.

'Well, yes, actually. Ironic anyway. Bit of a scoop for the boys in Fleet Street, wouldn't you say? A military unit that doesn't exist, quartered in a house that's uninhabited, prepares an assault on an empty building where no hostages are held. What you might call a negative option, eh?'

Riordan grinned. 'You could say that. What we have to do is find out where there *are* hostages . . . and then go back to square one and plan an assault to get them out of there.'

'Alternative action,' Brod said. 'With the whole of East Germany to search, where precisely would you suggest we start?'

'At the conference centre,' Riordan replied promptly. 'They send people there to take in food every day, remember. And again from time to time to pass messages to the interpreter. We'll be waiting inside next time. And – it may take several bites at the cherry, according to how far away the real hide-out is – we'll simply follow them when they leave.'

'Easy to say,' Van Eyck objected, 'but how do we get inside again, assuming there's no power cut?'

'I'll take one man with me and use the service tunnel again. And don't ask me how I make the main building, where the tunnel starts,' Riordan said, seeing that the Dutchman was about to speak again. 'The other five will create a diversion to draw away the attention of the cordon.'

'And if the terrorists you want to follow leave with the connivance of the security personnel?'

'Another diversion – or the same one continued. We'll arrange a system of signals.'

'Jolly good show,' Nelson-Harmer said lazily. 'Wouldn't

it help a bit, just the same, if we had answers to some of the basic questions?'

'Such as?'

'Well, for one thing, old boy, back to the Biblical conundrum: What shall it profit a man? ... and all that. There has to be a point, and a pretty strong one I should say, to this complex charade. Given that hostages have been taken and are held, who benefits from the fact that the locale has been secretly changed?'

'The terrorists?' Christal said.

'I said secretly, old chap. I can see that it could be an advantage to them if they admitted the hostages had been spirited away. Yah! Try and catch us now! But what good does it do them, keeping that building cordoned off – with or without the knowledge of the security force? It doesn't increase the blackmail leverage. It wouldn't if the move was no secret. They've got the bloody hostages anyway. Their lives are equally at risk in either case. Frankly, I fail to see the point.'

'Me too,' Riordan said. 'Meanwhile, before we start to put the alternative plan into operation, I'm going to call our fail-safe number and talk to our agent. He'd better get the OK from his principals before we begin planning moves in the light of the changed situation.'

O'Kelly wasn't at the number Riordan had been given. Or an any rate he was not available. The mercenary leader spoke to his old comrade-in-arms and O'Kelly's archivist, Beverley Hills.

'I'll pass it all on, old lad,' Hills said. 'But you'd better give me a rundown on the new plans – so far as you know them now, that is.'

'They're too fluid for a rundown,' Riordan told him. 'All I can do is give you the bare outlines for the moment.'

'Fire away.'

'We'll be in the outposted block next time they send a spokesman and a guard to speak with the interpreter. When they leave, we'll follow them. As soon as we discover where they go, where the prisoners are, we'll fight our way in and get them out. End of story.'

'Oh. And how do you propose to do that – follow them, I mean?'

'We'll work that out when we see how they get there.'

'So how will *you* get there. Into the block, I mean.'

'I've already found a way,' Riordan said guardedly.

'Don't you and your men risk being spotted by the security teams? If you follow them outside the block?'

'No more than the kidnappers would, if they were seen coming out. But I don't believe they would be seen. Surely the cops would question *anyone* they saw who looked halfway like someone leaving that block?'

'I imagine so, yes. So how do you think they do get in and out?'

'No idea. But we'll find out. And there'll be some kind of diversion arranged, just in case they should cross the police line.'

'Ah. What kind of diversion?' Hills asked.

'Something to attract people's attention,' Riordan said.

'I see. Yes . . . well . . . If that's all you can tell me at the moment . . .'

'I'll want O'Kelly's go-ahead before I fix anything definite. After all, this is a different script from the one we were booked for. I wouldn't want to rock any boats.'

'Quite. Well, I'll pass on everything you've told me and let you know . . .'

'I shall want to talk to O'Kelly personally before I initiate any action,' Riordan insisted. 'Let's be quite clear about that.'

'Just as you say, squire. No dealing with the underlings, what!'

'You don't have to get stroppy. The captain was the man who hired me, that's all.'

'No offence, Colonel. Just leave it to me.'

'Where is O'Kelly at this moment? Is he here in Berlin?'

'I really couldn't say. He's in contact; he phones in.'

'This number I call – it's a Berlin number: does it switch automatically through to Paris? Or is it what it seems to be?'

'It reaches us wherever we are.'

'Very well. Where are you then, you personally? Are you in Berlin?'

'Actually, I'm not supposed to say. Not far off, anyway.'

'Look, Hills, let's stop arsing around. This is no time for fencing. I'm serious.'

'I'll make sure Captain O'Kelly gets in touch, I promise. I mean soon. As soon as he makes contact, which should be later today. Tell me exactly where your chaps are holed up. I know it's in the old quarter behind the centre, but it'd help if you gave me the exact address, and when you'll be there. Be easier for the old boy to make speedy contact then.'

'It doesn't have a number and I don't know the name of the street,' Riordan said. 'I could show you on a map, but it's too difficult to explain on the telephone. There are too many damn lanes and alleys around there. Don't worry: I'll keep calling until I get him. Then we can arrange a meeting that suits both of us.'

'Quite,' Hills said.

Riordan had used a pay phone in a U-Bahn station. Wending his way back to the abandoned house, he pondered the conversation he had just had. Hills was intelligent. He was courageous – sometimes a little too daring for

112

his own good. More than once Riordan had been obliged to caution him when they worked together. It surprised him nevertheless to find that the young man – as he thought – was in the German capital. Was he there just for the hostage mission? Or did he have other undercover fish to fry? And why, if the former question was affirmative, had he seemed half the time to be stalling?

Riordan realized he knew very little of Seamus McPhee O'Kelly's postwar activities or how far his net of secrecy could be flung. The operation was already complex enough: he wondered just how much more troubled the waters in which he swam might turn out to be . . .

11

Riordan's 'diversion' had to be near enough the police cordon to engage its members militarily, but not so near that they could still keep watchful eyes on the whole of the isolated conference centre.

It must of course in no way be read as a possible assault – or even a feint – threatening the centre itself. There had to be a valid reason for it, a believable excuse wherever it took place.

With so little time to plan, Riordan's choice had to be a quick one. He decided the best explanation for an outbreak of violence, and gunfire if necessary, would be an armed robbery – or at least an attempted one.

With the city, even the Russian zone, still ravaged by shortages, no shops in this sector would offer enough worthwhile booty to tempt members of the underworld; the supposed aim of the operation would have to be money.

Eighty yards from the southern barrier set up by the security forces, the road forked, the right-hand street leading towards the River Spree and the demarcation line. Halfway along the first block, on the right again, a narrow cul-de-sac curved back towards the centre and the cordon guarding it – but cut off physically from them by a ruined church and a disused warehouse. On the street corner at the entrance to this alley there was a neighbourhood *Sparkasse*. This savings bank, Riordan thought, could be a credible target.

The advantage of the site was that although it was very near the cordon in a straight line, it could only be reached by going to the fork and doubling back.

'There are two security guards at the outer door,' Riordan told his team. 'I don't want you to get involved actually inside the bank. You must give the Vopos time to call up reinforcements before you rush the place. They have walkie-talkies with them. You exchange shots and then, when the guys from the cordon arrive, you retire gracefully, OK? That should give us plenty of time to make the central block.'

'Exchange shots?' Van Eyck echoed. 'You mean just that? No dusting the original guards?'

'Not unless your own lives are in danger. This is just a diversion. We don't want any complications – like an all-stations call on a murder case.'

'And you want I should liberate the transport first?' Aletti asked.

Riordan nodded. 'Something that's not too flash, but unusual enough to draw at least casual attention in this area,' he said. 'One of those Volkswagen vans. Something like that.'

'And after that we get out of there fast, abandoning the transport far enough away to play safe, but not too far from this quarter?'

'Right. And make your way back here separately. At ten or fifteen-minute intervals if you can.'

'How long must we wait before you show?' asked Brod.

'I wish I knew,' Riordan said. 'But it had better be quick if they're going to start wasting hostages by the end of this evening.'

Although he was second in command of the team, Pieter Van Eyck was an individualist, a marksman, a loner by choice when it came to battles. Riordan appointed Sergeant Crawford as leader of the diversion squad. The tough ex-soldier's experience of urban guerrilla fighting ranged from Anzio to Arnhem, from the hell of Caen to the factory floors in Karlsruhe, where he had once silenced a squad of Panzer Division grenadiers single-handed after a running fight among the smashed freight cars of a railway marshalling yard. Apart from his personal courage, his fearless determination invariably communicated itself to the men working with him. With Riordan that day, he strolled up to the site by a circuitous route to inspect the terrain, explore possible escape routes and estimate the most advantageous points from which a believable raid could be staged.

Crawford would take Van Eyck, Brod and Christal into the attack, leaving Aletti as cover at the wheel of the getaway vehicle. Nelson-Harmer was to accompany the mercenary leader during his attempt to track down the terrorists when they left the conference centre.

Food was delivered to the hostage wing late every afternoon, the trolleys with their covered hospital dishes being taken in lifts to the fifth floor of the main building and transferred to two men at the end of the walkway, after which they were returned with the empties from the previous meal. (Riordan wondered what they actually did with the uneaten food for more than twelve people: he had seen no sign of it on his own visit to the wing, not even a lingering suspicion of cooking smells. He assumed the same two men would remain there until the rendezvous later with Dagmar.)

The arrival of the trolleys was to be the signal for Crawford's diversion to begin. During it, Riordan and his companion were to make a dash for the main building. Between this and the arrival of the interpreter they hoped to pass through the tunnel and gain the wing – only this time the ascent to the operative level would be made inside the block and not perilously via a pipe in the air-shaft and a dizzy ledge.

Everything went according to plan at the start of the operation. The green police van with its motorcycle escort arrived beside the command car in the centre of the cordon at the appointed time. Two trolleys were wheeled down ramps. The uniformed driver and his mate, again escorted by the motorcyclists, who were now carrying Bergmann sub-machine-guns, wheeled the trolleys to the main building's entrance. The glass doors slid open; the trolleys and the men pushing them vanished inside; the policemen with the SMGs remained on guard outside.

Riordan and Nelson-Harmer crouched behind a dilapidated board fence on the edge of a bomb-site at the end of a cobbled lane snaking into the old town. Riordan drew the pin of a small plastic grenade with his teeth, swung back his arm, and hurled the missile eighty yards into another patch of waste ground, at the exit from another alley, where a collection of empty oil drums, iron bedsteads and battered dustbins stood waiting to be removed as scrap. The cleansing of the devastated city was still a priority in all four of the occupied zones.

The grenade exploded among the scrap metal with a sharp, cracking concussion and a burst of brown smoke. Before the sheared fragments had finished clattering against the wall of an adjoining house and into the street, Riordan had thrown another, repeating the din.

Along the line of the distant cordon there was consternation. A Soviet officer and two police captains involuntarily started towards the formal garden. Two civilians – Russian newspapermen perhaps? – and several soldiers ran in the

117

direction of the double explosion. Nearer at hand, the guards in front of the main doors sprinted for the alley, unslinging their Bergmanns as they zigzagged across the open space.

It was then that there was an eruption of gunfire – single shots alternating with the stutter of automatic arms – from beyond the ruined church on the far side of the cordon. Crawford was answering the signal as ordered.

Once again the security cordon was taken by surprise. Officers and men in the line wheeled around to stare at the church. Someone bellowed orders. The runners about-turned and headed for the fork in the road. The guards with the Bergmanns halted, stared around, and then made for the command car as the invisible exchange of shots continued.

Riordan and the Nigerian dashed for the glass doors, hurling themselves flat as they slid apart. They crawled across the lobby to the emergency stairs. In the basement boiler room, where the gunfire was no more than a distant rattle, the iron inspection plate still stood where Riordan had left it, leaning against the wall by the open hatch that led to the service tunnel.

Twelve minutes later, the two men emerged into the air-shaft at the foot of the hostage wing. A light rain had begun to fall again, streaking the soot on the white-tiled walls.

'Pretty well par for the course, old boy, wouldn't you say?' Nelson-Harmer said. 'I mean, everything as planned – and it's only now that the bally things start to go wrong.'

'Positive thinking, that man!' Riordan grinned. He produced a bunch of skeleton keys given to him by Brod and strode across to the locked door on the far side of the shaft.

The door creaked open with a push after the third key he tried.

There remained something curiously menacing about the deserted building. No hostages fearing for their lives sweated on the upper floors; no evil captors, gloating over their prisoners' discomfiture paraded, guns in hand. The guards at the fifth-floor stairhead, if they bothered to stay in that part of the building at all until Dagmar's arrival, were probably chatting and smoking an illegal cigarette rather than keeping their weapons trained on possible rescuers.

And yet . . . and yet . . . was the sweat dewing Riordan's own upper lip as he led the way up the cold concrete emergency staircase no more than the chill effect of the approaching dusk, the lowered temperature of the unused air in the unlit passage?

When they reached the fourth floor, he eased open the pass door and they stole out on to the landing in front of the lifts. Light outside the wide windows was fading. Here and there among the dun façades beyond the formal garden indoor lights already gleamed. The sounds of gunfire had long ago ceased, and now only the persistent drone of cargo planes approaching Tempelhof and Gatow overlay the subdued rumble of the divided city's approaching night.

According to the indicators, all the lifts were on the ground floor. From the storey above there was no evidence of occupation . . . and then came a soft footfall, something that could have been the clink of a bottle against a glass, the rise and fall of a male voice.

'Not on the landing: they're inside the conference suite,' Riordan murmured.

'Is there anywhere we can hide up there?'

'Not on the landing, no. The walkway leads directly into it. But however they get out, it can't be upwards, and there's certainly no exit from that floor, I can tell you. Wherever the secret exit is, they have to go down to it. It's up to us to follow once they pass this floor.'

'Couldn't they use the walkway and go down inside the main building, bypassing us altogether?' Nelson-Harmer asked.

'They could,' Riordan said. 'But it's glassed in. They'd risk being spotted once the floods were on. I reckon we can ignore that possibility. If I'm mistaken ... well, we'll bloody well have to come back another time. I can't see anyone else trying to break in here and rescue the non-existent hostages in the next twenty-four hours.'

'What about the threat to top one of them if their terms are not met by tonight?'

'In my experience,' Riordan said, 'threats of this kind are invariably followed – at least the first time – by an extension of the deadline. It's the old cat-and-mouse game, keeping the opponent on tenterhooks. It's a risk we have to take, that everyone has to take.'

'Including the poor bloody hostages,' Nelson-Harmer said soberly.

Riordan nodded. 'Including the poor bloody hostages.'

The thickening dusk outside yellowed. On the floor above, lights were being switched on. Away to the north, the entire façade of a Soviet high-rise block blazed to life storey by storey, a concrete ocean liner riding a swell of slate roofs.

'We might as well be comfortable,' Riordan said. He crossed the landing and dropped on to the bench beside the lifts, pulling back the slide of his Browning to lodge a round in the breech.

Nelson-Harmer joined him. The gloom shrouding the landing brightened suddenly as the floodlights below were activated.

'If you ask me,' the Nigerian said, 'this is a pretty rum situation for a so-called soldier of fortune to find himself in. Full of sound and fury, as the jolly old Bard said, but signifying damn-all.' He shook his head. 'Very rum indeed.'

'It's a dirty job,' Riordan said, 'but someone's got to do it.'

Even perched on a shattered window embrasure of the ruined church, Christal couldn't really see exactly when the food trolleys vanished into the conference centre. Street-lights, telephone poles, the swing of a demolition crane and billows of smoke from a bonfire someone was trying to light in a weed-infested garden all obstructed his view. There was no doubt, however, about the double thud of Riordan's grenades, which was the definitive signal for the diversion to commence.

As the members of the distant cordon scattered and ran, Christal fired two shots into the air from his Russian Stetchkin automatic and jumped fifteen feet to the ground. He scampered through the overgrown churchyard, vaulted a rusty gate and hurried to the dark-blue Volkswagen van that Aletti had parked with the engine idling not far from the corner where the *Sparkasse* was located.

The VW had been 'liberated' from a municipal car park behind the local town hall. He hoped the flashing amber light on the roof and the dark, windowless body would give an impression, at least at first, that the vehicle was some kind of official transport.

As soon as Christal swung aboard through the open rear door, Aletti backed up fast and reversed into the cul-de-sac running alongside the savings bank. Traffic was light: bicycles, scooters, an occasional taxi, Isetta bubble cars and Messerschmitt three-wheelers adapted from the jigs producing the Perspex-covered cockpit compartments of fighter-bombers. The few pedestrians were on the far side of the main road, where the local food shops were.

The two guards outside the bank, one on either side of the revolving doors, lounged idly against the walls, cradling their SMGs. They favoured the stolen van with a disinterested stare as Aletti squealed it to a halt fifty feet away. Inside, the mercenaries pulled on their black wool Balaclavas and readied their weapons.

What they had not bargained for, what nobody could have foreseen, was the arrival of a second van, an armoured one with a bulletproof windshield, which careered into the lane and stopped with a judder immediately opposite the revolving doors of the savings bank. A team from the national security directorate was delivering the day's takings from the local state department store.

'Shit!' Crawford hissed. 'Of all times for those bleeders to stick their sodding noses in!'

'What do we do?' Van Eyck asked from behind him.

Crawford was sitting in the front seat beside Aletti. He turned around. 'Play the cards we're fucking dealt,' he said. 'There's nothing else *to* do.'

'Rush them as planned?' Christal asked.

'Let them show themselves in front of the bloody armour,' Crawford growled.

The rear doors of the armoured van opened. Two uniformed guards jumped to the ground, carrying heavy sacks chained to their wrists. The driver remained at the wheel. The bank guards formed up to escort the men with the money. 'Let the buggers take in the first load,' Crawford ordered.

The four men went into the bank. The mercenaries waited, ready to spring out of their van at any moment. Christal was holding the unlatched rear doors closed with one hand. Crawford kept his eyes on the driver of the security vehicle, who leaned his head against the armoured partition separating the cab from the strongroom and lit a cigarette.

A woman walked out of the bank, stuffing a purse into her shopping bag as she negotiated the revolving doors. She crossed the main street and went into a butcher's shop. A bus stopped. Two elderly men and a schoolgirl with a satchel alighted.

Light winked as the doors of the bank began turning once more. 'Christal, Brod, cover me when I make for that sand bin,' Crawford hissed. 'You stay here, Aletti, with one finger on the starter and one around the trigger. You fire when you think it's necessary. Mister Van Eyck, you knock out the rear window and use that machine to make them keep their fucking heads down, sir.' He gestured towards the Dutchman's Husqvarna.

Van Eyck nodded. 'Will do,' he said. He shifted his grip so that the butt plate of the rifle faced the glass.

The two security men emerged from the revolving doors, followed by the two bank guards. 'Now!' Crawford yelled.

He shouldered open the passenger door and leaped into the street, spraying slugs from his machine-pistol as his feet hit the tarmac. Brod and Christal were underneath the van hosing 9mm rapid fire around the armoured vehicle. Van Eyck shattered glass as instructed and loosed off three very careful shots. One struck an SMG carried by one of the bank guards, the second creased the biceps of a security man without seriously wounding him, and the last splatted against the wall half an inch from the head of the other guard, stinging his cheek with chips of stonework.

The volume of noise in the quiet street was astonishing. Since Crawford and his men had no intention of going anywhere near the bank, and the sole aim of the diversion was to draw the attention of the cordon isolating the conference centre, the machine-pistols were without their silencers. The appalling clatter of Crawford's Bergmann and the hoarse, deeper detonations of the VZ-23s of Christal and Brod, punctuated by the single menacing coughs of the Husqvarna, shattered the late-afternoon calm as effectively as an artillery barrage.

Brakes screeched in the main road. A woman screamed. Somebody inside the bank shouted a warning. And then the guards, taken totally by surprise, reacted and their own MP-38s added to the ferocious clamour.

Crawford was haring towards a galvanized sand bin with a sloping top, one of many placed at convenient street corners so that the city authorities could strew the icy streets in Berlin's cold winter. He flung himself down behind it as the first volley from the defenders screeched over his head.

Now that the initial impact was over, they were acting as they had been trained to do. The man whose machine-pistol had been struck was flat on his face behind one of the wheels of the armoured van, firing his revolver. His fellow guard, who had escaped Van Eyck's near miss, blasted furious short bursts from the vehicle's roof. The unhurt security man had leaped in between the open rear doors, prepared to defend the remains of the cargo with his life, and the one who had been winged, sitting at first with a hand clasped over his bloodied arm, was also now shooting with a revolver. The driver, crouched secure behind his bulletproof door, raised himself from time to time to loose off three and five-shot bursts in the general direction of the attackers.

The mercenaries' van rocked on its springs under a hail of bullets. Glass tinkled from the smashed headlights, the windscreen erupted in a fountain of toughened granules, the amber light exploded. One of the tyres, and then another, deflated with a sigh.

Swerving crazily from side to side, Aletti sprinted for the sand bin. Brod and Christal increased their rate of fire viciously to cover him. And then Van Eyck, seeing the security driver raise himself abruptly upright to aim his Bergmann at the fleeing man, regretfully downed him with a single shot. The man folded forward over the lowered window, his outflung arms letting the MP-38 fall to the ground beneath the unseeing gaze of a third eye which had appeared in the exact centre of his forehead. The half-smoked cigarette was still clinging to his lower lip.

Aletti tumbled to the ground beside Crawford. 'Christ, man, why the fuck did you do that?' the sergeant exclaimed. 'Get yourself bloody killed, you will!'

'I should remain in that flaming colander?' Aletti panted. 'Thank you very much! Kraut workmanship, did somebody say? That heap is but fragile, I am telling you; the bullets they skim through like red-hot knitting needles already. Why even the Dutchman is lying beside Brod on the ground. As it is, I lost the heel of one shoe. Five dollars the pair, they were, at Macy's.'

'Well, you can help immobilize another piece of Kraut workmanship now,' Crawford grinned. 'But don't waste rounds on the bodywork. And whatever you do, keep the slugs away from the wheels.'

'Why should I do that, when there's a man he's trying his best to kill me behind each?' Aletti demanded.

'Because we're going to steal his bleeding van, ain't we?' Crawford said. 'That's why.'

Dagmar was later than usual that evening, presumably because of the gun battle behind the church. The terrorists upstairs had been getting restive. Riordan and Nelson-Harmer had heard the pacing feet, an occasional burst of conversation, as their impatience manifested itself. Certainly it seemed a long time before they saw the girl and her escort appear in the glare of the floodlights below and head for the main building.

Soon afterwards, light footsteps tap-tapped along the walkway overhead.

Riordan stole to the stairway and opened the pass door. The voices were quite loud, louder than they had been when he himself had played escort to the interpreter the previous day. Dagmar's tones were measured, placatory, the kidnappers' hectoring.

'Can you by any chance identify the language they're speaking?' Riordan whispered.

'Oh, yes,' Nelson-Harmer replied casually. 'It's a dialect, an obscure one, from the Muslim sector of the ancient kingdom of Benin – that's to say the northernmost part of Dahomey, between my country and Togoland.'

'An odd place to be sending ransom specialists to Berlin.'

'Not really. Like most places in West Africa, they'll be screaming for independence, for freedom from French and British colonial rule, any day now. Your specialists will probably be rebels, planning to overthrow the government with a *coup d'état*, and the chaps they want let out of jail will almost certainly be political activists. That's why they'll have been put away, for the colonialists are not completely daft.'

'Yes, but . . . why Berlin, of all places?'

'Because of the trade conference, old chap. Lots of colonials there, not to mention fellows with a direct interest in the area. There must have been a deal of lobbying done, to say nothing of the spectre of Soviet aid if the West won't toe the old line.'

'Yes, I can see that. But what I don't see . . .' Riordan paused. He held up a warning hand.

Heel-taps along the walkway were audible once more. Dagmar was on her way back to the police escort in the main building.

'Right,' Riordan murmured. 'This is where we hold our breath, count to ten and keep our fingers firmly crossed.' He held the door wide open, pushed Nelson-Harmer through, and added: 'You take the stairs, keep ahead if you can, but in any case check which floor they take below. I'll stay here and watch the indicator in case they use a lift.'

The Nigerian nodded. Moving incredibly lightly for a man of his size, he sped down into the dark.

Riordan eased the door shut. He heard other doors closing on the floor above. The indicator light beside the lifts glowed. A discreet whine of hydraulic machinery announced the arrival of a lift from below. The illuminated pointer spun around the dial. The number five lit up.

Riordan was already on the stairway, stealing down three at a time. He dare not take another lift, even after the terrorists had left their own: the tell-tale sounds were too distinctive.

Through the fabric of the building, he heard the lift gates close. There was a heavy click, and then the descending whine, increasing, then diminishing in volume as the car passed close to the stairwell.

At the second floor, Riordan dashed through the pass door to glance at the indicator. The pointer continued to sink until the zero lit up . . . and remained lit. He heard the slide of opening gates. The light went out.

Riordan frowned. The terrorists had left the lift on the ground floor. But there was no exit that way; even the windows were small – and permanently shuttered.

Nelson-Harmer was waiting for him at the pass door. 'They went thataway,' he announced with a grin, sweeping one long arm to the right.

'Towards the front of the building? But that's . . .'
Riordan shook his head. It didn't make sense. 'Did they
have anything with them?' he asked suddenly. 'Were they
carrying . . . ?'

'Empty-handed. Except for cigarettes.'

'I should have checked,' Riordan said. 'But if the fifth
floor is as pristine as it was when I came before, that
certainly explains one thing.'

'Namely, O King?'

'The food. How they get rid of it. It's so simple, I never
saw it.'

'I have to confess, squire, that I'm still in that state
myself.'

'A charade, Teddy; an elaborate fake. There are no
hostages here, as we know, so they don't need any food.
And if no food is needed, why bring any? All that's
necessary, for the outside world, is again a pretence —
the pretence that food is being delivered and eaten, and
the empty dishes taken away.'

'And so?'

'So, in my view, the covered dishes so carefully delivered
with their police escort are in fact empty. And it's the
same dishes, still empty, which are taken back later in
the guise of yesterday's consignment. The problem of how
to dispose of the unwanted food no longer exists, because
there is none.'

'Yes, but surely, that implies . . . ?'

'Exactly. The cordon, all the security people involved
with it, do in fact know that the hostages are not here
but somewhere else. They're all in on the conspiracy. The
Comrades are playing along with the Devil!'

'Christ!'

'Quite. Now where did those colonial activists go?'
Riordan looked out across the ground-floor lobby, which

was lit dimly by reflected floodlight filtering through the slats of the shuttered windows.

'Right again at the end of the passage,' Nelson-Harmer said.

The passage passed between tall rows of shelves tightly packed with files. The right turn led them past more deeply spaced shelves of unpainted wood bulging with ledgers, daybooks, bundles of documents tied with string and more files, most of them boxed now. The atmosphere in the narrow corridor was choking, the desiccated air stale and laden with dust.

Riordan swallowed an urge to clear his throat, to cough. 'Just as I thought,' he whispered. 'The lower floors of this wing are used for storage. Some kind of archive, I guess: the stuff here looks as if it goes back years.'

'In a conference centre? Archives recording what, one wonders?'

'All the tosh spouted by delegates maybe,' Riordan suggested. 'Although judging by press and radio reports you'd need a sight more than four floors to preserve the gems of wisdom uttered just at the four-power Control Commission meetings, let alone international conferences.'

'Do I scent a cynic here?' Nelson-Harmer enquired.

The passage turned again ... and stopped ten feet further on, blocked by an outer wall and another shuttered window. The reflected light was much brighter here. A thin current of air stirred the floating dust. Riordan stole up to the window. It was closed but not locked. Very gently, he twisted the latch. The current of air strengthened. The steel-framed window swung inwards with a slight squeak.

'Well I'm damned!' Riordan said. He tried the double shutter: each leaf swung silently outwards.

One after the other, the two mercenaries clambered through and dropped to the ground outside. Lights flashed overhead, red and white, as a plane rumbled in on the approach to Tempelhof. 'I don't believe it!' Astonishment tinged Riordan's voice once more. Gratefully, he gulped in mouthfuls of the moist night air. 'Who would have thought it could be that simple?'

Crouched below the open window, they were shielded from the watchers behind the blazing floods by a four-foot ornamental bush at the limit of the formal garden. In the hard ground between the window and the bush was set a circular manhole cover.

'We follow?' Nelson-Harmer murmured.

Riordan nodded. Cautiously he closed the window, re-latching it by pushing the blade of his commando knife between the frame and the steel surround. He slipped the knife back into the sheath at his ankle and slid the shutters into place. Nelson-Harmer had already levered the cast-iron cover from the circular concrete shaft below.

The ground shook. Another aircraft, even lower, roared overhead. Once it had passed they could hear, faintly from the yawning shaft, the sound of running water.

Riordan switched on the hooded torch. He saw a vertical ladder with shining steel rungs attached to the wall of the shaft. 'Act Two, Scene One,' he said. 'The entrance to an underground sewer.' Grasping the top rung, he lowered himself into the shaft.

His companion followed, easing the manhole cover silently back in place above his head. 'You did say sewer?' he muttered when they were some way down the shaft.

'I did.' Riordan's whisper echoed hoarsely off the curved concrete wall, half lost in the whispering rush of water below. 'But the term, especially in a city, is used to indicate *any* drainage outflow, any conduit designed to carry away used liquid. It is not necessarily excremental.'

'No shit!'

'Precisely. There's a pretty noxious smell drifting up from below, but it's the stink of staleness, of un-hygiene, of bad ventilation. If it was the other thing, we couldn't survive without masks, believe me. And the terrorists certainly couldn't present themselves as spokesmen if they came this way: the girl would run before they were within twenty feet.'

'Well, that's a relief,' Nelson-Harmer said. 'Of one kind if not, er, of another.'

There were thirty-two rungs in the ladder. The feet were set in a square of cement from which four steps led down to a ledge running away in each direction beside a channel of rushing water. The sound of the water was very loud now, but not noisy enough to drown a distant splashing and stumbling, a murmur of voices which accompanied a winking pinpoint of light far off to their left.

'Lead, kindly light,' Riordan said. He stepped down on to the ledge. It was perhaps nine inches wide – a little less precarious than the one in the air-shaft of the building above them. The channel was two feet deep, but the swirling current, which occasionally swept a fast wave over the ledge, was not especially murky when Riordan shone the torch down.

For an instant he played the beam on the walls and roof of the sewer. It was flat-arched, built of crumbling, age-old brick. Away in the dark distance, faint shafts of light slanted down from gratings in the streets above. 'Like the catacombs below Paris,' Riordan observed. 'Probably Roman in origin.'

He led the way, moving cautiously in the direction taken by their quarry.

It was a strange and dreamlike pursuit, both the hunter and the hunted moving at a snail's pace, the slightest sounds swelling suddenly to an ominous roar, the swift rush of water diminishing at times to a gurgle. From time to time, as they passed beneath the light from a grating, street noises and the rumble of traffic penetrated their subterranean odyssey. Once they heard a violent argument break out between a man and a woman invisible in the night above.

They lost all sense of time. Tiptoeing here, flat-footing there, sometimes wading a few yards, Riordan had long ago ceased trying to compute the distance they had travelled. They were passing beneath the ninth grating when Nelson-Harmer muttered: 'Poor sods! Thank goodness *we* don't have to do this twice a day. Frankly, I imagine . . .'

He broke off with a gasp. Rotted cement at the edge of the walkway had crumbled beneath his weight, toppling him into the stream and projecting him violently against the far wall of the tunnel.

The stumbling splash, the ringing impact of the gun he was holding against the brickwork and his involuntary smothered curse filled the arched sewer with tell-tale echoes.

Riordan had already blacked out the torch, but he was too late.

There was an angry shout – not so far ahead as he would have expected – and then a vivid orange flash imprinting the tunnel brickwork instantaneously on the dark. And the shattering roar of a heavy-calibre handgun. A powerful beam lanced down the sewer towards them.

'Don't shoot – *duck*!' Riordan yelled, flattening himself against the wall.

But Nelson-Harmer, the ace marksman, his gun already in his bruised hand, was quicker still to react.

He had fired twice – vicious whipcrack shots from the Stetchkin automatic – aiming at the flash and light beam, before the words were out of Riordan's mouth.

They heard a keening cry, a splash heavier than any in

the tunnel so far, something unintelligible from a second voice. The torch arched through the air and dropped into the channel.

Submerged but still glowing it was rolled along by the force of the current, the drowned beam playing now this way, now that, to illuminate the surface or swing reflections across the dripping walls. By the time the torch reached the two mercenaries, the racing water it lit was running a smoky red.

'Act Two curtain!' said Nelson-Harmer shakily.

12

The hijacking had been deceptively simple, perhaps because it had passed so quickly. Crawford, fearless as ever, had taken advantage of a lull when two of the opposition were obliged to reload at the same time. He had dashed across the narrow cul-de-sac and thrown himself down behind an iron bollard outside the bank on the street corner. The bollard, which was over a foot wide at the base and tapered to a ridged boss at the top, had probably been used once as a hitching-post for horses. It was not wide enough to give complete cover, but the curved stem would deflect anything but the most minutely accurate shot aimed at the projecting shoulders of a man lying flat behind it. From here, Crawford was in a position to enfilade the security men by the armoured van.

For a short while an inferno raged along that stretch of pavement. The security men, exchanging a murderous fire with Crawford only inches above the cobbles, were also in peril from the crossfire directed at them from beneath the van on the far side of the lane. Aletti, at the same time, sprayed across a deadly hail at waist height to force them to keep their heads down. And Van Eyck, who had joined him behind the sand bin, blasted off single shots, gouging chips of granite from the pavement in front of their faces.

Confronted by such a barrage, the defenders had no choice. A second man had been hit in the shoulder.

Dragging him with them, they retreated into the bank entrance, shifting crabwise among shards of glass from the shattered revolving doors. Here they should be safe — or safer — until the arrival of reinforcements, which must be imminent.

But it was then that Crawford, profiting from a pause in the cannonade and the screech of ricochets from the curved surfaces of the bollard, had shouted his final orders.

'All right, lads: this is it. Alex, dump the driver and take the wheel. The rest of you, pile in any way you can, shooting as you run.'

Shooting, they ran.

Aletti hauled the dead driver down from the lowered window of the cab, wrenched open the door, and scrambled up inside. The Volkswagen engine clattered into life. Van Eyck, racing behind him, fired the Husqvarna from the hip to down the security man left in the back of the van to guard the remaining sacks of money. It was a lucky shot, shattering the man's knee. The Dutchman dragged him out groaning, and propped him up as a shield while Brod and Christal rounded an open rear door and leaped inside.

Aletti slammed the gear lever into reverse and raced the engine. The van began to roll backwards. Van Eyck lowered the wounded man as gently as he could to the pavement, shielded now by the second open door. The other two mercenaries pulled him up inside. The cumbersome vehicle rocked towards the street.

It was then that Crawford, rising from behind his bollard, jumped for the step on the passenger side of the cab. And it was then too that the bravest of the security guards, stepping out from the bank entrance, stood in the centre of the pavement and spewed out the entire magazine of his Bergmann in one lethal burst.

A deadly 9mm hail from that flaming machine-pistol

cracked across the sergeant's back like a leaden whip, almost cutting him in two. His outstretched arms, so nearly grabbing the door handle, jerked wide; catapulted into the road, he lay on his back like a broken doll, his sightless eyes staring at the grey sky. Beneath him, rivulets of blood etched a spider's web of crimson between the stone-cold cobbles.

Aletti wrenched the wheel of the armoured van around to send the vehicle skidding backward into the main street.

He stamped the brake flat against the floor, forced the unsynchronized gear lever into first and trod on the throttle pedal. The rear wheels spun on the greasy tarmac, finally gripped, and the van shot forward. The bodywork shook as a volley of shots, fired by the men from the police cordon alerted by the sound of gunfire, splatted uselessly against the rear doors. Advancing from the fork in the road, they dropped to one knee and loosed off a second withering barrage of SMG fire. The van staggered again, appeared almost to shake itself, then accelerated ferociously out of range. It careered left on two wheels at a junction, scattering vegetables and fruit from an upturned barrow, zigzagging away on a cobbled surface criss-crossed by pre-war tramlines.

Aletti knew the security men had called for help on the radio: the rasping voices had been clearly audible, distorted by static, over the shooting outside the bank. The speaker beneath the dashboard still vibrated with agitated questions from the local dispatcher. He was determined to get clear of the area before mobile reinforcements got a fix on the vehicle.

But although they were still invisible, it was clear from the dispatcher's terse voice over the radio that pursuers were closing in on the fugitive VW. Whichever way Aletti twisted and turned, doubling back from street to avenue to square, the points of reference quoted invariably, in their geographic sense, suggested the remorseless tightening of a net.

'. . . Skalitzer Strasse towards the river . . . south on Kottbuser Damm, Sonnen-Allee, Eisen Strasse . . . back north-east now, past Treptower Park to Wiener Strasse . . . The émigré revolutionaries are reported to have crossed the river . . . it was at first thought they were heading in a general direction eastwards, towards Lichtenberg and Karlshorst, but they have turned again . . . They have been reported [the dispassionate voice tinged now with excitement] driving north-west on the Rummelsburger Strasse.'

Aletti was flinging the heavy vehicle around a traffic circus not far from the Soviet war memorial when they saw the first of the pursuers. The green-and-white police patrol car was blocked by a bus at the exit from a side-street when they shot past. Seconds later they heard the raucous blast of its siren. Aletti wrestled the van all the way around the circus, skidding perilously close to Moskva saloons, motorcycles and another bus before plunging into the side-street from which the police car had emerged. He snaked through a second street market, shot through a red light in front of an army lorry and narrowly missed a file of children on a pedestrian crossing at a broad crossroads. But still the see-saw blare of the siren, louder now, raced behind them.

'We have a sighting. Hauptstrasse, direction Friedrichs-hain . . . Car B-17 in contact; Cars B-12 and A-6 to converge left and right in support . . . Alerting Car D-9 at Alexanderplatz . . . Alerting Car D-9 at Alexanderplatz . . .'

Aletti turned west and crossed the river again.

The second police patrol car appeared as they roared beneath a bridge carrying the S-Bahn over the road. It flashed past in the opposite direction, braked fiercely, and spun round in a U-turn. In the driving mirror, Aletti saw it catch up with Car B-17. Side by side, passing on both sides of traffic islands, blasting other vehicles out of their way, they pursued their prey.

Despite Aletti's skill at the wheel, the armoured vehicle was no match for the two police Mercedes. They formed up thirty yards behind and stayed there, waiting for a wider stretch of road. There was no point in their wasting ammunition: the VW's rear wheels were too well protected, and the bodywork was impervious to anything less than a rocket grenade or an anti-tank gun.

Their chance came when a third patrol car appeared ahead. Seeing the approaching cavalcade, the driver braked hard, hauling his vehicle around with tyres screaming, to block the road broadside on.

Aletti had no choice: he threw the van into a ninety-degree turn – and found himself in a broad, tree-lined avenue, heading west.

At once the two Mercedes roared up alongside, swinging their heavy bumpers one after the other against the VW's rear-wheel covers.

The van staggered, lurched, staggered again. Aletti corrected as it slewed sideways, then spun the wheel as the patrol cars crashed into it once more. The steel bodywork groaned with each impact.

The pass door between the strongroom section and the cab was open. Van Eyck sat next to Aletti. The scared faces of the other two were crowded into the opening behind them. 'Maybe we better should junk this jalopy and run for it?' the Dutchman suggested.

'Affirmative,' Aletti said. 'Just so I can make it far enough ahead we have the space to run.' He swore as the van almost tipped over under a particularly heavy double assault.

The avenue was running between buildings now: bomb-blasted façades with the blackened scars of flame streaked upwards from each blank window. On the right, a narrower street forked off diagonally to run downhill. Aletti swung the VW into the opening.

'But, Alex . . .' Van Eyck was staring anxiously through the windscreen. 'This lane leads down to the river – and there's no bridge.'

'I know it.'

'Yes, but . . . ?' The Dutchman glanced over his shoulder, then at the outside mirror. The Mercedes, three of them now, were close behind.

'It just happens I know this road,' Aletti said. 'I study maps, you know; I familiarize myself.'

'I am sure you do. Just the same . . . ?'

'Look. Open your door and hold it nearly closed with your two hands, OK? You two' – he glanced over his shoulder – 'unlatch the rear doors, but hold those too almost closed. I'll do the same with mine. There is a step in the road, you see; a big step. When we hit, you throw open those doors and dive out. Right?'

'And then?' Christal asked anxiously.

'If we survive, we scatter. Below this step are bomb-sites still; ruined houses; you know. Together or separately we make our way to the tavern, for the RDV with Riordan, as arranged. You follow me?'

'I am not seeing that we have too much choice,' Van Eyck said.

The lane turned a corner. The slope steepened. Between the ravaged roofs below, the river gleamed cold and grey.

There was indeed a step at the foot of the hill: the road stopped at the top of a ten-foot wall. Steps led down on either side. And below the wall the road, or a continuation of it at a lower level, slanted on for two hundred yards to the waterfront.

Aletti had reckoned on enough speed to shoot the gap, counting on his skill to keep the van upright and manage it to a standstill once it hit the road, with all the damage such an impact implied.

What his maps had failed to show him was that the Russian occupation authorities had considered the step a danger, and before they turned their attention to the restoration of the warren of dilapidated houses below, they had minimized that danger by barring the road along the top of the wall with a cast-iron railing between heavy concrete posts.

The van, with all four wheels locked and streaks of rubber lining the roadway behind, was travelling at some thirty-five miles per hour when it hit the railing.

It shot the gap all right. But upside down and somersaulting, after the nose had ploughed into the cast-iron with an appalling crash and the whole vehicle had reared up vertically to cartwheel over the barrier. Still inverted, it flew a further fifty feet before thumping down on its roof with a concussion that brought masonry tumbling from the façade of the nearest house. During that flight, the hinged bonnet had broken free and flapped away like a metal bird, a quantity of heavy sacks had fallen from the open rear doors, and a number of figures – the driver of the leading patrol car was sure of this – were seen to leap at various stages from different parts of the doomed vehicle.

It was impossible to prove this, however. Because within seconds of the impact, and long before the nearest policeman could leap down the stairs, petrol from the ruptured tank had streamed on to the overheated engine and the whole wreck had erupted into an incandescent ball of fire. By the time the police could get near enough the blazing debris to investigate, the area below the wall was filled with choking black smoke and any survivors would long ago have vanished among the crumbling walls of the waterside ruins.

13

Captain O'Kelly arrived at the rendezvous exactly on time, as was his habit. Although he was wearing a heavy tweed Norfolk suit, with thick woollen stockings below the breeches, and a narrow-brimmed Tyrolean hat with a feather in the band, nobody could conceivably have mistaken him for a German. His silver hair and pink face, witness to the daily application of hot towels, along with startling blue eyes and a certain brusqueness of manner, placed him at once and irrevocably in a narrow curve of territory between the Temple, Smith Square and Jermyn Street.

The rendezvous – that down-at-heel tavern not far from the mercenaries' safe house – was fuller than it had been when Riordan met Brod. A group of beer-swilling workmen from a nearby factory occupied most of the bar; several slatternly women obliterated their poverty with schnapps and other less salubrious potions; there were a number of lone males. The place was quite busy. But there was no sign of Riordan or his men.

Van Eyck and Aletti were the first to arrive, almost twenty minutes after the appointed time. The Dutchman was limping. Both sported more than one strip of sticking plaster. O'Kelly made no move. It had been agreed that any communication must appear to be the result of chance – as between any drinkers in a bar after a glass or two.

O'Kelly's fierce eyebrows nevertheless rose another inch with the appearance of the third latecomer. Brod was covered from head to foot in white brick dust, his face was streaked with blood from a gash in his forehead, and one arm was in a sling.

'Bloody construction workers,' he mumbled to no one in particular. 'On piecework, they are. The more they get done on a shift, the more they get paid – and the hell with any poor sod unfortunate enough to get in the way.'

'What happened, mate?' One of the workers at the bar swung around.

'Happened?' Brod raged. 'I'm only passing this bloody bomb-site where there's a demolition crew at work, knocking down the ruins so that they can put up another monument to socialist realism . . . and this bloody crane-driver just swings his fucking iron ball and sends a five-storey wall crashing down on the pavement the moment I cross the flaming street . . .' He spat on the sawdust floor and shook his head. 'If it hadn't been for this Englander soldier on furlough' – he indicated the dishevelled Christal – 'I'd still be beneath a hundred tons of rubble, waiting to be posted missing my bloody self.'

Christal was dusty but otherwise apparently unhurt. 'Just managed to grab him in time,' he muttered in his bad German.

O'Kelly mentally chalked up a plus sign. He had no idea what had really happened, but the scene had been well played; more importantly, it left the door wide open for communication between the arrivals and those already in the tavern: it would be as normal for O'Kelly, Van Eyck and Aletti to start talking to them as it was for the drinkers propping up the bar. Very soon the place was loud with sympathetic complaints.

'Foreign workers, of course. They're drafting them in by the thousand. Poles, Hungarians, Lithuanians even!'

'No regard for other people; all they want is the cash.'

'Believe it, I was talking to some character he came from *Bulgaria*!'

'. . . the real men lost their lives trying to save the Fatherland.'

'You should have gone to the Commissariat and claimed damages . . .'

'It's the same everywhere: they tell me that even in the West . . .'

'I don't know what things are coming to. A man can't even . . .'

'Things were better when the country was run by . . .'

'Sssssssh! You want to get on the wrong side of the Stasi?'

'What happened?' O'Kelly asked Van Eyck in a low voice after he had loudly joined in the condemnation of the workers supposedly responsible for his condition as well as Brod's. They moved a little away from the raucous commentary along the bar.

'We lost Crawford,' the Dutchman whispered. He bit his lip, shaking his head slowly. 'It was terrible. Awful. Things went so well, and then, suddenly, he was . . . gone. Destroyed.'

Events had moved so fast after the death of the big sergeant, so chaotic had been the succeeding chase and its sequel, that the survivors had been too traumatized even to mention the drama. Stunned by Crawford's loss, they had dared neither express their shock nor examine their feelings. 'Tell me about it,' O'Kelly said gently.

Using very few words, Van Eyck reported Riordan's planned 'diversion' and what had followed it from the moment Christal heard the grenade explosions to the spectacular destruction of the armoured van and his own escape and arrival at the tavern. 'And whether of course it was successful – or worthwhile – we shall not hear until the colonel returns with his report.'

'You must remember,' O'Kelly said, 'that I'm completely in the dark. I . . . happened to be . . . in East Germany myself. I got a message to RDV here with Riordan at a certain time. I arranged to do that. I came here. But I haven't the ghost of an idea how the hostage situation has developed, what stage you've got to . . . or anything else for that matter. For the last couple of days the papers, at any rate the local ones, have contented themselves with brief "nothing to report" pieces.'

'I'd rather you heard the whole story from Riordan himself,' Van Eyck said. 'But, in the nutshell, no hostages are being held in the conference centre, maybe none ever have been, and it seems the Soviet authorities are not only aware of this but are also playing some part in the deception.'

'Good God! You mean the Russians are actually working with these damn terrorists?'

'Not necessarily, no. Just turning the Nelson eye. Because perhaps it may suit them, politically, to have certain hostages out of the way awhile. We already know they do not exactly move the earth and heaven to get these people released.'

'Good God!' O'Kelly said again.

'But perhaps we may know more when Colonel Riordan does come,' Van Eyck said. 'If he has been able to follow the two kidnappers who come to the centre, and maybe find out where they *do* hold these people.'

'I should certainly hope so,' O'Kelly said.

But it was another hour before the mercenary leader finally showed, and most of the drinkers had left, leaving O'Kelly and his four companions awkwardly noticeable as foreigners in the tavern.

Riordan was alone. He nodded to O'Kelly, as though to a chance acquaintance, and felt safe enough to greet Brod, since they had at least been seen together in the same bar before, and survived the murderous hit-and-run attack of the BMW driver only half a block away.

'What happened? Why the fancy dress?' he asked Brod, jerking his head at the dusty and damaged façades of Van Eyck, Christal, Aletti and the Austrian himself.

Brod told him, adding the details, so far as he had seen them, of the loss of Crawford.

'I'm very sorry, both on a personal level,' Riordan said soberly, 'and on the level of this particular mission. The man is . . . was . . . irreplaceable.'

Brod nodded. 'Every war inflicts its casualties. What about your own sortie? Did the diversion work? Did you and Nelson-Harmer get into the building unseen? Were you able to . . . ?'

'Not here,' Riordan interrupted. 'We're already too conspicuous. There's a beer hall on the far side of the roundabout at the end of this street. Teddy's there already. Be there in ten minutes and shake his hand as if you were old friends. Tell the others to come, one before and the others at five-minute intervals. My news can wait until then.' He grinned, tapped Brod on the arm, and drained the beer he had ordered. Seconds later he had left the tavern without a glance at the others.

The beer hall was brawling with late-evening drinkers. In the background, an accordion blared over the hubbub of voices. Although it was a warm night, the wide windows were misted up.

By the time O'Kelly and the six mercenaries had manoeuvred themselves into adjacent booths it was nearly midnight. Between noisily exchanged pleasantries of the sort that could occur between any group of compatriots finding themselves together unexpectedly in a strange country, they exchanged their respective stories. Much of the material had to be repeated, often in bits and pieces, for O'Kelly's benefit.

Before Riordan got to his own account of the terrorists' pursuit along the sewer and the gunfire which terminated it, Aletti had silenced the exchanges with an observation which had escaped everyone else. For some time he had been trying to get in a word. His chance came during a sombre appreciation of the talents of Sergeant Crawford. 'He was a good man,' Riordan said. 'And, like the song says, a good man is hard to find.'

'There's the corollary too,' Nelson-Harmer put in.

'The coro . . . the what?' said a bemused Christal.

'Corollary. The other side of the coin,' the Nigerian explained. 'A good man is hard to find – but also a hard man is good to find. And the old sarge was as hard as they come.'

'He won't be too hard to find for the Comrades,' Aletti lanced into the conversation at last. 'At least so far as his identity it is concerned.'

There was a sudden silence in the two booths. On the far side of the huge circular bar somebody had begun to sing. 'What do you mean, Alex?' Riordan asked at last.

'His disc,' Aletti said. 'He wore one of those oval silver ID bracelets on a chain, remember? I happened to notice it on the plane.'

'And so? It happened to have his name on it? So what?'

'He must have got it when he was still serving,' Aletti said. 'His name was on it, sure. But so was his rank, his regiment and his army service number.'

'Oh, shit!' Riordan said.

'Exactly,' said O'Kelly.

'I don't see that it matters,' Christal complained. 'What

the hell – it was an army ID tag. So what? He demobbed nearly three years ago, didn't he? He was retired, for Chrissake.'

'Matters?' O'Kelly repeated, his voice rising half an octave. 'What does it matter, you say? Just put yourself for a moment, young man, in the position of a Russian press officer whose job is to glorify the Comrades and blacken the West. What a piece of good fortune, what a golden bloody opportunity!'

'I don't see that . . .'

'Listen, lad. They don't have to link it to the hostage situation, which they're playing down anyway. Your "diversion" can stand now as an operation on its own . . . and on a plate as far as they're concerned! What do we have here, from their point of view?' O'Kelly demanded grimly. He ticked off the points on the fingers of one hand.

'We have initially a dastardly attack by armed brigands on a People's Savings Bank. The assault is beaten off by the courageous resistance of Soviet guards, aided by their plucky East German Communist associates, one of whom is killed and two wounded. Finally, when the murderers abandon their vile plan and flee, one of them too is killed . . . and it turns out that he is a non-commissioned officer in the army of another occupying power.'

'*Was* a non-commissioned officer,' Christal corrected.

'Doesn't matter from the propaganda point of view,' O'Kelly said. 'The attack will be presented as a criminal attempt by unruly elements of the British military occupation forces, with or without the complicity of their superiors. Probably the latter: they don't want to – they don't *need* to – make it too far-fetched.'

'But they could say that about any underworld manifestation, any terrorist gang operating in their zone,' Van Eyck protested.

'They could *say* it, yes,' Riordan cut in. 'But they couldn't prove it, and nobody would believe them anyway. This time, though, they will be able to prove it – or appear to be able to. Because of that damn ID tag.'

'Yes, but . . . I mean, the bloody British will deny it flatly. They'll . . .'

'Of course they will, Piet. They'll say, perfectly truthfully, that there are no "unruly elements" in the Soviet zone or anywhere else; that they have no trace of any Sergeant Crawford since he left the army three years ago. But then they would say that, wouldn't they?'

'They may not allow the British authorities near enough to read the number,' O'Kelly said. 'They may not even release the name – at first. They're a pretty devious crew, after all. They may simply produce the tag as evidence, and then sit on it hard. But that'd be quite enough to convince the world press, especially in the uncommitted countries, and provide a hearty slap in the face for the Brits, a bone for the other members of the four-power Commission to pick . . . and a splendid propaganda coup and political scandal for the Russkis to gloat over.'

'Which is exactly what we're being paid to avoid,' Riordan said.

'So, like it says in the exam papers, what does A do?' Nelson-Harmer asked.

'We must get the ID tag back,' answered Riordan.

The morgue in that district of the Soviet sector was in a basement behind the Rathaus, the town hall. It was flanked by a red-brick building whose courtyard was used by the local police as a motor pool, and a restored block housing suites of new offices, most of them occupied by Party functionaries, commissars transplanted from Moscow and experts in making the simple appear complex.

Riordan and Christal surveyed the entrance from a dark doorway across the street. It was three o'clock in the morning. The red-brick building was in darkness; only three windows in the office block — on the first, third and ninth floors — showed lights. The sky was clear, bright stars eclipsed every few minutes by the landing lights of airlift planes trundling supplies into Gatow, Tegel and Tempelhof. A chill wind blew scraps of paper and empty cigarette packets along the gutter.

'There are blackout doors at street level,' Riordan said. 'With a night clerk and a guard to see that he stays awake on the far side. We have to surprise them from inside the building so that we can prepare an entry into the morgue from the area. Do you think you can make that third-floor window — or rather the dark one next to it — up the outer face of the block?'

Christal was silent for perhaps three minutes, his ready eyes taking in every detail of the pipes, cornices, ledges and sills webbing the façade in the wan glow of the sodium street lights. Then he nodded. 'Piece of cake. 'Course it depends on the latches of the unlit window. How long it takes to get in, I mean.'

'Sashes,' Riordan said. 'You can slip in a knife-blade.'

'Tickety-boo. But come to think of it, how the hell do you happen to know all this? If you don't mind my asking.'

'I was here earlier this evening,' Riordan said. 'Looking around.'

'No kidding. But of course . . . you never did get around to filling us in on what happened when you tailed them two terrorists from the centre, did you?'

'It's not a story you're likely to believe,' Riordan said.

He drew Christal further back into the shadows as a green-and-white prowl car, with lights flashing, turned into the far end of the street. The car skidded to a halt outside the red-brick building. One of the rear doors opened. They heard an exchange of words, a burst of laughter, and then the door slammed. A dark figure ran into the courtyard. The car accelerated away, turning left at an intersection. The rasp of its exhaust faded, died. Two minutes later a light came on in one of the first-floor windows of the block.

'You were saying?' Christal prompted when the street was silent again.

'I can't go into it all now,' Riordan said, 'but, briefly, we followed the terrorists into a kind of underground tunnel, a culvert, they rumbled us, there was an exchange of shots and one of them was killed.'

He paused, squinting up into the sky. An orange glow silhouetting the rooftops in the west had dimmed and then vanished. A power cut in the American zone had killed Tempelhof's landing lights.

'And then?' Christal said.

'We reckoned it was safe to assume the survivor wouldn't necessarily know there were two of us too. It was a chance worth taking anyway. I told Teddy to continue tailing the guy, to let himself be spotted when they surfaced, and to allow the guy to lose him.'

The cat burglar chuckled. 'He ain't exactly the most anonymous man you ever saw, our Ted.'

'They came up through a manhole in a side-street,' Riordan said. 'The guy was running now. I crammed on speed too, took the next manhole and tailed Teddy. He let the guy dump him in an all-night café and cigar store – in one door and straight out past the toilets at the back.'

'Amateur stuff,' Christal said.

Riordan nodded. 'I was waiting for him. He led me a couple of blocks and sneaked into another bar, only this time he took a seat; he joined two men in a booth at the back. Since he'd never set eyes on me, I chanced it again and moved into the next booth. The place was crowded – the sort of smoky dump where you find late-duty tram drivers on their way home, night maintenance men, taxi drivers and whores who didn't click. It was noisy as hell too, so I didn't have a hope of hearing what these characters were saying. But I could watch without seeming too nosy – and what I saw . . . well, like I say, you wouldn't believe it.'

Riordan paused again. A heavy aircraft, planing in to land with floodlights blazing from the leading edge of each wing, had zoomed up again at the last minute to circle the darkened field. Behind the two mercenaries, glass panels in a doorway rattled as the thunder of four engines under full boost shook the ground.

'Sometimes,' Riordan said, 'coincidences are too much. Maybe they happen to guys like me because we move around a lot, have to learn to keep our eyes open all the time, can't afford to miss a trick. Whatever, what I was seeing in that all-night bar would have meant nothing to me . . . if it hadn't been for the fact that I happened to know both the men the terrorist was meeting. Or at least know who they were and what they did.'

The rooftops were silhouetted once more. A fainter glow this time as supplementary generators activated the emergency lights. The circling heavy aircraft had landed and another was already on its way in.

Riordan said: 'There was a lot of gesticulating, hand-waving and shrugging of shoulders and that sort of thing. I guessed the terrorist was explaining what happened to his mate and why. He was the type you might expect: swarthy, with dark, receding hair, very bright eyes, and a bushy moustache. It was the other two who gave me, as the French say, furiously to think. Or, rather, the fact that they were together, in that place, at that time. That they were together at all.'

'So who the hell were they? Truman and Stalin?'

'Not quite. But about as likely. One of them,' Riordan said slowly, 'was a KGB officer called Piotr Peniakov – or at any rate that's what he was called when I met him in a Helsinki POW camp during the Russo-Finnish war. The other was Klaus Frodenburg, one of the leading theatrical agents in Berlin.'

'A theatrical agent . . . ? But what the fuck . . . ?' Christal's astonishment was almost comical.

'Right. A KGB officer hobnobbing with a terrorist in a hostage situation was weird enough. But as you say, what the fuck could someone in the entertainment business be doing there?'

'You found out?'

'I think so. The Russian seemed to be leading the conversation. He was putting all the questions. That was normal enough. But the crunch came when they all appeared to run out of words. That was when Frodenburg shrugged, glanced at the KGB man – who nodded – and produced a briefcase from under his seat. He unstrapped it, took out an envelope, and gave it to the terrorist. The guy opened the flap, took a dekko inside that, made some remark . . . and then got up and walked out.'

'Did you see what was inside the envelope?'

'A wad of bills,' Riordan said.

'Christ! The Aussies have a phrase, don't they: "You wouldn't read about it in a book!" But how the hell *did* you read that?'

'I reckon there's only one explanation fits *all* the facts,' Riordan said, 'given that the whole conference centre set-up is a fake. Our kidnapper is no terrorist at all but an actor – employed, via Frodenburg, by the KGB to impersonate some dyed-in-the-wool villain who could convince the world press of his villainy. He looked like an Iranian or perhaps a Kurd. I might guess one of the reasons they chose him was exactly because he spoke that dialect that was Greek to almost everyone else.'

'Just go on,' Christal said. 'And don't any fucker wake me up.'

'I'd imagine further,' Riordan said, 'that all the so-called terrorists who have actually been seen are equally . . . well, spurious.'

'Spurious? You mean like phoney?'

'I do. Probably actors hired through the same agent. There need not have been more than half a dozen at the most. Maybe even less, judging from the low profile the kidnappers have kept.'

'I have just one question,' Christal said.

'Shoot it to me.'

'Why? Why the fuck bother? What's in it for anybody, anywhere? All this complicated sodding claptrap: who's really on the make here?'

'That sounds more like five questions,' Riordan said. 'For my money, two points will cover them all. One: who stands to gain? The Russians: there really are hostages held somewhere and it suits them politically to have some of these people temporarily out of the way. Two: why all this complex charade? Answer: because the hostage situation, if it's successful, deflects attention away from the strength of that Soviet interest.'

'Are you telling me that this whole bloody thing has been masterminded by our . . . ?'

'For the moment, Danny, I'm telling you nothing more.' Riordan was looking at the illuminated face of his watch. A plane, very low overhead, flew in towards Tempelhof. 'It's more than an hour since they changed shifts across the road. Enough time for the new men to lower their guard a bit, maybe start feeling a little sleepy. And time enough for us to make our move.'

'I'm on my way,' Christal said.

'You know what to do?'

'Make it to the room next to that lighted window on the third floor, put the cop you tell me guards the files in there to sleep, put on his uniform and take the stairway down to the lobby. Then I step out and surprise the two there long enough for you to make your entrance, OK?'

'Perfect. And the signal?'

'I shout "*Achtung!*" as I make my entrance.'

'That's my boy.' Riordan grinned in the darkness. The idea of Christal, wearing a stolen uniform and, yelling "*Achtung!*", being mistaken for a German policeman was hilarious. But split-second timing was vital, and that instant of burlesque should give Riordan himself the opportunity to burst in and get the drop on the night clerk and his guard while – hopefully – they were still turned around to confront the apparition from within.

'I'll see you,' Christal said. As yet another freight plane rumbled overhead, he dashed silently across the street and crouched down on the dark side of a bus shelter there. When he stood upright again, the suction pads were strapped to his elbows and knees and he wore his soft-soled climber's boots. He vaulted nimbly over an iron railing and approached the wall of the block.

From the doorway, Riordan watched him climb, marvelling at the man's skill and agility. Even knowing he was there, it was at times difficult to make him out among the shadowy pipes and projections on the moonlit wall. Christal shinned up a pipe, traversed a chimney breast, swung out sideways to grasp a ledge, hauled himself up and reached for a console below one of the second-floor bays. From here he launched himself across six feet of bare wall, the only space over which, for two heartstopping seconds, he had to rely wholly on the grip of his pads and soles. Catlike, he balanced on a ledge as he tensed to jump for another pipe.

Headlights lanced the gloom of the street. Christal froze. A Russian scout car packed with soldiers in uniform careered into view, roaring towards the office block. In the doorway, Riordan held his breath. A security patrol . . . or troops returning to barracks after a night on the town?

Christal was spread-eagled on his ledge, visible on the wall's one bright, uncluttered, moonlit patch as an insect pinned to a board. If you happened to be looking that way.

The scout car was open, like an oversize jeep with the top down. Were the soldiers looking? Thankfully not. They were singing – a drunken chorus of some mournful melody from the steppes. The car passed the building and swung out of sight around a corner. The voices dwindled away, swallowed by the pulse of the city night.

Christal leaped. Riordan heard a scrape of metal and a muffled clang as he clung to the pipe. Seconds later he was hunched down on the sill of the target window. There was no visible reaction from behind the illuminated pane alongside.

A very faint creak of wood . . . a momentary flash of reflected moonlight as bright glass moved . . . and the cat burglar had vanished inside the building.

Riordan was aware that the incessant drone of aircraft landing or taking off had ceased. In the silence he fancied he could hear the thumping of his own heart. The silhouette of a man wearing a peaked cap appeared in the lit window. An arm swept up in a beckoning gesture. Riordan counted slowly to a hundred, then crossed the road.

Outside the block's double entrance doors, he drew his Browning automatic and pulled back the slide. He stood, listening, just back from the crack between the two doors.

In the distance, an early U-Bahn train rattled along rails. Somewhere, there was a sudden burst of music, quickly stilled. No sound was audible from the far side of the doors.

And then, chilling in its expectedness, the strong but reedy voice of Danny Christal.

'*Achtung!*'

Riordan drew back his right foot. His leg shot forward to thud with stunning force between the doors at the level of the lock. He sprang forward as the doors crashed open, hurling himself into the lobby with the Browning out-thrust, his whiplash voice rapping out the time-honoured threat: 'Put up your hands, fast, or you're dead!'

The scene that confronted him on the far side of the bleak lobby etched itself into his mind. It was to remain there a long time. Three figures in arrested motion: a Soviet infantryman, halfway to his feet, frozen with one hand outstretched towards a Tokarev sub-machine-gun propped against a wall behind the desk; Christal at the entrance to the stairway, absurd in a uniform three sizes too big for him but the gun in his hand steady as a rock; the night clerk half turned in a swivel chair, backed up against the desk.

The clerk was a woman, a sullen, heavily built, short-haired type of the kind seen sweeping the streets or driving Moscow buses. Even as Riordan came to a halt, her hand was reaching for the phone on the desk.

'*Nyet!*' Riordan yelled. 'This is ungallant, I'm sorry, but it's necessary.' He strode forward and tapped her behind the ear with the butt of his Browning. The woman folded sideways across the desk, then rolled out of her chair and subsided to the floor.

Christal meanwhile, with the most economical movement but surprising force, had rabbit-punched the guard, who collapsed against the wall, knocking the SMG sideways, and slid down behind the desk.

'That uniform,' Riordan burst out, swooping to catch the weapon before it fell. 'That's a Russian Intelligence major's! What the hell . . . ?'

Christal spread his arms. 'Search me. You said a Kraut cop. But this was the guy watching the files.' He shook his head. 'He fell hard.'

'I'm not surprised, looking at the size of his uniform,' Riordan said. 'You better strip that off and change with the soldier here.'

'Just my luck,' Christal complained. 'Reduced to the fucking ranks again! A bloody private this time.'

'At least you won't get court-martialled,' Riordan said. 'I'll see if I can get into that gear myself.'

The peaked Soviet military headwear, with its absurdly wide circular top, sat uneasily on their heads, but otherwise they looked reasonably convincing as an officer and his escort. Christal shouldered the Tokarev and they made their way downstairs to the basement.

The area was narrow but uncluttered. It was separated from the outside of the morgue only by a low wall topped by an iron railing. Voluminous Russian greatcoats made the crossing of this awkward, but once they were over it was no problem for Christal to force a storeroom window and let them in.

They crept through to the entrance lobby and rattled the outer doors as if they had just unlocked them, then walked boldly to the anteroom outside the chamber reserved for the dead. A thickset man in a white laboratory coat, drowsing over a desk on which stood a box telephone installation, pushed back his chair abruptly as they marched in.

'*Herr Major*!' he exclaimed. 'I am sorry. I did not think . . . that is to say, I was not expecting . . .'

'We do not work office hours in my division,' Riordan barked. 'It is expected that minor officials – especially minor ones – should respect the same devotion to duty.'

'Yes, sir. Of course,' the morgue attendant stammered, his florid features paling under the harsh neon lights. 'It was just that, for a moment . . .'

'Enough. The commissar shall hear of your dereliction.' Riordan spoke Russian with a Finnish accent. He hoped that when he made the double switch – affecting to speak German with the accent of a Russian occupier – the disparity would not be too evident. 'Now . . . a criminal was delivered here by the security police. At the end of the afternoon.'

'Oh, yes, indeed, sir. An Englander involved in a bank robbery. They said that he had . . .'

'Take me to him.' Anxious to please now, the attendant was thinking of anything but accents. 'If the Herr Major would come this way . . .' he mumbled, opening double doors leading to the cold-storage department.

'Stay here, Oblomov,' Riordan snapped over his shoulder, unwilling to subject Christal to too close a scrutiny under those lights.

Still standing by the entrance doors, Christal sprang to attention, clicked his heels and murmured what he hoped might sound like a Russian affirmative. Riordan followed the attendant through the doors.

Three sides of the bare room, with its tiled floor and central drain hole, were occupied by the long, deep drawers in which the dead awaited burial or post-mortem inspection. An examination table, complete with the basins and soakaway tubes necessary for autopsies, stood above the drain. The stench of formaldehyde cloyed the refrigerated air.

The attendant stood with a hand resting on the outside of a drawer in the centre row of three on the far side of the room. 'If the Herr Major would care to step over here . . . ?'

'I do not wish to view the body,' Riordan said hastily, reluctant to see what a full magazine of 9mm Parabellums, fired at five hundred rounds per minute, had done to the frame of his sergeant. The drawer had already begun to move. 'It is the effects that interest me, what the man was carrying.'

'Of course.' The drawer slid closed. 'They have of course been removed. All is accounted for, doubly signed and listed on this bulletin.' The attendant unhooked a small clipboard from the handle of the drawer. 'A second copy was removed by the police.'

'Read it to me.'

The attendant fished a pair of steel-rimmed spectacles with circular lenses from his overalls' pocket and settled them on his nose. 'Regrettably,' he said, 'there was nothing that could be done with the clothes. They were much too . . .'

'Quite. Read me the rest.'

The man cleared his throat, then recited in a singsong voice:

'Two Swiss-manufacture climbing boots, unmarked; one eighteen-carat gold signet ring, monogrammed BC; a silver neck chain bearing a small silver effigy believed to represent the Judaeo-Christian Saint Christopher; a silver identity bracelet bearing a military inscription . . .'

'Ah, yes: the famous bracelet,' Riordan muttered.

'. . . one flat-bladed knife in a leather ankle sheath; a

packet of "Full Strength" Capstan cigarettes containing nine unsmoked cigarettes, three stubbed butts and a Ronson metal lighter; one Browning-style automatic pistol with a full magazine; three twenty-four-carat gold crowns, one severely damaged, possibly by a bullet penetrating the head as the body fell.'

My God, Riordan thought. They even remove the teeth! In such a way are we stripped of all personality in the total anonymity of that final dark. The unsmoked cigarettes, the professionally husbanded stubs that would leave no evidence, the fetish saint secretly worn – all removed, all docketed, filed and taken away. No rings on the hand that knocked at the door.

Aloud, he said: 'I wish to examine these articles.'

The attendant's jaw dropped open. 'But . . . Herr Major . . . that is not possible. I cannot . . .'

'I order you to produce them immediately. At once.'

'Sir, it is not possible. They are no longer here.'

'No longer . . . ? Then where the devil are they?' Riordan shouted.

'They were taken by the Intelligence colonel,' the attendant gabbled. 'He signed for them. Everything is in order. They will be quite safe. He is to keep them for the officers from the Propaganda Abteilung who will come tomorrow.'

'Oh, yes,' Riordan said, changing key rapidly. 'I forgot the colonel might get here before me . . . Where did you say he was keeping them?'

'Why . . . in the PA filing centre, of course. Up on the . . .'

'On the third floor of the building next door, naturally,' Riordan cut in swiftly. The man's eyes had flicked momentarily upward and he reckoned the hunch was worth playing.

'Yes, sir. Of course. You need not worry. The colonel will be there all night, and they will doubtless be in his safe.'

'Very good. We shall visit him now. Oblomov, open the main doors. And as for you' – he threw a piercing glance at the attendant – 'make sure you remain awake for the remainder of your tour of duty.'

'*Jawohl, Herr Major,*' the man said.

Christal jerked open the latch of the self-locking outer doors and they strode into the night. The doors hissed shut behind them.

The sky was full of aircraft again. Riordan wondered idly why Crawford's Bergmann machine-pistol had been missing from the list of his effects. Which black-market channel would be handling the weapon now?

They went back into the office block through the doors he had so recently kicked open. The night clerk and the guard were still laid out on the floor. 'We'll drag them into the stairway, close the doors and get back into our own clothes,' Riordan said. 'Then – I'm afraid it's a bit of a lumber for you, but at least it's inside this time – you're on your way back to the hard man on the third floor!'

Christal grinned. 'If a thing's worth doing once, it's worth doing twice,' he said.

14

One of the most frequently quoted aphorisms in France, customarily invoked in cases of accident, misfortune or loss, is *Jamais deux sans trois* – Never two without a third. The fact that truisms, like contraband, can cross frontiers was proven yet again in Berlin, on the night Barry Riordan determined to retrieve the identity tag from the body of his dead sergeant.

Christal had been philosophical about the necessity to return a second time to the Russian filing centre on the third floor of the office block next door to the morgue. In fact a third visit was required.

The reason of course was the safe.

'I never noticed the fucker first time around,' the cat burglar confessed when he returned to the office with his leader. 'But then I was here to nick the bloke's bloody uniform, wasn't I?'

'Not to worry,' Riordan said. 'We didn't know there *was* a safe, and certainly not that Crawford's bracelet would be in it. The thing is, can you crack it?'

The safe was very old, extremely large – and very solid. It stood half immured in a wall between two stacks of steel filing cabinets. The guardian, who was also very large and solid, but not that old, sat in his long-legged underwear, roped to a chair in front of a table equipped with a PBX manual telephone exchange. His eyes were closed and he snored slightly over the wide band of sticking plaster circling his thick neck and gagging his mouth.

Christal walked around the projecting parts of the safe, tapping here, stroking there. 'Not a hope,' he said, shaking his head. 'This kind of caper ain't my bag, honest. I'm no peterman. I ain't saying I ain't used a mite of jelly in my time – when the haul was certain and the premises unoccupied. But you'd need a sackful of the stuff to bust this one . . . and probably start World War bloody III into the bargain.'

'Right,' Riordan said. 'We can't afford noise, even if we had the stuff. There was a light on the ninth floor, remember. It's out now, but whoever it was is still there, because nobody's left the building since you got in: if they had, there'd have been a hue and cry when the couple in the lobby were missed.' He stared again at the safe, with its heavily moulded corners and iron curlicues. It was dark green, with the paint worn away to show dull metal over some of the smooth projections. 'There's that huge keyhole, of course . . .' he said.

'No,' Christal told him. 'Key's probably in the left-hand drawer of that table. But it's only to help you swing open that bloody great door once the combination's been entered. Some models, you fuck up the combo if you mess with the key first.'

'So it's crack the combination . . . or nothing?'

'Yes, sir.'

'In other words . . . Brod or nothing?'

'I reckon.'

Riordan sighed. 'We'll have to risk it. Go get him, Danny. Quick as you can. I'll hold the fort until you return.'

Christal nodded. He fingered the butt of his Stetchkin. 'Give our friends downstairs another friendly tap on the way out?'

'You'll find this easier, safer and surer,' Riordan said. He pulled up the hem of his black roll-neck sweater and fished a small, flat cardboard box from a pocket in the money belt around his waist. He handed the box to Christal. It contained a miniature phial with a black rubber membrane sealing the neck, and a diminutive hypodermic syringe in a cellophane wrapping.

Christal took the box. He grinned. 'Mickey Finns for two coming up,' he said. 'See you.' He left the office, closing the door silently behind him.

Would he have the sense to change out of the ill-fitting uniform and collect his own clothes when he attended to the night clerk and the guard? Riordan wondered. Or would he accept that rapidity was everything and chance meeting a Russian patrol on his way to contact Brod? Maybe he should have given Christal specific orders on that. Forget it, he told himself. You're the guy who's supposed to know how to delegate!

He switched off the lights and moved to the window. Behind him, the unconscious Russian snored in his bonds. Soon Christal appeared outside the entrance to the block. Still wearing the Russian military cap, he had thrown the greatcoat over his own inner garments. The machine-pistol was once again slung over his shoulder. He crossed the street and hurried away.

Riordan chuckled. 'Smart boy,' he murmured aloud. 'Best of both worlds – if luck is with him!' He settled down to wait.

It was going to be tight, however quickly the burglar could get Brod to the block. Already, the eastern sky above the roofs of the houses on the far side of the street appeared to be paling slightly.

The drone of incoming and outgoing aircraft wavered but never ceased. Occasionally a patrol car or a lorry passed the block. In the distance, early trains shunted. A night-worker rode homewards on a bicycle.

The sands of sleep denied were gritting beneath Riordan's eyelids by the time Christal returned with the safe-breaker, although in fact it was less than forty minutes since he set off from the block. From his vantage-point in the darkened window, the mercenary leader had missed their surreptitious arrival below.

Suddenly, silently, the door swung inwards and they were there.

'No lights,' Brod whispered. 'I can concentrate in the dark. Just show me where it is.' A thin beam of illumination slanted down from the masked torch in his hand.

Riordan took his arm and guided him around the table and across the room. 'Here. Between these two rows of files.'

The beam of light played over the rugged surface of the safe. 'Oh,' Brod chuckled. 'An old Brumann & Esterhazy, Model Nine. We're old friends.'

'You can open it?'

'If I cannot, nobody can,' Brod said without a trace of vanity or irony. He was just stating a fact.

He knelt down in front of the safe, inserted the earpieces of his stethoscope, held the business end against the steel door and reached the long, thin fingers of his free hand for the dial of the combination lock.

For what seemed a long time there was no sound in the room but heavy breathing. It was interrupted only occasionally by the faintest of clicks from the interior of the safe, a murmur of annoyance or satisfaction quickly smothered by the cracksman. Once there was a louder, more definite snick as a tumbler fell.

It was just after this that the captive Russian regained

consciousness, gurgling behind the plaster gag and creaking the chair as he strained against his bonds.

Brod unshipped the stethoscope and turned around. 'Frankly,' he said, 'one could do without any further manif on the part of that agito.'

'Right,' Riordan said. He stepped towards the prisoner, held out his handgun butt forward, and said: 'One more sound, just a single sound from you, and you get a second helping of this.'

In the dim torch beam, light glinted on the metal framing the butt – and on the furious glare blazing from pale-blue eyes above the sticking plaster. Far from obeying Riordan's order, the Russian Intelligence officer began a loud and unintelligible roaring behind the muffling gag, at the same time rocking the chair frantically back and forth so that the front legs crashed repeatedly against the wooden floor.

Riordan raised his gun arm, but Christal forestalled the blow. 'Upstairs, downstairs, what's the bleeding difference,' he said. 'This is the one thing they learned me in that fucking unarmed-combat course!' For the second time that night, a scientifically placed rabbit punch silenced an adversary. It was delivered just in time. A soft red glow was pulsing now on the fringe of the torchlight.

A pilot lamp flicked on and off above one terminal on the PBX box.

Riordan didn't hesitate. Stifling a curse, he pressed down a lever on the switchboard and picked up the handset. 'Listening,' he said in Russian.

The mercenaries held their breath. Faintly, they could hear an authoritative voice quacking in the earpiece. 'Understood,' Riordan said, and replaced the handset. The red pilot was extinguished.

'The Propaganda Abteilung, or whatever the Soviets call

it,' he said tightly. 'Their man is coming to collect "the material in the safe".'

Christal broke the silence. 'When?' he croaked. And then: 'Just that? One man?'

'Fifteen minutes,' Riordan said. 'And they didn't say, but he's bound to have an escort.' He turned to Brod. 'Can do?'

Dawn light was now diluting the gloom in the torchlit office. In its pale, cold illumination they saw the Austrian's elaborate shrug. 'It depends,' he said. 'One more tumbler. Now shut up.' He bent back towards the safe.

The tension in that room as they waited was almost tangible.

Five minutes passed . . . seven minutes, eight . . . Tiny clicks. A scrape of metal. A breath caught.

Trains clattered along the S-Bahn. A lorry's engine roared. Riordan felt the thumping of his heart shake his entire body. His throat was dry, and there was nothing they could do – nothing but wait.

Ten minutes . . . eleven . . . twelve . . .

'Got it!' Brod's triumphant cry shattered the silence and drowned the final decisive clunk within the safe. The massive door swung open.

Riordan's torch showed up ledgers, bundles of newly minted – but now outmoded – Reichsmarks, a small box file, several documents in Cyrillic script bound with red ribbon.

There was also a large brown envelope closed with wire which ran through a wax seal. Riordan snatched it out and slit it open with his commando knife.

'I think they're here,' Christal called from the window.

Down in the street below, motorcycle engines stuttered into silence. Crawford's effects were strewn across the table. Riordan pocketed everything identifiably British:

the cigarettes, the Ronson lighter, the signet ring (the hallmark would identify its place of manufacture), the St Christopher, the tell-tale ID bracelet of course, and even the gold crowns (they could be matched to Crawford's jaw. And, possibly, somewhere, a dentist's chart with a name and number. The KGB was nothing if not efficient).

Riordan ran to the window. A Zil limousine and a Zastva staff car were angled into the pavement below. Two uniformed outriders leaned their machines on their stands.

'We'll take the stairs,' Riordan said. 'Danny, call all the lifts to this floor. That'll give us a couple of minutes while they call them down again. Junk the cap and greatcoat; keep the shooter.'

'I brought up your own clobber,' Christal said from the door.

'Great. I'll leave the greatcoat and jacket here, change the trousers once we're clear.

Brod was at the window. 'Guy in civvies has got out of the limo,' he reported. 'Fur collar and fur hat. Two offos from the staffer. They're at the entrance. Two guards with SMGs left to guard the door. Christ, talk about cutting it fine . . . !' There was sweat on his forehead.

'Don't panic,' Riordan warned. They could hear the lifts whining upwards. 'We're the ones in a hurry. So far as the Russkis are concerned, until they see this office it's just a routine call. No urgency, no sweat, no need to be on the lookout . . . at first. By the time they're wise to what happened we'll be away.'

'But . . . the guards on the door?'

'There's a back way out. Danny found it earlier. A yard with bins full of shredded papers, discarded film stock. And a wall with a door in it. They have no reason to cover the rear . . . yet. They may not even know there should be a night clerk on duty.' He took Brod by the arm. 'C'mon, soldier: let's go.'

Slipping through the pass door to the emergency stairway, the three mercenaries heard the heavy click of contacts as the lifts were summoned back to ground-floor level. They were passing the first floor when gates clanged shut and one of the lifts began to rise again. By the time the shouting started, they were through the yard and out into the lane beyond.

Three blocks away, they slowed down. Ahead of them, a wide, curving avenue led to the roundabout and then the tavern, the lane and the bomb-damaged house which had become their secret base. The sky was no longer clear: dawn had brought low clouds, scurrying from east to west. The eastern horizon, nevertheless, still glowed a fiery red.

'"Red sky in the morning . . .",' Riordan began, stopping halfway through the proverb as a Dakota banked steeply over the Russian zone and then settled into a glide path heading for the runway at Gatow. The undercart thumped down as the freighter seemed to skim the rooftops on its approach.

'Who was it supposed to be warning?' Christal asked. 'The red sky, I mean.'

'Shepherds,' Riordan said. 'Though I'm not so sure . . .' He stopped again. 'That's no romantic sunrise,' he said slowly. 'The red light's reflected *downwards* from the *under*side of the clouds.'

'It's kind of pulsating too,' Brod said. 'Brightening and then fading, almost as if there was . . .'

He broke off. Riordan had started to run.

They needed to go no further than the roundabout.

The lane was choked with fire engines and a turntable jetting foam. Fat hoses from a water-cart snaked across the cobbles. Axe-wielding men in bright helmets smashed at the door above glistening puddles blushing a ruby red.

It was already clear, though, that their safe house was doomed beyond recall. Flames streamed from each gaping window, and a column of fire, blazing through the shattered roof, was whirling sparks high up into the tower of black smoke looming over the quarter.

'We got away – through the rear entrance and across the waste ground.' Nelson-Harmer had materialized beside them, his soft voice barely audible over the roar and crackle of the inferno. 'It was a near thing, just the same. They lobbed an incendiary through one of the holes in the roof for starters, and I'm pretty sure someone was in there later with a bloody flame-thrower. Nice people, eh?'

'What did you save?' Riordan asked.

'Bugger all, old man. The pistols we carried, one of the Bergmanns, and what we wore. It was rather urgent, if you see what I mean.'

Inside the burning house, a heavy beam fell, sending a fresh stream of sparks cascading through the savaged roof. The murmurs of excitement swaying through the crowd gathered outside the tavern and jamming the far end of the street swelled momentarily to a roar.

'Place is completely gutted, of course,' the Nigerian said. 'Everything else – weapons, supplies, maps, gear, ammunition, the lot – went up in smoke. Folks outside had a hell of a time for a while, listening to all that 9mm stuff going off. To say nothing of the odd grenade.'

In the distance, approaching police sirens and ambulance bells could be heard over the hubbub animating the area.

'Not so secret after all,' Riordan said.

15

During the first week of the Berlin Blockade, the RAF's No. 46 Group was required to organize from among the sixty Dakota aircraft available a daily total of 161 sorties, which would fly four hundred tons of urgently needed supplies into the beleaguered city. Forty four-engined Avro York transports, which were faster and carried a bigger payload, would be added within the next few days. Airfield controllers at the inner end of the access corridors were ordered to prepare for a landing rate of one plane every four minutes.

In the same period, with longer distances to cover, the 102 C-47 transports of the USAF 60th and 61st Troop Carrier Groups flew in an astonishing fifteen hundred tons daily from the southern part of Germany.

Flying boats which landed subsequently on the Havel lake, and civil aircraft from British Overseas Airways, British South American Airways and twenty-three charter companies, added to 100 sorties daily by the Yorks, soon greatly increased these figures. At the height of the airlift the amount of supplies flown in each day was equivalent to that carried by twenty-two trains, each of fifty freight cars.

There were innumerable troubles to be overcome. The most important of these were inadequate airfield facilities, the lack of the most modern approach aids, the difficulty of maintaining an even flow of arrivals when planes flew at differing speeds, and crew fatigue. In the initial weeks of the blockade the number of US personnel alone assigned to airlift duties rose from 1300 officers and 3600 men to 2400 officers and no fewer than 7500 airmen.

American Shooting Star jets and British Tempest fighters were on hand to protect the transports and keep the corridors open if necessary. And, as a moral deterrent, a force of B-29 Super Fortresses was transferred to Europe for 'exercises'.

'As you know,' Captain O'Kelly told Riordan and his men, 'these planes are capable of delivering atomic warheads over huge distances. What you don't know, and the Russkis, thank Christ, don't know because it's the world's most closely guarded secret, is that only two atomic bombs actually exist at present. They were made in case a couple more might be needed to flatten Japan – and then stored. There'll be more coming, but at this moment the situation is ultra-sensitive.

'I'm feeding you all this because it has a crucial bearing on your mission. The name of the game, of course, is politics. And the politics in question relate to nothing less than our wartime ally's determination to steer the world, shall we say, off course. To the left.'

'Are you telling us the Comrades aim to run the whole sodding planet?' Christal asked.

'That's one way of putting it,' O'Kelly said.

'The extension, globally, of spheres of influence might be another,' Riordan said.

'Exactly. There are rumours, pretty strong ones, that Chiang Kai-shek's Nationalist forces are about to be over-run by the Reds in the Far East. Imagine the propaganda impact if the whole of China falls into Communist hands! We hope to beat their damn blockade here, but just suppose they did starve us out of Berlin? Yet another propaganda victory. Add to this the possibility of vastly increased Soviet influence – perhaps even Communist control – in the Middle East, Suez and West Africa . . .' O'Kelly shook his head. 'Well, you can see why it's absolutely essential that we crack the hostage situation wide open and release these johnnies before it's too bloody late. If those three areas were to turn left, by God, Western Europe would be, to all intents and purposes, encircled.'

They were sitting in a corner café at the western end of the Kurfürstendamm, only three hundred yards from the Grunewald woods and the lake where their plane had made its spectacular forced landing. Bad weather had turned the stream of incoming aircraft into a trickle: the sky was overcast; rain drummed on the canvas awning above the café entrance and splashed ankle-high from the pavement outside.

There was very little traffic. Many of the shops were closed. The market gardens supplying the city's fresh fruit and vegetables all lay in the Russian sector of Germany and deliveries to the Western zones had been brusquely terminated. Pedestrians hurrying with bent heads past the café towards the nearest bread queue displayed tense expressions above their turned-up collars.

'Of course it's vital to get them out,' Riordan said. 'Nothing has changed from that point of view. What has changed – completely – is the actual situation. Both from our angle and theirs. We arrive here with the idea that we're faced with the standard hostage scenario: a group of people held prisoner at gunpoint in a closed urban situation, their release to be balanced against specific terms. We anticipate something like the standard answer to that problem: isolation, militarily, of the location; infiltration and contact with the prisoners; negotiation with the terrorists, drawn out if possible, in the hope that they, as well as their hostages, will begin to suffer stress reactions; finally, ideally, a successful raid. With no casualties.'

Riordan drained his tankard of beer and raised a finger to summon a waiter in a long white apron. It was as gloomy inside the café as it was on the once-bustling street outside. In the wavering candlelight – there was, as so often, a power cut – his craggy face was grim. 'Instead of that,' he said, 'what do we find? No hostages are held in the location cordoned off by Communist security forces. The only terrorists we have seen are in fact actors paid to play that role. The entire charade is known to the Russian occupation authorities, who certainly know about the actors, even if they are not actually paid from KGB funds.'

The waiter came to the table with a tray of tankards, set them down, and removed the empties. Riordan nodded his thanks and the man went away. The round table at which they sat was the only one occupied. Two workmen sipped schnapps at the bar.

'So much we have found out,' Riordan resumed. 'Against, I may say, considerable opposition. My car was bombed within two hours of the original briefing in Paris. Brod and I escaped a hit-and-run attempt here. Shots were fired at us as soon as we were installed in the hotel. And now our base has been burned down and all our weapons and supplies destroyed. Every conceivable obstacle has been put in our way . . . and despite the fact that we have survived, all we have done is come back to where we started, proving nothing but negatives.'

'The one positive point that remains,' O'Kelly said, 'is that there really *are* hostages . . . somewhere.'

'Oh, sure. We even know who they are.' Riordan permitted himself a wintry smile. 'But before we can do anything about them now, there are a few questions which must, in my view, be answered.'

174

'Like where the buggers are?' Christal said.

'Well, that of course. That's number one. But the way I read it, we'd be a lot nearer the answer to that if we could settle some of the others first. Like what is the *real* object of the kidnapping? Is it really to obtain the release of terrorists from jail? For money? For concessions in some of the world's hot spots? And, following that, who actually are the kidnappers? Who holds the hostages, wherever they are? And, perhaps most importantly, who is it that knows what we are doing almost before we do it – and tries every way there is to stop it?'

'That's number one for me,' O'Kelly said. 'It's . . . I mean I can't understand it. It makes no sense. And yet . . .'

'A leak,' Riordan cut in. 'From the beginning. Someone, somewhere, on the inside. Either they pass information on, or they organize themselves. They don't *want* those poor sods released. Not by us anyway. Tell me, Captain, apart from ourselves and your own office, who knows anything at all about this mission? Who knows it even exists?'

O'Kelly passed a hand over his thinning silver hair. 'Well, that's it. I mean this is a *secret* operation. I've always insisted on that. My principals made it a condition that nobody knew.'

'These principals – the Foreign Office? The PM? Members of Parliament? Could they have informed Military Intelligence, for example? MI6?'

'No way. The whole point was that the security services should not know. It mustn't be tied in to the UK in any way. The PM wouldn't know. MPs certainly not. Your fees come out of secret funds, which don't have to be accounted for specifically. The FO is the only possible . . . but as they were the ones insisting on secrecy, I can't see . . .'

'There are plenty of British security people here in Berlin. If by any chance there was a Foreign Office leak, is it possible that they might, through some departmental rivalry, be responsible?'

'Not to the extent of attempted murder, good God no. I've heard of them shopping cowboy operators to the Russkis for political gains or as part of some swap. But not this.' The silver head shook decisively. 'In any case, no FO leak could possibly be detailed enough to allow anyone to pull . . . what they've tried to pull. Dammit, I don't know what you're planning myself half the time!'

'The consignment of weapons and supplies you had delivered? If the unit they came from was really on the ball, could any of the security bods have caught on? Especially if they were planning some cowboy operation in the Eastern sector themselves? Maybe even another rescue attempt?'

'Unlikely. They'd never get permission to run such an operation. If they could, there'd have been no job for you to do.' O'Kelly coughed. He drank from his tankard. 'As it happens, no unit was involved in the supply of the, er, material you mention.'

Riordan laughed. 'OK, OK. You went to the black market, the underworld. Good for you. That's secret after all. Can you do it again?'

'Not very easily,' O'Kelly said. 'Somebody owed me a favour. The debt has now been discharged. But I'll try.'

'One other question,' Nelson-Harmer said. 'It seems to me of some importance. Whoever it is that's pulling the wool over the world's eyes on this hostage thing, do they know that we know the conference centre scenario is a fake?'

'I think they must,' Riordan said, 'after the little adventure you and I shared in the sewer. Otherwise why would we have been there?'

'Talking of which,' Van Eyck asked, 'what about the

second guy in the sewer – the one Teddy killed? Was he an actor too?'

'I would think not,' Riordan said. 'I don't see a theatrical agent, or even the KGB for that matter, supplying a hired actor with a firearm – especially as the guy fired on us first. I would guess he was, well, one of them. Sent along as a kind of chaperon, to keep an eye on the actor and see that he played his part convincingly.'

'Them?'

'Yeah, that's the rub, isn't it? Who?'

'So you're saying there are at least *some* terrorists?' Christal asked.

'Maybe.'

'You're being evasive, old man,' Nelson-Harmer said. 'Is there something concealed up the strategic sleeve?'

'In a way, yes,' Riordan admitted. 'It's just a wild idea. A hunch if you like. I think this whole rigmarole may be one hell of a lot simpler than we've allowed for. I don't believe there *are* any terrorists, anywhere. I don't believe there ever have been . . . I think the so-called ransom demands are as phoney as the conference centre set-up, made deliberately unacceptable to gain time. I believe Western negotiators have been denied access to the Russian zone because there is in fact nobody to negotiate with.'

'Just a minute!' O'Kelly interjected. 'Are you saying that . . . ?'

'I'm saying not only that the Russians are aware the scenario is faked but that they faked it themselves, that nobody but the Soviets has ever been involved. I believe they have simply sequestered the three or four men the Western powers particularly want released, and that they intend to hold them until the Reds have taken over in those countries.'

'Well, that's a thought,' Brod said. 'It's certainly the

kind of operation the KGB might mount – another kind of disinformation really. And the other eight or nine hostages . . . ?'

'Window-dressing. Because the important ones must believe they're being held to ransom by obscure terrorists. Otherwise, if they knew it was really the Russians, they'd be yelling their heads off once they *were* released.'

'Seems a hell of a lot of trouble, just to keep a handful of guys penned up for a few days,' Christal said.

'The rest of the world has to believe the hostage story too,' Riordan told him. 'That way, the Soviets can't be blamed for keeping these men away from their countries at a critical time. Skulduggery – to twist around the famous phrase about justice – may be done, but must not be seen to be done.'

'Well that's an alternative explanation of the facts as we know them,' O'Kelly said. 'A pretty convincing alternative too.'

'But where exactly does it leave us?' Van Eyck asked.

'Exactly where we were,' Riordan said. 'With a mission to complete. We have to find out where these people *are* being held, and then go in and get them out.'

'But – Christ! – if it's the Comrades holding them rather than a small band of terrorists, they could be anywhere in the whole of East Germany. In the whole bloody Soviet Union for that matter.'

'Exactly. That's why we have to act right now, before it's too late. I believe, you see, that they are still relatively near – because the Russians might need after all to produce them at short notice if their scenario is to go on being believed.'

'But we're still faced with someone on the other side, on *some* other side, who's determined to stop us, and who seems to know in advance every move we make,' Nelson-Harmer objected.

'Correct. That's the last question to be answered.'

'Is it the bloody Russkis? Are *we* at the wrong end of their fucking sights too?' Christal said.

'Maybe. Either them directly, or persons unknown paid by them or sympathetic to their aims. Our first task is to establish which.'

'An excellent plan,' Van Eyck observed. 'How precisely may this be started?'

'As to that,' Riordan said, 'I have a couple of alternatives of my own to try out.'

16

She was wearing the West German equivalent of the Christian Dior 'New Look' that was all the rage in London and Paris: a flowered, bell-shaped skirt reaching halfway down her trim calves, with a wide suede belt and a hyacinth-blue top with a scooped-out neckline. The brim of the shallow straw hat perched very straight on her head was decorated with a spray of forget-me-nots. The style, developed as a contrast to the austerity of mannish wartime fashions, suited her hourglass figure. She looked stunning.

Riordan stood behind her chair. 'May I join you?' he said.

Startled, Dagmar Harari glanced swiftly over her shoulder. He was smiling. 'Well, yes,' she said doubtfully. 'I suppose so.'

'You are not waiting for someone?'

'Er, no. Nobody in particular.'

'Good.' Riordan pulled over a chair from a nearby table and sat down opposite her. 'I hope they are paying you the full Equity rate as well as your interpreter's fee,' he said conversationally.

She stifled a small gasp. And then, toying with a long-stemmed glass of white wine, she murmured with lowered eyes: 'How did you find out?'

'It wasn't very difficult,' Riordan said. 'I happened to be following someone – a man I thought was a terrorist but who turned out to be an actor. I saw this man paid by a theatrical agent I recognized, in the presence of a Russian officer. When he left the all-night bar where this took place, I followed him again. He came to this café . . . where he met you. You had a meal together.'

She bit her lip. 'I see.'

'After that,' Riordan said, 'it took no more than a telephone call the following day to establish that you too were on the books of the Frodenburg agency. That you were in fact in on the conference centre deception.'

'It's just a job,' the girl said defensively.

'An odd one for a cabaret artist down on the books as "soubrette and comedienne".'

'I have also worked as assistant to an illusionist,' she said with a flash of spirit. 'Who are you anyway? A policeman? Someone from the Western security services?'

'Not exactly,' Riordan said. 'Let me get you another glass of wine.'

'Thank you. It's not very good, but anything's better than going back to that dreadful ersatz coffee after all this time.'

Riordan called over a waitress.

The café was a large one, just across the road from the Tiergarten U-Bahn station, with a *Weinstube* and beer hall down below. It was very crowded, perhaps because of the rain still gusting in squalls across the wide street outside.

Riordan rubbed a clear space in the steamed-up window with his sleeve, staring out at the distant skyline silhouette of the Brandenburg Gate. 'What a contrast,' he said, 'to find all the gloom over here, and all the good food and bright lights beyond that arch in the Eastern sector. What brings you to this particular café in the West?'

'I agree that the fun and games are normally on this side,' Dagmar said. 'But the situation is so tense now, and

181

people are so scared of another war, that there's a demand for something, anything, to cheer them up. Cabarets and small satirical fringe theatres are springing up all over the place. Berliners can always laugh at themselves, you know. I come here because the place is a favourite haunt of the writers and directors who put on these shows and . . . well, you never know.' She drank some wine. 'Does that answer your question? You haven't answered mine.'

'It doesn't answer all my questions,' Riordan said. 'Am I right in thinking you were offered this job because you happened to speak the particular dialect your actor friend speaks . . .'

'That's right. We lived in Turkey once. When I was little.'

'. . . and that this obscure dialect was chosen because it was virtually unknown? So that nobody overhearing your conversations with the supposed kidnapper would understand your fake dialogue? And the terrorists themselves wouldn't be identified with any existing activist group?'

'I guess so. Why do you want to know? You still haven't told me who or what you are.'

'The name is Riordan. Barry Riordan. Let's say I have an interest in seeing that certain members of the hostage group are freed before their countries go up in flames. As you say, it's just a job. Like yourself, I'm paid to do it.'

Riordan drained his glass and summoned the waitress again. 'There's one thing you could tell me without in any way compromising your duty to your employers,' he said. 'The man with the gun who accompanies your actor friend when you meet apparently to hear the kidnappers' latest demands – is he an actor too?'

'Oh, no. It's not always the same one. I think they're probably Russians. They speak German with a very strange accent. The one with us last night was kind of creepy.'

'That's what I thought.' Riordan allowed his gaze to rest on the girl for a moment. She really was very attractive. The blue top was fashioned cleverly, loosely, from heavy grosgrain silk, cut in such a way that the folds suggested – without actually revealing – the fullness of her breasts. Riordan found the calm stare of her wide violet eyes as unsettling as he had the first time he met her.

'When we met,' she said, as if reading his thoughts, 'you told me that you were concerned with the Control Commission. And that your friends were businessmen, lawyers, and so on. Then there was the shooting incident and you all left. The friends, I suppose, are really working with you?'

'Yes,' Riordan said after a short pause. 'Look, I'm going to trust you. I need help and I think you may be able to provide it.'

'Try me,' Dagmar said.

'I'm assuming four things right away: that you had nothing to do with what you call the shooting incident, that you don't drive a BMW 328 convertible, that you are not a pyromaniac – and, most importantly, that even if you are paid with Russian money, you have nothing but that job in common with the people who hire Frodenburg.'

She smiled. 'Quite an assumption. Supposing those beliefs to be true, how do you imagine I can help you?'

'I must find out where these hostages really are. You may, without knowing it, be able to give me a lead. Have you ever been asked, as part of your interpreting job, to go anywhere but the conference centre? Either to speak your Turkish dialect or Russian?'

She shook her head. 'Never. But I think Tufik may have.'

'Tufik?'

'Habib Tufik. My actor friend. I think he was asked to

183

go out of town once. Somewhere south-east of the city. I remember vaguely that he told me he had to teach another actor a few sentences in the dialect.'

Riordan mastered his growing excitement. 'That must have been an actor posing as a terrorist to convince the hostages themselves. Could you . . . do you think you could possibly find out where Tufik went?'

'I could try. I know where he will be this afternoon.'

'I can't tell you how grateful I'd be. Just for trying,' Riordan said, 'I'd be happy to offer you the most splendid dinner the new Deutschmark can buy.' He grinned. 'And as for a successful try . . .'

The glance from the violet eyes was level. 'Very well. Meet me at eight o'clock at Die Insel – that's a restaurant-cabaret overlooking the river at the end of Franklin Strasse. I will see what I can do.'

'It will be a pleasure – either way,' Riordan said.

Was he mistaken – could it have been the last sip of wine or had there really been a moist glisten on that full lower lip as she rose to smile goodbye?

Die Insel – The Island – was a smart place to take fashionable West Berlin ladies if you had enough money to pay the black-market prices. A striped awning in blue and white was hooped over the modest, brass-handled mahogany door when Riordan climbed the short flight of steps above the pavement that night. It was still raining. The cloud cover was very low, and the absence of noise from incoming and outgoing aircraft was as noticeable – and almost as menacing – as the wavering drone of approaching squadrons itself.

Inside, the place was all deep-blue fitted carpet with ivory panelling picked out in gold. The restaurant was a series of interconnected alcoves, none of which held more than three tables. Somewhere a pianist improvised dreamily on Western themes derived from Cole Porter, Jerome Kern and the Gershwins, and there was a discreet tinkle of cutlery and good glass beneath the subdued hum of conversation.

Well-fed men in dark suits and women wearing cocktail dresses drifted on and off a tiny dance floor. At first Riordan was worried that his high-necked white silk sweater and sober jacket might not be considered formal enough for such a sophisticated retreat, but he was ushered without comment to one of the smaller alcoves, where Dagmar was already installed.

She was dressed in a strapless black velvet sheath that set off to perfection her rich curves and creamy skin. A wide velvet band around her neck was accented with a single large amethyst the colour of her eyes. Riordan fell instantly for her welcoming smile. He kissed her hand before he sat down.

There was only one other table in the alcove. It was unoccupied. Through a window beyond it, he could see the dark water of the Spree festooned with long strings of loaded barges, immobilized by the Russian clamp-down on river traffic.

Dagmar made no reference to the reason for their meeting until after they had ordered. Riordan went with the tide, discovering in himself an unexpected talent for small talk. In the soft light from the one small lamp illuminating the table, her eyes were slumberous and the slightest of shadows separated the slopes of her breasts.

He learned that Die Insel was the spiritual home of the satirists Günter Neumann, Tatjana Sais and their theatrical troupe, who doubled up Berliners daily with a radio show known as *Die Insulaner* – The Islanders. The background to the series – a reference not lost on listeners in both West and East Berlin – was that, for some reason nobody could fully understand, the city had become entirely surrounded by water.

The meal was admirable. 'Please order anything you want, anything at all,' Riordan said grandly. There was a wad of bills in his pocket and it wasn't his own money. What the hell, Archie! What the hell . . .

They ate quenelles of pike that were as soft as sleep, roast duck with a caramel sauce, and crêpes Suzette. After one questioning glance in his direction, Dagmar had told the wine waiter to bring a *Beerenauslese* Graacher Munzlay, the most delicate − and the dearest − of the dry Moselles on the list.

Riordan was in a mood almost to laugh when at last she said solemnly: 'I feel I'm taking the whole of this evening on false pretences.'

'Never,' he said.

'Yes, yes. Really. I did see Tufik, you see. He *was* taken out of town. East and south, as I thought. On the Frankfurt-an-der-Oder autobahn at first, and then for fifteen minutes on a country road. But he was blindfolded the moment they left the autobahn. He has no idea where they ended up.'

'It's a start,' Riordan said gallantly. 'How did he get there?'

'He was taken by one of the men who comes to the centre with him. I think they went in a hired car.'

'The work I'm doing,' Riordan said, 'is contracted to me through an agent. I never see the people who actually pay the bill; I'm not even one hundred per cent sure who they are. The agent takes care of all the details: briefing, logistics, supplies, checking on policy decisions. You work through an agency too. Are the . . . mechanics . . . of what you and your friends do arranged in the same way?'

'I suppose so. What exactly do you mean?'

'Specifically, would the car taking Tufik and his guardian out to wherever the hostages are have been hired through the Klaus Frodenburg agency? Or do you think – from your own instructions – that it's more likely the Russian officer who contacts you would have arranged it himself?'

Dagmar shrugged. 'I have no idea. I suppose Klaus could have done.'

'It was just a thought.'

'While we wait for the coffee,' she said, 'would you care to ask me to dance?'

Riordan pushed back his chair. 'Nothing would give me greater pleasure,' he said truthfully. He rose to his feet, offering her his arm.

Steering her past the next alcove, he saw that it was entirely filled by a single large table around which half a dozen uniformed British, French and Russian officers were dining with flashily dressed and over made-up German girls. Among the men, he noticed with some surprise, was the KGB officer, Peniakov.

There was laughter at the table. The Russian was recounting some anecdote which seemed to appeal particularly to the French. It was clear that he recognized Dagmar, for he stopped in mid-sentence the moment he saw her. Then, as his gaze passed to her escort, he frowned and his eyes narrowed. I know that face. Somewhere, sometime . . .

Riordan leaned towards him, smiling. 'A far cry from Helsinki, Piotr!' he said pleasantly.

They passed on, leaving the Russian staring after them.

The pianist had been joined by an electric guitar and a bass, and they were stroking their way through a slow version of *Where Have All The Flowers Gone?* Riordan put his arm around Dagmar and eased her on to the crowded dance floor.

The lighting was dim, the air hazy with smoke, redolent of expensive perfume, cigars, the aroma of rich food cooked in wine – and perhaps the faintest hint of sweat from one or two of the scantily dressed women. Like many well-rounded girls, Dagmar was exceptionally light on her feet; and like many continental girls she enjoyed the physical contact of dancing. It was, Riordan thought as he steered her expertly between the close-packed couples, like manoeuvring a piece of thistledown.

Thistledown with a thigh between his knees.

She laid her cheek unselfconsciously against his. He could feel the pulse in his wrist throbbing against the bare skin of her back.

'Good lord! What a bally coincidence! Fancy seeing you here, squire.'

The voice, with its exaggerated English drawl, came from immediately behind them. Riordan swung Dagmar around.

It was Beverley Hills, Captain O'Kelly's archivist and Riordan's own former recruit. Hills was sitting at a table on the edge of the dance floor. He was wearing a white tuxedo and a black tie. The two sober-suited middle-aged men with him looked like high-powered business executives. There was a bottle of champagne on the table and another in a silver ice bucket on a stand. 'Didn't expect to see you among the fleshpots, old man,' Hills crowed, flipping back a lock of hair from his eyes. 'Thought you'd more likely be tugging at the old ball and chain . . . over there.'

'Oh, well,' Riordan said lightly, 'you know the old saying: all work and no play . . .'

'Well, you're certainly no dull boy tonight!' Hills said with a leer in Dagmar's direction.

Riordan swung the girl into an intricate reverse turn that

took them to the far side of the floor. 'Who was that?' she asked, removing her cheek for a moment.

'Just someone who worked for me,' Riordan said, 'once.'

'I don't think I like him very much.'

'I'm not sure that I do. But one can't always choose one's associates. He's a marvellous shot. King's Prize at Bisley. Probably a little tight.'

The cheek was nestling once more against his own. 'Do you know,' he murmured in her ear, 'that more than anything else in the whole world, I would like to go to bed with you. Now.'

He heard a small exhalation of breath. Her belly swung against him and he could feel through the velvet dress her pubic mound grinding over his own hardness. Then she was leaning back against his arm, smiling with her eyes. 'Yes,' she said. 'I do know. And I think I would like that very much. Perhaps you should ask for the bill and we can leave?'

The bill was astronomical. He left a huge tip and asked the waiter to call them a taxi. All the lights went out, leaving the restaurant in darkness.

Over the expected chorus of groans and catcalls, Riordan said: 'The only thing is . . . well, I don't know where to take you. Obviously we can't go where my friends are. I wouldn't want to embarrass you by suggesting your hotel – and anyway there are other reasons why I would rather not return there. I'm not sure . . .'

He stopped. A cool finger had been laid against his lips.

'No problem,' she said. 'Just listen to the band.'

'The band? They're still bravely playing through the power cut – except for the electric guitar of course – but I don't see . . .'

'Listen to *what* they are playing.'

He laughed suddenly. 'I see. Of course. *There's A Small Hotel*?'

'Exactly.'

The taxi was waiting at the kerb below the steps. Dagmar was about to give the driver an address when Riordan halted suddenly, gripping her arm. There had been a flurry of movement ahead of them.

'What is it?'

'There,' he said. 'On the roof of the cab.'

A pale shape dropped to the ground, streaked across the street, and vanished into shrubbery bordering the restaurant car park. 'It's only a cat,' she said. 'Probably enjoying the heat rising from the engine, poor thing. The Berlin evenings stay cold quite late in the year.'

'You saw it? Was it by any chance a white cat?'

'I couldn't possibly say. Not in this light, without the street-lights. Why? Does it matter? It certainly wasn't a *black* cat. Do you worry about luck?'

'Not at all. It was just . . . Oh, just a thought. Forget it. It's of no importance.' He opened the taxi door and helped her in.

The cabbie started the engine and they rolled downhill towards the river.

He reached for her. 'There's one thing I have to say,' Dagmar murmured.

'Say on, my beauty.'

'It may seem . . . I don't want to sound forward or presumptuous, and I'm not one of those girls who take a yard when you offer an inch, but at the same time I don't want there to be any misunderstanding. OK?'

'I'm listening,' Riordan said.

'Well. It's true that I love to — what's that ugly word the British use? To fuck? Yes, I love to fuck. And I only fuck with those I really like. But if I go to bed with you tonight and it's lovely, and I go to bed with you again and it's still lovely, that doesn't in any way whatever confer proprietorial rights. It doesn't make me "your girl". I may have slept with someone else in between, and I shall certainly sleep with someone else afterwards. I love to make love but I also love, as the Americans say, to play the field. Is that understood? Or does that make me a monster?'

'You mean like no strings?' Riordan said, reaching for her again. 'Baby, it looks like you and me were both cast from the same mould.'

He pulled down the wired top of her strapless dress and her breasts fell into his hands like ripe fruit.

17

Riordan had been obliged to break in using the crude methods of the amateur burglar. There was no time to collect Christal from the seedy Kreuzberg hotel where the mercenaries were now lodged, and he doubted whether he would need the very specialized talents of Brod. In any case it had been almost five o'clock when he stole out of the room he shared with Dagmar.

The rain was falling more heavily now. Some of the streets were awash, and the night was alive with the splash and gurgle of drainpipes and guttering. Below the Kottbuser bridge, he could see as he jogged across that the sluggish surface of the Landwehrkanal was pitted by the downpour.

There were still more than a dozen blocks to cover, but at this time on a wet morning, with fuel strictly rationed, there wasn't a hope in hell of finding a cruising taxi. The U-Bahn wasn't running yet. He would have to cover the whole distance on foot.

Electricity had been restored, and the wide streets stretched glistening and deserted in every direction. Tempelhof was a glare in the sky less than a mile away but no planes lumbered down through the low cloud and the city was eerily silent beneath the pelting rain. Within minutes Riordan's lightweight topcoat was soaked through and his sodden trousers clung clammily to his legs.

The target building was a red-brick nineteenth-century block, miraculously spared by bombs and shells. Judging by the number of brass plates beneath the columned porch, most of its eight floors were occupied by office suites. And even if some of the apartments were residential, there was no night porter: he could see through frosted glass that the entrance lobby was in darkness.

A cobbled lane ran behind the building, separated from the yard by a high brick wall. There was a door in the wall but it was locked.

Riordan drew back two paces. There was no time for the niceties of lock-picking, even if he had the instruments. He was going to have to take chances on noise the whole way through. He launched himself forwards, shooting out his right leg so that his heel thudded against the door just below the handle. The door burst open with a splintering crash.

For an instant, he paused. No voice shouted. No light shone suddenly out from the dark façades on either side of the lane. No footsteps clattered and no police whistle blew. He slipped inside the yard and pushed the door to.

A fire-escape zigzagged up the rear wall of the block, but above the shadowy second floor it was brightly illuminated by the lamps in an adjoining street. Not worth the risk. Early workers in the houses on the far side of the lane could be getting up at any moment: a man on the fire-escape would be advertising a cat burglar as clearly as a neon sign. He would take a second chance and break in on the ground floor.

The rain drummed loudly on a double row of dustbins below the lowest flight of the fire-escape. He bit his lip. The bins would have to be put out: that probably meant that cleaners would be arriving in less than an hour.

He scrambled up on to the most solid-looking lid and rammed his elbow through the glass of a small window.

No burglar alarm shrieked, but the smashing of the pane, lost outside in the clatter of rain on galvanized iron, would have been uncomfortably loud in the block's interior. He waited a moment, then thrust his arm through the hole.

The window had a latch, but no locks screwed into the frame, he noticed with relief. That meant he wouldn't have to push out the remaining shards of splintered glass. He twisted up the latch, swung the window wide, and climbed inside.

He was in some kind of storeroom. His pencil torch showed him shelves of cleaning material, mops and brooms hanging neatly from hooks. He eased open the door and found himself in a passage that led to the entrance lobby. Here, thick carpet covered the floor; he smelled furniture polish, and a suggestion of yesterday's cigar smoke. That could be bad: it meant the place was well looked after. Maybe some of the apartments were residential after all.

The building's single lift was non-hydraulic. It was of the ancient, open-cage type, moved up or down by hauling on a thick padded rope passing through the car, over a wheel at the top of the building and then to a counterweight which rose and fell in the shaft.

The offices of the Klaus Frodenburg Theatrical Agency were on the fifth floor. Riordan had no time for stairs. He opened the curved mahogany doors of the lift, stepped inside, eased the doors shut, and pulled on the rope. The car rose smoothly, silently upwards.

So far, again so good. Lifts of this type usually groaned and protested like a brass-framed bed with a spring mattress. This one was clearly maintained in splendid condition. Perhaps the agency took more than the normal ten per cent from its clients?

The offices were at the far end of a long corridor. The torch showed him that the solid double doors were secured with an ordinary mortice lock . . . No specialized arrangements. But then there would be nothing but papers to steal in a theatrical agency anyway. Why go to the expense of fitting sophisticated locks?

There was one long-stemmed passkey Brod had given him which the Austrian swore would open any standard mortice lock – provided the user knew how to handle it. Riordan had once spent more than an hour trying to memorize the different twists and turns and other manipulations which could be employed. He produced the key now and began experimenting with the various combinations as far as he could remember them.

He supposed it had been a smart move on the part of the KGB to recruit an agent from the Western sector to supply the personnel needed. It certainly minimized the chances of a leak in the Soviet zone – and the risk of an overzealous journalist stumbling on the secret of the deserted conference centre. After all, he himself had followed a similar line of reasoning when he transferred his men to the West and arranged the last rendezvous with O'Kelly. Until they knew where the hostages actually were, there was no point leaving the rescue squad in an area where they were vulnerable both to Russian action and to the machinations of whoever was trying to write them off before the rescue even started.

It was ten minutes before he mastered the precise manoeuvring of the key and the tongue of the lock drew back with a heavy click. Moisture seeping from the soles of his shoes and dripping from his drenched clothes had darkened the carpet with a tell-tale patch of dampness where he had crouched. He shrugged. There was nothing he could do about it. He pushed open the door and went into the office suite.

There was an anteroom with a receptionist's desk, half

a dozen upright chairs and a low table stacked with film and theatre magazines. Beyond this was a secretary's office crowded with grey steel filing cabinets. Three telephones flanked the PBX exchange on the desk. Frodenburg's inner sanctum was furnished with deep-buttoned leather armchairs and a walnut cocktail cabinet. Framed and inscribed photographs of past and present show-business stars smiled down vacuously from the walls. The massive glass-topped desk held nothing but a single telephone and a virgin blotter. Riordan reckoned that what he was looking for would be – if it was anywhere – in the outer office. He returned to the filing cabinets and started to pull out drawers.

Contracts . . . bills . . . records of legal proceedings . . . taxation figures and accountants' reports . . . papers relating to the lease of the offices. The sixth cabinet contained personal dossiers on the agency's clients.

There was a fat file on Dagmar Harari, but it told Riordan nothing she hadn't already mentioned herself. He was surprised to see how much she was being paid for her work at the empty conference centre. Details of various employers – language schools, business conferences, an occasional cabaret or theatre – were filed in a separate folder, with cross-references to Accounts and Contracts. There was no cross-reference for her current work, simply a pencilled comment: 'PP – Verbal. Accounts check with KF.' PP was presumably Piotr Peniakov. Frodenburg – KF no doubt – was hardly likely to list the KGB as the employer of his clients.

Habib Tufik's dossier was leaner than the girl's. Where there would normally be a contractual reference, his current work was again annotated with the same pencilled comment instructing the accounts department to refer any queries to the boss. There was, however, a typed note on the last page of the file. It read: 'See also Accounts for Expenses.'

Riordan's breath quickened. Could this be the lead he so hoped to find?

He wasted ten minutes riffling through a dozen different accounting headings in five different cabinets. There was no mention of Tufik in any of them. And then suddenly he realized: the actor wouldn't have paid for the hired car himself when he was taken out of town to meet the hostages; the bill, if it was not paid by the KGB, would have been settled by the agency. It would surely be filed with other office papers, as something to be recovered from the actual employer when the final settlement was made.

Riordan began feverishly to search for accounts headings that might list recoverable disbursements. He tried the taxation files. Perhaps such sums were deductible under postwar company law? He found nothing.

It was by chance – thinking of business trips and the entertainment of clients at places like Die Insel and visits to Hamburg, Paris and London – that he looked out Frodenburg's personal tax file.

And there it was.

On the top page of a thick sheaf of papers, a single sheet bearing the line: 'PP/Tufik: settled on account by agreement. Recover.' It was dated less than a week previously.

Stapled to this sheet was an invoice from a Berlin car-hire company. The bill, which was countersigned twice and stamped 'Paid', itemized: 'Driver Schultz. Mercedes. Two passengers Berlin Centre – Siegsdorf. One way. Pick-up 13h.30. Driver to return unaccompanied. 39km.'

Riordan's pulse was racing. His eyes ached from too much concentration on lines of typescript read by the light of a tiny torch. But he had found the place.

Siegsdorf.

SOLDIER OF FORTUNE 9

He searched the shelves and found a road map. Yes, there it was. In very small letters: a village near a canal, on a minor road south-east of the city. The nearest town of any size was Storkow.

Riordan replaced the file, shut all the drawers, left the office and re-locked the door. Dawn was already lightening the sky outside the landing windows. He hurried down the corridor, turned the corner . . . and stopped.

The lift was no longer at the fifth floor.

Did it return automatically to street level like some hydraulic lifts? Or would it only move if somebody called it?

He peered through the bars. Five storeys below there was light in the lobby: he could make out the bulk of the car blocking out part of the entrance.

So the lift had been called down. Why? Surely because somebody wanted to rise.

Who? Cleaners? A resident? Some kind of security check? Police, alerted by somebody who had heard him breaking in? Or seen the torch flashing behind the fifth-floor windows.

Whatever the explanation, he couldn't risk being found on that particular floor. Not with that damp patch outside Frodenburg's door. In his soaked condition, no bluff could talk him out of that. He ran for the pass doors and sprinted up the emergency staircase.

On the top floor, he pushed through the doors and ran for the lift shaft. Eight floors below now, it was difficult to make out anything at street level in detail. But the rope controlling the lift was vibrating. Very slowly the wheel at the top of the shaft had begun to turn. The rope moved.

Somebody was bringing the lift up.

It was then that the light in the lobby caught the

distinctive gleam of brass. It was no more than a glimpse, but it was definitive to Riordan's trained eye: buttons, belts, buckles. Uniform. *Russian* uniform – in the West?

No time to ask questions. If by any chance it was Peniakov . . . But how could it be? No matter. Riordan had to get out fast. Just in case it was.

There was a maintenance hatch at the very top of the shaft. He opened it, climbed through, and dropped to the massive slab of the counterweight as it began to descend and the lift rose up.

Riordan clung to the greased outer strand of the rope with one hand, keeping his balance over the gaping void with difficulty. The Browning automatic was gripped firmly in the other.

The lift continued its relentless advance. As he was lowered towards it, he could see through the latticed grille of the roof that there were two men inside. And, yes, they were wearing Russian greatcoats with the peaked and flat-topped army cap. Each held a revolver.

The space between the ironwork outer wall of the shaft and the rear of the cage was limited. Clearly it was ample for the passage of the counterweight, but it was going to be a tight squeeze – possibly a dangerous one – for the man perched on top of it.

Riordan tensed as the cage approached, flattening himself as far as possible beside the cable. The two Russians had their backs to him, staring left and right through the doors as each landing sank past. If they were heading for the fifth, the counterweight should have passed and should be well below the floor of the lift before they emerged. He hoped there was an inspection hatch for maintenance engineers at each level.

The domed roof rose past the lower edge of the weight. The rear of the car was just clearing the toes of his shoes.

He sucked in his breath and held it, feeling his shoulders scrape the shaft wall.

They were level: the lift, the Russians, the weight and Riordan himself. Then, as the weight continued to sink, there was a sudden metallic rattle, a wrench that almost pulled him off his perch and spilled him into the void, and a shout from one of the Russians.

The buttons of Riordan's topcoat had caught in a criss-cross of ironwork at the rear of the cage. The coat burst open, ripped down the back and was wrenched off him as he fought to keep his position on the weight. The right-hand half, with the buttons still entangled, rose with the lift, dragging the sleeve off his arm and tearing the Browning from his grasp. The gun, loaded, cocked, and with a round in the breech, fired as it hit the bottom of the shaft four floors below.

Fortunately for Riordan, the Russian hauling on the cable in the car, doubly surprised by the discovery of an outside passenger and the echoing gunshot, continued for a moment to jerk frantically in the same direction. Instead of descending to bring Riordan back within range, the lift went on shooting upwards.

They had crossed, evidently, at fourth-floor level. By the time he felt the weight vibrate beneath his feet and the cage shuddered to a halt, he reckoned the Russians would be at the fifth . . . and he would be suspended between the second and third. Would they leave the lift there and try to shoot him down through the bars of the shaft? Or would they hurry the car back down to return him to their level?

Well, that was a choice that Riordan could make himself. He stepped off the counterweight and transferred himself to the grille walling the shaft. He heard a gabble of Russian from above. And then the roar of heavy-calibre handguns.

Slugs winged obliquely down the shaft, ringing against ironwork and rattling the grille. Ricochets screeched off into space. But from that height the angle was too acute for accurate shooting: a web of bars and crosspieces and angles of ironwork made a clear sight impossible. Riordan ignored the danger and looked down. Against the light rising from the entrance lobby he could see that there was indeed an inspection hatch perhaps fifteen feet below him. Agile as a monkey, he swarmed down towards it. The gunfire ceased. Now he was top dog.

Because here the stairs did not encircle the lift shaft. They were for emergency use only, and were at the back of the building. If the Russians used them, he would have almost a three-storey lead, out of sight and out of range all the time; and if they brought the lift back down to street level, the time lag would give him very nearly as great a head start. A further advantage was that he was familiar with the ground floor: he knew where he was going and they didn't.

He levered open the hatch, climbed through, dropped to the second-floor landing and ran for the door leading to the stairway.

The pounding footsteps were still a long way above when he ran into the storeroom, clambered through the shattered window, and dropped on to the dustbins and into the yard.

He pulled open the door in the wall and stepped cautiously into the lane. As he did so he felt the pluck at the sleeve of his jacket at the same time as his ears registered the soft thunk of a silenced automatic. The subdued muzzle flash came from a dark doorway to his left.

Peniakov?

It had to be. And of course, seeing that the entrance doors had not been forced, the KGB man would naturally rush round to cover the rear. Riordan turned right and sprinted the fifty yards to the lane's entrance, weaving to each side and slightly varying his pace as he ran. He heard nothing but the clatter of his own footsteps and the labouring of his breath, but the gunman was still firing: brick dust from the wall peppered his hand, and once a bullet struck sparks from the cobbles between his racing feet.

Turning the corner into the street, Riordan risked a quick glance over his shoulder. It was Peniakov all right. He was standing in the middle of the lane now, clearly visible in the reflected street-lights, still in evening clothes, crouched with his pistol held in two hands.

He made no attempt to follow his target. There were people in the street now, and even the KGB knew their limits. Five minutes later, Riordan sank gratefully on to a wooden seat in a southbound U-Bahn workers' train. The windows were streaked with rain and the roofs of the city shone against the grey sky, but the airlift was in operation again: he saw the wide wings of a four-engined Avro York gliding down towards Gatow in the west.

Apart from shooting in the street, and gunfire in a private block, it was pretty daring of the KGB, he reflected, to bring uniformed Russian soldiers into West Berlin on such a mission. It made him feel comfortable just the same: it underlined the importance to the opposition of Siegsdorf: it proved that his own impromptu mission had been more than worthwhile.

Leaning his head back against the window, he closed his eyes to shut out the daylight. For the first time since he left the hotel, he permitted himself to think of the girl he had taken there. Could she have tipped off Peniakov that he was likely to break into the offices of the Frodenburg agency? Had he been foolish to follow up a gut reaction and trust her?

He hadn't decided to attempt the break-in until she had

reported to him at Die Insel. And since then she had never left his side until they went to bed. Had she run to a phone when she was supposed to be in the hotel bathroom? It was possible, but it didn't seem likely. Had something she had said before that evening tipped off the KGB officer? Less likely still. And it had to be remembered after all that Peniakov's table had been in the next alcove to his own at the restaurant. Was it possible that he had overheard part of their conversation?

What the hell. Whatever the answer, even if they knew he knew, the name of Siegsdorf was now etched into his mind. The rest was no more than a matter of logistics.

So far as the girl was concerned ... well, a raincheck? Was that really necessary? For the moment, his recollection of her was limited to the turmoil of her hungry mouth, her plump lower lip between his teeth, hot tongues embracing ... and the scalding clasp of her body wrapped around his urgent thrusts.

Dagmar had not been asleep when Riordan eased himself from the bed and stole out of the hotel room. She allowed him time to leave the premises and then rose herself, drawing aside the curtain from the darkened window to watch his lean, muscular figure stride away down the street.

Smiling the slow, secret smile that women reserve for the remembrance of satisfactory physical complicity, she moved to the bathroom and ran hot water into the tub. The man really was a very good lover.

Fifteen minutes later, fully dressed again, she flung a short silver-fox coat over the backless velvet dress, left some money on the dressing-table, and went quietly downstairs. A night porter raised a sleepy head and smiled as she appeared. 'Thank you, Günter,' she murmured, leaving a fifty-mark note on the edge of the desk.

The man sprang to his feet and hurried across the small entrance hall to unlock the revolving doors for her. Smiling still, she walked out into the night.

A block away, a pay phone stood outside a post office. Dagmar dialled a number and spoke a few words, then left the kiosk and withdrew to a recessed doorway at the next crossroads.

Ten minutes later a black Mercedes saloon angled into the kerb. One of the rear doors opened and Dagmar got in. The car swung into a U-turn and accelerated away. It passed through Schöneberg, traversed the Potsdamer Strasse and skirted the Tiergarten. Finally, having crossed the river via the Spreeweg bridge, the driver turned north-west and stopped outside a large residential property in a quiet, tree-lined avenue.

Tall wrought-iron gates, swung open by uniformed sentries, admitted them to a semicircular driveway which led to a pillared portico. The car stopped there. Dagmar got out and ran up the steps into the mansion. The uniformed man at the reception desk was not at all sleepy; nor did he smile. 'On the first floor, Fräulein,' he said briefly. She nodded and crossed the black and white marble floor of the lobby to a shallow, curving stairway.

The room, at the far end of a long corridor, was almost in darkness. She was dimly aware of several desks strewn with papers, of charts and maps on the wall, of the smell of sweet tobacco.

The room's only occupant, a pipe-smoking man with a big, dark moustache, sat beneath a green-shaded lamp in his shirtsleeves. He looked up as she came in and laid his pipe down in an ashtray on the desk. 'Well,' he said, 'you took your time.'

Dagmar smiled. 'I was enjoying myself,' she said.

18

Van Eyck went to Siegsdorf. Riordan knew that for himself it was impossible: they knew now who he was; why he was in Berlin; and what he looked like. And they knew — they must know — that he had found out that this was where the hostages were. Peniakov could draw on the entire resources of the KGB's Berlin station to keep the place staked out, on permanent watch for him. Until the hide-out had been located and the attack planned, it would be crazy for him to show his face.

The Dutchman spoke good German. A tall, thin man with ash-blond hair, he was the least likely among the group to attract unwelcome attention.

His job, however, was not going to be easy. Siegsdorf was a tiny village and a stranger would be noticeable. In addition to this they had no idea even of the hide-out's approximate position. Or in what type of building it might be. Tracked down by Brod, his memory sweetened by a hundred-mark stimulant, the driver of the hire-car revealed that he had not taken Habib Tufik and his companion to a specific address: they had simply transferred to another car on the outskirts of the village — a Volkswagen.

Had either of his passengers at any time during the journey been blindfolded? *Mein Gott*, no! the driver said. He wouldn't stand for that kind of caper in his cab.

'But — Christ! — they may not be in Siegsdorf at all,' Van

Eyck complained. 'With a full tank, the VW has a range of almost two hundred miles. They could be anywhere in the whole of the bloody Brandenburg *Land*.'

'Let's not exaggerate,' Riordan said. 'If that was the case, why use a hire-car to drive them that short distance out of the city? Why blindfold the actor so far from the target? In any case he was back in Berlin that evening for the routine visit to the conference centre. I'd look for some large place in the surrounding country – an abandoned castle, a warehouse, a disused school even. There are twelve of the poor sods, remember. Maybe, as a kind of double bluff, a property before you get to Siegsdorf. Don't forget, though, at that time they'd no reason to keep a special watch; the whole world believed the hostages were in East Berlin. Nobody was looking anywhere else, let alone in Siegsdorf.'

'OK. So how do I get to this cultural gem of the East?' Van Eyck asked.

'You travel in a hire-car of course,' Riordan told him.

Siegsdorf lay at the southern edge of the huge plain separating East Germany from the River Oder, which formed the Polish border. It was a riverside village in a barely undulating area of farm land pitted with small lakes, strewn along the low ridges with dark patches of woodland. The main street was interrupted by a single intersection – a muddy lane ending in a wharf.

Van Eyck arrived on foot, having paid off the chauffeur at a bus stop on a main road a mile out of town. He was wearing lederhosen with thick woollen stockings and an embroidered Bavarian jacket. The rucksack on his back contained specimen jars and transparent envelopes. If anyone asked, he was a naturalist researching rare insects, butterflies and aquatic plants in the marshes bordering the river and the lakes.

Nobody did ask; the natives were not friendly. Neither were they particularly unfriendly – just sullen and uncommunicative, the real lumpen, Van Eyck thought acidly.

He killed a couple of hours circling the fields outside the village, then found a room in a lakeside inn half a mile away. He ate a meal of sausage, beer and bread that was already stale on the outside. There were no other patrons. When he had finished, he returned to the lobby. The boy who had served him was sprawled in a chair behind the reception desk, half asleep.

'I'd like to find the bar where the foreigners go,' he said.

'Foreigners?'

'The Arabs. Those who buy a lot of food. I thought you might know where they go.'

'Why should I know? I'm not in the business of selling food.'

'Well, since you have the only tavern in the town . . .'

'What of it? I mind my own business. There are no Arabs here.'

Van Eyck returned to the village. The rain had stopped, but low clouds still raced across the sky. Beyond a footbridge, three figures in long overcoats stared at him from the steps of an unused cinema. Further away, a male choir sang Russian songs on a radio that needed new batteries. A gust of cold wind carried the odour of inefficient drains.

There was a bar at the exit from the village, a single room at the back of a yard adjoining a vacant church. Two women with plastic handbags sat at a table. There were three labourers grouped around some kind of pinball machine, and two gangling youths talking to the bartender. One of them had a cheap Spanish guitar slung across his back.

Clearly, it would be impossible to start any kind of conversation here, especially if it involved asking questions.

Van Eyck drank a glass of beer and left. As the door closed behind him he heard the conversation, which had ceased the moment he entered, start again. One of the women laughed shrilly.

Half a dozen teenage children loitered by the cracked cement basin of a dried-up fountain. One of them threw a stone as he passed, not so near that he could take exception but close enough to be a gesture. He thought there might have been somebody watching him from inside a half-open barn door.

Van Eyck left the village and headed south. He found three large buildings within a mile. The first looked promising – a grey stone façade in a grove of beech trees, at the end of a rutted, overgrown track. But the mansion was roofless, the windows blank or boarded up, the interior walls cracked and mildewed. Ancient scorch marks blackened the crumbling staircase and saplings grew through the conservatory floor.

Van Eyck's second choice was an abandoned farmhouse half hidden in a fold between two hills. But there were no tyre tracks along the muddy drive and the greenhouses were empty. Rats scurried away when he forced open the warped door and trod across the rotted flooring of the entrance. Apart from a broken table, the house was as empty as the barns. Clearly the place had been uninhabited for years.

The third possibility – a corrugated iron shed some two hundred feet long – was surrounded by rusting harvesters, harrows and hay rakes, inches deep in yellow mud. It turned out to be a granary.

Van Eyck returned to the village. By the time he reached it, darkness had fallen. He passed through two pools of light from wrought-iron lampposts – one at each end of the village. The shops were already closed. There was a glow from behind some of the shuttered windows, and several times he heard snatches of radio music from a military band. 'The Eastern workers' paradise!' he muttered aloud. He went back to the inn.

The same boy sat with his feet up on the desk. He was reading a Western movie magazine. 'Can I get a drink here?' Van Eyck asked.

The youth looked at him but did not reply.

'A drink,' the Dutchman repeated. 'Something to drink?'

'You want water? There is water in your room.'

'No, I want a *drink*. Schnapps, akvavit, brandy. Even beer.'

'There is a bar in the village,' the boy said.

Some kind of Pils was served with the evening meal – sausage again, with potatoes soaked in grease and watery salad. Afterwards he went up to the room. It was narrow and bare, with plaster walls that crumbled in places and cracked linoleum on the floor. The water that trickled into the marble basin was brackish. There was no lock on the door.

When he awoke in the morning, he saw that his rucksack had been searched and the specimen jars, which he had prudently filled with plant samples, insects and butterflies the previous day, examined.

It was very cold. He had slept badly, woken once by what sounded like a long military convoy passing through the village, and again, much later, by a furious argument between a man and a woman in an adjoining room, speaking a language he did not recognize. From the window, he saw as he dressed that wisps of fog had drifted in from the river to veil a line of trees on the far side of the country road. Hunched figures with agricultural implements over their shoulders trudged past on their way to outlying fields. Some of them were dressed in parts of discarded army uniform, greatcoats with the insignia and badges of rank removed, forage caps.

Downstairs they gave him coffee and a boiled egg. Van Eyck took his rucksack and stepped out into the damp, chilly morning. This time he walked away from the village, in the direction of the main road to Berlin. In twenty minutes the only building of any size that he passed was a concrete bunker that seemed to be used as some kind of cafeteria. A closed lorry was parked by the roadside, and burly women in headscarves bustled around trestle-tables preparing a midday meal for the workers in the fields.

Van Eyck tramped past onion fields, a swell of grassland, a hawthorn grove. A bus crammed with schoolchildren overtook him. Two men in dungarees rode towards the village on bicycles. Once, on the far side of a slight rise, he heard the puttering of a tractor.

Five minutes later he turned right and took an unmetalled track curving away towards the river. Grass grew in patches along the middle of the track, but the undergrowth and weeds on either side had been flattened by the passage of many wheels, and the muddy surface here and there was engraved with the overlaid marks of different tyres.

From the roadway, a watery radiance overhead had suggested that the sun might break through by noon, but here among the marshes the fog was thicker. Visibility was at most fifty yards, and bushes, trees, a fallen elm which had broken a gate, swam out of the obscurity in bewildering variety: a presence, a blur, an image forming a recognizable shape – to be as quickly obliterated by the wreathing mist behind.

At one point, crossing a stretch of open marshland, Van Eyck lost the track altogether. He was waist-deep in rushes, heading away from the nearby burble of running water, when he heard the singing.

At first he thought it must be some kind of aural hallucination – a trick of the wind, sighing through the reeds, distorted by some vagary of the heavy, humid atmosphere.

Then, as he moved further away from the stream, he thought, no – I *can* hear singing. A male choir again.

A radio? Out here in the marshes? In the fog?

Impossible. It was then that he accepted for the first time that the singing he heard was real. A group of men, not very far away, were belting out the German melody known in England as *O Come, All Ye Faithful*.

But why? And where?

Van Eyck turned his head first one way, then the other, to allow his ears to vector him in on the sound source.

Soon he was back on the track. Trees crowded in on every side. The singing grew louder. He passed a Volkswagen van parked in a clearing. The actor, Tufik, had been transferred to a VW van. So what – there were dozens in every town in Germany. Even so . . .

Beyond, the fog parted to show him two cars drawn up beneath the dripping trees. The first was a black Mercedes saloon. It was the second that set his heart thumping. A Zastva limousine with Russian plates.

A harsh voice, surprisingly near, was bellowing orders. Abruptly, the singing died away, faltering into silence.

Van Eyck was face-down on the sodden earth, worming his way into that silence. He was at the water's edge, prone, among the rushes.

Then suddenly the fog rolled aside and a shaft of pale sunlight slanted down between clouds to reveal what he knew he should have been looking for all along: the leaden waters of a lake, perhaps three-quarters of a mile across, and no more than two hundred yards offshore, an islet on which stood an abandoned church.

A Romanesque basilica, the church had three domes above a triple apse and an impressive bell-tower. It had evidently been the site of a battle or skirmish at the end of the war: the red sandstone walls were gashed by shell bursts, pitted by automatic fire, and one of the domes had collapsed. Fallen statues lay among the undergrowth threatening to submerge a flame-blackened porch. But it was, without doubt, where the singing had come from.

Parting the thick stems of the rushes, Van Eyck saw that the islet was linked to the shore of the lake by a causeway buttressed with granite blocks. Changing his position cautiously, he made out two men half screened by a clump of bushes at the nearer end of the causeway. They were in civilian clothes, but each carried a sub-machine-gun slung over his shoulder. In a gust of wind that rolled away more of the fog, he heard a murmured conversation.

The sun, brightening, now struck a metallic gleam from the barrel of a gun held by a third man, lounging by the church porch on the island.

Van Eyck eased a notebook from his rucksack and began to make detailed notes of the church's architecture and the layout of the site. He rose to his feet and backed away. Within an hour he had circled the lake and made a plan, roughly to scale, of the entire target area.

He walked the seven miles into Storkow, where at least there was traffic and shops were open and there were people on the streets. By an open-air vegetable market he found a pay phone and called the fall-back number in Berlin which had been given to them by O'Kelly. The captain was not there but Beverley Hills took down the details of the island church and its position on the lake, advising the Dutchman to rejoin Riordan in the city as soon as he could.

Van Eyck boarded a bus bound for East Berlin and left it at the junction where the lane branched off for Siegsdorf. The sun was out now, and the fields and woods, steaming in the sudden warmth, stretched peaceably away on either side. When he returned to the inn to pay his bill and collect his belongings, the police were waiting for him.

19

From the East German Geographical Institute, a newly created body charged with a detailed survey of all the Third Reich lands now under effective Soviet control, Riordan obtained a 1cm = 1km map of the Siegsdorf subdivision. Later he returned to the Institute to consult a larger-scale *Länder* survey of the Storkow-Fürstenwalde Regional Planning authority, which offered a field by field – almost ditch by ditch – view of the village, the lake and its islet, and the surrounding marshes. On this map, the church was marked as 'disused military barracks'.

'This is the most obvious target I ever saw for a dual assault,' Riordan said to Nelson-Harmer. 'Land, sea, as it were, and maybe even by air, if Piet's description of the church tower is accurate and Danny can climb that high.'

'Is the river leading to the lake navigable?' the Nigerian asked.

'According to the depths indicated, yes. For anything flat-bottomed, at any rate. It's a tributary of the Spree, up-river from Berlin.'

'So we land on the island from a motor boat and rush this causeway at the same time – maybe with a little diversion from our tame bat in the jolly old belfry?'

'That's about the size of it,' Riordan said. 'But we *must* contact the hostages first. If the church is down as a barracks, there must have been a unit garrisoned there during the war. Which means the interior will have been much modified to provide living quarters, a galley, offices, guardroom – that kind of thing. We must have an accurate picture of the layout. And in any case some kind of signal has to be agreed with the prisoners. Meanwhile, I'll alert the captain and ask him to – God knows how, if it's so secret! – to lay on the aquatic transport.'

But O'Kelly was not at the fall-back number in Berlin. Nor was Beverley Hills. A female secretarial voice told Riordan primly that the captain had been summoned to the embassy in the French sector. And, no, she had no idea when he would be back.

'What the hell's the old bugger doing at the French Embassy?' Riordan grumbled. 'Why is he in the French zone at all, for Christ's sake? I thought the whole lot of us were supposed not to be in Berlin at all.'

'We could at least take a shufti at the church while we wait.'

'You want to go? You're a good enough swimmer for cold lakes?'

'I did a bit once. I was with our Olympic team here in '36.' Nelson-Harmer grinned. 'I was about as popular as Jesse Owens.'

'Yes, and of course you know our prisoner potentate, don't you – the ruler of your West African neighbours?'

'Oh, good lord, yes,' Nelson-Harmer drawled. 'Fellow was my fag at the old school.'

Van Eyck was transferred to a Russian army command car in Storkow. On the way back to Berlin, he was questioned by a thin-faced officer wearing the uniform of a Soviet colonel. Two soldiers with Stetchkin machine-pistols guarded the exit doors at the rear of the vehicle.

'You will be sent to Moscow and tried, in public, as

an Imperialist spy,' the officer told him. 'A despicable attempt by the West – by fascist reactionary elements who have infiltrated Western political spheres – to sow discord among allies who fought together in the Great Patriotic War.'

'I have no idea what you are talking about,' Van Eyck said for the fourth or fifth time.

'Do not make the mistake of taking me for a fool,' Peniakov said. 'Why else would you – a known mercenary, a mongrel operator who acts only for money, one of the dogs of war – why would you be poking around on the outskirts of Berlin, worming your way towards a military installation . . . ?'

'I know nothing of this. I told you: *you* are making a mistake; I am a naturalist. I am researching certain rare species of marsh flora and fauna.'

'*Rare?*' Peniakov's narrow lips parted. His smile was no more than a rictus, a gash in the pale mask of his face. 'What do you take us for? Your stupid supposed specimen jars have been examined by experts. What do they find? Horsetails; Red Admiral butterflies; the smaller fleawort; *Riccia fluitans* – what the British call floating crystalbane. All found in abundance throughout northern Europe!'

'Every species has its variants,' Van Eyck said. 'It is the examination of sub-species, differing very little from the basic version, which lends my current research its . . .'

'Don't give me that,' the Russian growled. 'I say again: what do you take us for, that you dare to insult our intelligence by expecting us to . . . ?'

'It might help if one knew who "us" was,' Van Eyck interrupted.

'That is immaterial. We are here to find out who *you* are.'

'Look, I already said, I don't know how many times, that I am . . .'

'A Dutch naturalist? Yes, yes, I know. Seven times, to be precise. That is what you will tell the judges at the trial in Moscow. And I will tell them that you are a spy.'

'I was carrying no weapons, no camera, no binoculars – none of the spy's equipment,' Van Eyck said mildly.

'You will have been by the time the evidence is presented.'

'I see. Like that, is it?'

'Exactly like that. But I do not think you do see.' Peniakov leaned forward, the thin smile in evidence once more. He tapped Van Eyck on the knee. 'Listen, my friend. What we have been saying is for the public, the newspapers. It has nothing to do with what you Westerners love to call *facts*. We both know perfectly well that you may be Dutch, but you are certainly not a naturalist. We both know that, equally well, you are no spy. I think we both know that whatever I choose to say about you in Moscow will be believed, irrespective of what may or may not have happened in Siegsdorf today. No. Wait!' He held up his hand as Van Eyck was about to interrupt.

'I am speaking to you in English because these oafs' – he nodded towards the two guards – 'do not understand the language. So. The world will hear the two versions I have outlined, each of them bogus. But there is one other thing we both know that the world will not be told.'

Peniakov paused for emphasis. Then he said: 'You are working with the renegade mercenary, Riordan, through the man O'Kelly. Somehow you have stumbled upon our little . . . subterfuge . . . concerning the "hostages". You have even discovered where they really are. And you are being paid to free them.'

Van Eyck said nothing.

Peniakov said: 'You will not free them. What can you do? A hired assassin, a cat burglar, a safe-breaker, a greaseball mechanic, a nigger – and yourself, a prizewinner at amateur target shooting!'

'You list our specialities,' Van Eyck retorted, stung into speech by the sneering contempt in the Russian's voice. 'You forget that we happen also to be veterans of a number of military operations. Which we have survived.'

Peniakov ignored the interruption. 'You have the effrontery to set yourselves up in opposition to the massive weight of the people's authority,' he said. 'A puny band of hired cutthroats? The only professional soldier among you is dead, and he was retired.'

'An authority,' Van Eyck said, 'which hasn't the guts to admit to the bare-faced kidnapping of political opponents, but puts the blame instead on some illusory terrorist organization, by implication with Arab connections. Just who was it who used the word "effrontery"?'

Peniakov laughed. He seemed genuinely amused. 'Remember Clausewitz,' he said.

'Oh, I often do. Every morning before breakfast.'

'War is politics continued by other means, eh? Well, you would do well to remember that precisely the reverse is also true. Especially today.'

Van Eyck refrained once again from comment. He was both astonished and alarmed by the extent of the KGB officer's detailed knowledge of Riordan's operation. Even down to the c.v.s of himself and his companions. It explained up to a point the continual appearance of obstacles designed to hamper that operation. But the leak must be very close to home.

'I tell you,' Peniakov was saying, 'that I am so confident of our supremacy, convinced to such an extent of your own impotence, that I am not even bothering to remove our . . .

guests ... from the hideaway you have discovered – even if you did manage to telephone the news to your employer before you fell into our hands.'

Van Eyck suppressed with difficulty a start of surprise. How in God's name had the man known that? They couldn't have every telephone in East Germany bugged! To cover his confusion, he said: 'Since we are talking cards-on-the-table, my Russian friend – and talking of impotence – you didn't do so very well, did you, with your plan to use the military identity of the soldier who was killed to embarrass the other occupying powers?'

Peniakov shrugged. 'The proletariat remain proletarian. One minor success in a train of disasters, illegally obtained. Burglary, after all, is not an edifying trade.'

The Dutchman was smiling. He said nothing.

'You will not, I am afraid, be able to hear of the humiliating destiny we plan for your wretched group,' Peniakov said, 'because you will be in prison in Moscow, awaiting trial. Under medical treatment, shall we say, before you are schooled in what to say at that trial. However' – the voice lowered, the glance sliding towards the impassive guards – 'there may be a way to avoid that distressing journey East. If you are minded to be helpful.'

'Oh, no!' Van Eyck exclaimed. 'You're not trying to *turn* me, are you? We agreed that I wasn't a spy, so how can I be turned?'

'Perhaps not. It is possible, however, that you can be bought,' the KGB man said evenly. 'You are, after all, a mercenary, are you not?'

Before Van Eyck could reply there was a screech of brakes and the command car slewed to a brutal halt. The two of them were hurled forward against the partition separating them from the driver's cab; the standing soldiers

218

sprawled on the armoured floor, their machine-pistols skidding away from their clutching hands.

'What the devil . . . ?' Peniakov cried angrily, picking himself up.

A small hatch in the partition slid aside and the driver's face appeared. Somewhere, Van Eyck could hear men shouting.

'My apologies, Comrade Colonel,' the driver said. 'A sharp curve . . . and the road appears to be blocked immediately ahead.'

Captain O'Kelly was ushered into a comfortably furnished first-floor office, where he sank into a leather-covered armchair. Through the tall windows he could see an errant sunbeam shafting through a gap in the low clouds.

The young women behind the desk, he noted with approval, was agreeably rounded – a fact emphasized by the trim cut of the light-blue uniform she wore. No badges of rank were visible on her shoulder-straps or the forage cap set on her short, dark hair. Her smile was wide. 'The Commandant will not keep you long, Monsieur,' she said huskily. 'Perhaps, while you wait, I could offer you some refreshment? A pink gin, is it not?'

'Now that,' O'Kelly said warmly, 'is what I call efficient Intelligence.'

The Commandant proved to be a tall man with a lean, tanned face and a dark, drooping moustache, beneath which his mouth formed a surprisingly boyish smile.

'This meeting, *mon capitaine*,' he said when he had checked that O'Kelly had been provided with a drink, 'is so informal as to be non-existent. No record has been kept of your visit; you were not checked in and you will not be checked out. No notes will be taken while we talk and the discussion will not be minuted.'

O'Kelly cleared his throat. 'Fine,' he said. 'Er, what exactly are we here to talk about? If it's not too grave a breach of security to tell me.'

The boyish smile widened still more. 'Fournier, Jean-Jacques,' the Commandant said, holding out his hand. 'We have asked you to come here, of course, to discuss the work of one of your clients.'

O'Kelly shook the hand. The Frenchman's grasp was firm and dry. 'One of my clients,' he repeated, and the phrase was not formed as a question. 'I see. I imagine I need hardly ask which?'

'I think not. No names, as your countrymen say, no back drill.'

'*Pack* drill actually,' said O'Kelly.

'Ah. And I had always wondered what the damned thing meant. As a *militaire*, one is ill informed.'

'I doubt it,' O'Kelly said, looking around the room. Through the nearest window, light flashed as the Perspex nose of a low-flying Dakota passed through the rays of sunlight.

'Landing at Tegel,' the Frenchman observed. 'We have the field fully operational now.'

'Just so. Now – about my nameless client?'

'A man of considerable expertise and unblemished reputation. I will be brief,' Fournier said. 'My charming colleague here' – he indicated the girl at the desk – 'happened to become aware that he was in Berlin with . . . a somewhat unusual collection of companions. My colleague, one of our most assiduous agents, soon pieced together a hypothetical scenario not unconnected with certain quasi-political dramas which have been playing recently upon our local stage. The scenario assumed that your client was here to put right certain wrongs – without in any way compromising those who employed him.'

220

'And so?'

'I must explain here,' Fournier said, 'that the purpose of this meeting is purely informative. My government makes no requests, it offers no help, it has nothing to discuss or negotiate, officially or unofficially. We cannot in any way whatever become involved. We cannot even be seen to be interested, in the same way that your own government . . .'

'Not mine, actually. The British.'

'I beg your pardon. Yes, of course. Nevertheless,' the Frenchman continued, 'it has been felt that it would be no bad thing if your client, through yourself, was made aware that unofficially his work is approved – even if it cannot actively be assisted. After all we, like your . . . that is to say the British, have the most cogent diplomatic reasons for seeing certain, shall we say detainees, liberated as soon as possible. The country ruled by one of them, as you know, was until very recently a French mandate, and we still have an important series of mineral and petrochemical concessions there. It would be a tragedy if these were to fall – in the case of a contrary political climate – into alien hands.'

'What you are telling me,' O'Kelly said, rising to his feet, 'is that you've found out what we are doing, that you're not going to put any obstacles in our way, indeed that you approve in principle – but you're damned if you're going to do anything to help. Right?'

'I would not argue with that reading,' Fournier said.

'OK. Noted. And thanks for the tip-off. Meanwhile, felicitations for a fine piece of deductive work to Mademoiselle . . . ?'

'Harari,' the girl said. 'Dagmar Harari.'

*   *   *

Nelson-Harmer, at dusk, with his dark face framed by the rubber helmet of a black wetsuit, was virtually invisible. Emerging from the cold waters of the lake, chest-high in rushes and reeds, he squelched cautiously towards a muddy bank forming the shoreline of the islet. Above this, perhaps sixty or seventy yards distant, the Romanesque bulk of the abandoned church was silhouetted against the darkening sky.

He lay prone on the bank, allowing his senses to accustom themselves to the sounds of the approaching night – a rattle of reeds as wind stirred the branches of nearby trees, a plop and swirl as some aquatic animal launched itself into the water, far-away voices murmuring. He could just hear, a mile to the south, the faint rumble of traffic on the main road to Storkow.

And, suddenly too close for comfort, the tread of boots on a hard surface.

Face-down among damp greenery, he held his breath. Two men, walking purposefully but not in a hurry. He judged the surface to be concrete, asphalt or macadam: there was no crunch as each foot fell. A perimeter track then, circling the marshy islet?

Raising his head as soon as the footsteps passed, he was still able to identify the outlines of twin figures in some kind of loose battledress, the spiked silhouette of shoulder-slung weapons.

So, not unexpectedly, the hide-out was patrolled. How often? By how many units? At what intervals?

Pulling himself half upright, the Nigerian scrambled across the track – macadam, as he had guessed – and crouched down in a clump of bushes to wait.

'They've no special reason to be wary,' Riordan had said. 'They won't know that Piet's discovered the island, even if they know we probably got on to Siegsdorf as a general area. But *you* must be particularly careful: we want the full gen on their m.o. And they must on no account know that we know it.'

Well, Nelson-Harmer thought, he had the whole bloody night to find out, didn't he? Stealthily, he stripped off the wetsuit. Beneath it, he wore a skin-tight black ski-suit made from a thermally efficient fabric developed by scientists who had once worked with O'Kelly in Naval Intelligence.

The initial difficulty, in the dark, was to distinguish one couple of guards from another. Voices were useless to him: they were all speaking a language with which he was totally unfamiliar. He assumed this was the same dialect as that used by Habib Tufik and the interpreter girl, but he did not believe these were actors; he guessed they were selected soldiers from one or the other of the Soviet provinces nearest to Turkey, perhaps between the Black Sea and the Caspian. It was, after all, as Riordan had pointed out, essential that the hostages continued to believe they were in the hands of terrorists rather than units of the Russian army.

Nelson-Harmer eventually identified the different pairs by gait, body language and tone of voice. There were three patrols operating at any one time; they passed at seven-minute intervals, always in the same direction; and the complete tour took twenty-one minutes. Assuming they marched at an average of three miles per hour, this meant that the circumference of the perimeter path was . . . well, never mind, that could be established later. In the light of a miniature torch, he scribbled notes on a pad, returning the torch, the pad and an indelible pencil to a waterproof pocket in the wetsuit. He stowed the suit beneath a hawthorn bush, waited for a patrol to pass, counted off three and a half minutes on the luminous dial of his watch, and stole after the soldiers along the macadam pathway.

Lights had been showing for some time now within the church – not directly through the arches of the ruined windows, but diffused from some source or sources within the outer fabric of the building. It was clear that a secondary structure had been erected inside the original tall framework of the basilica, presumably when the place was transformed into a barracks.

Before he could investigate this, Nelson-Harmer found that an enclosed space, a kind of exercise yard, had been organized as an open-air extension of the chancel. It was about fifty yards long, lozenge-shaped, and completely cleared of bushes and vegetation. A quick duck down to find a sight-line against an illuminated window showed him that the yard was surrounded by a chain-link fence about fifteen feet high and curved in at the top. Evidently this was designed to stop people getting out rather than getting in. Perhaps the barracks had been used as a Russian army jail? Or had the yard been purpose-built for the hostages?

Maybe a look through one of those glassless church windows would offer an answer.

He hurried ahead. Checking the compound had delayed him enough to be within earshot of the following patrol. Now he was level with the church itself. Past the triple apse with its three undamaged domes, he dodged off the path and crouched down beside the first buttress supporting the south transept.

The patrol passed. In the diffuse light, he saw that the soldiers were concentrating on the lake shore rather than looking inland. Once they were walking below the nave, Nelson-Harmer started to scramble upwards. The lower part of the transept wall was ornamented with three Lombard bands – contrasted ridges of sandstone projecting from the brickwork. Above these a double line of blind arcades was recessed. From the upper row, he was able to pull himself up on to the slanting sill of a savaged window embrasure.

Perched there, he saw that the entire inner fabric of the basilica – stalls, screens, pulpit, choir, reredos, galleries – had indeed been ripped away. In their place, sheathed by the massive thirteenth-century outer walls, three single-storey corrugated iron structures had been built.

The largest of these took up most of the nave and was, he presumed, the old army dormitory, now used to house the twelve hostages. At right angles to this, in the transept, a partitioned hut was used partly as a canteen, partly for ablutions. The third building was in the chancel. The floor here, up half a dozen steps, was at a higher level, but the building had been raised further still and provided with wide glass windows overlooking the whole ground-plan of the church. This was clearly the nerve-centre, control room and guardhouse of the operation: behind the lit windows he could see two, if not three, figures moving. A smell of vegetables cooking rose with the steam from a partly open door at one end of the cookhouse-canteen.

So far, so good. Nelson-Harmer waited for a patrol to pass and lowered himself to the ground. He set off before the following sentries were due and made an entire circuit of the church.

There were no outhouses, no other buildings on the islet. An armed guard was positioned inside the entrance porch, and there were two more at the landward end of the causeway, revealed by a match flame and the glow within cupped hands of lit cigarettes. A fourth guard, he had already noted, stood just inside the main doorway.

There could, of course, be a whole battalion in the woods between the causeway and the Siegsdorf road. Here, with the six sentries, there were ten men on guard. Add, say, three more in the control room, and another couple in the kitchens, with certainly a couple of overseers. Seventeen chaps actually on the spot – and at least as many again who could be called up, because there had to be reliefs. Even under Soviet orders, people couldn't be worked twenty-four hours a day!

Unless you wanted to deal with anything up to forty defenders, then, any assault-and-rescue operation would have to be bloody quick. Go in, do the job, get out. A maximum of ten minutes, bearing in mind the terrain. Preferably five or six.

OK, what else had he noticed that might be of tactical use? Three things. The church roof had gone, along with most of the columns and arches supporting the part that covered the nave, although a group of rafters like the spars of a sunken ship still arched skeletally over the entrance. Apart from the main doors, all other exits had been bricked up except for one that led from the central apsidal chapel to the exercise yard. Finally there was the bell-tower. Unusually, it rose above the chancel rather than the entrance, and could be used as an observation post to overlook the yard. Or as an unexpected entry – Nelson-Harmer smiled – for a cat burglar. The tower seemed, as far as he could see, to be in good condition. Stairs led into it from the ambulatory, so it was reasonable to assume that guards would be posted there during daylight hours.

Returning to the hawthorn bush, Nelson-Harmer recovered the pad, pencil and torch from his wetsuit. Between the passage of sentries, he made copious notes, then added a diagram of the church interior and another detailing the layout of the islet as a whole, with an estimate of the distances involved.

He replaced everything in the waterproof pocket and went back to the church. Now he was faced with the more difficult and dangerous part of his solitary mission: the contact, at last, with the hostages.

From his original vantage-point in the ruined window, he had seen in the diffused illumination emerging from the barred shutters of the dormitory hut that a stone lectern still projected from the church wall beyond the building's flat roof. This could be reached by an agile man from the empty embrasure immediately opposite the one he was in. And although the steps leading up to the lectern had been removed, the drop to the ancient flagged floor was no more than ten feet.

Skilfully using the reeds, the bushes, and what ground cover there was, Nelson-Harmer — in the opposite direction to the sentries this time — circled the islet until he was opposite the north wall of the old church.

The overturned lorry lay broadside-on to the roadway, completely blocking both lanes, and adding to the confusion with a chaos of smashed crates from which several tons of onions, cabbage, apples, tomatoes and sugar beet had spilled. Judging from the black skid marks twined across the tarmac surface, the driver must have lost control of the articulated vehicle, taken the sharp bend too fast, run halfway up a steep bank, and then dropped back into the road with the lorry on its side.

If Van Eyck noticed that, according to the position of the wreck, the skid marks should have been on the *far* side, rather than the near side of the truck, he kept it strictly to himself. Nevertheless, the thought put him very much on the alert.

Momentarily, as the command car ground to a halt, he had considered making a grab for one of the guards' machine-pistols as they skittered across the floor, but Peniakov was far too quick for him. As the KGB man whirled around from the partition against which he had been flung, there was already a drawn automatic in his right hand. 'Not so fast, my friend,' he said, smiling. And then, to the discomfited guards: 'If you have quite recovered your equilibrium – and your weapons – take him outside and keep him covered. If he makes the slightest move, the slightest, shoot. The ankles and behind the knees. Is that quite clear? Even to your limited intelligence? I myself shall investigate this foolishness.'

Standing beside the command car with the 9mm muzzles of two machine-pistols less than a foot from his back, Van Eyck watched the Russian crunch across broken glass to the waste of vegetables where two embarrassed East Germans in overalls were trying to explain what had happened to Peniakov's driver and his mate.

'What is this nonsense?' Peniakov barked. 'We are on important business; a prisoner has to be delivered. The way must be cleared at once.'

Twisting a greasy cap between his hands, one of the Germans was stammering that, alas, with the best possible will in the world, this was not immediately possible.

'Ridiculous. Get that wreck out of the way. I will give you exactly ten minutes to clear a route for my vehicle.'

'If the Herr Comrade Colonel would kindly listen,' Van Eyck heard the man explain, 'the lorry is a twenty-tonner. Until a breakdown vehicle with a winch and a crane is here, nothing can be moved.'

'Get such a vehicle. At once.'

'A man has been sent. The nearest telephone is a mile away, at Löwenthal.'

'Use my command car and driver. Overtake the man.'

'Unfortunately' – the arms flung wide in resignation – 'the village is on the far side of the wreck.'

Peniakov was visibly reddening with fury. 'This side,

then. How far back is the nearest village with anything as efficient as a telephone?'

'Five miles. Perhaps six. I am a stranger myself. If the Herr . . .'

Peniakov choked him off with an explosive curse in Russian.

It was exactly at this moment that Van Eyck heard a dual gasp, a kind of suppressed double gurgle immediately behind him. He froze, agonizingly aware of those murderous guns. But the sounds were followed only by the slither and slump of two bodies falling to the ground. A limp outstretched hand appeared on the road beside one of the Dutchman's boots.

'Drop!' a voice hissed in his ear. 'Quick! Crawl under the command car.'

Van Eyck obeyed instantly. As he fell, he saw in a quick flash an unforgettable tableau, a freeze-frame from an action movie: two indistinct figures standing over the unconscious guards with the Russians' Stetchkins covering Peniakov; the KGB man, face distorted with rage, half turned with his gun arm outstretched; his driver and mate frozen in astonishment.

And, from behind the mounds of spilled vegetables, half a dozen more men in dungarees rising with handguns to menace the Dutchman's captors.

Peniakov had fired once, a sharp crack, aimed in a hurry, a shot that failed to score, before a warning voice cautioned him to drop the pistol if he valued his life. The gun clattered down among broken glass.

'All right,' the driver of the wrecked lorry said briskly in German. 'No harm will come to you if you behave. What we want is your command car. There's a little job we have to do in Storkow. A People's Bank, so called. It will be a useful getaway.'

'A band of degenerates,' Peniakov said through set teeth. 'Common criminals – ex-Nazi riff-raff, by God! – *daring* to steal a Soviet vehicle . . .' Rage finally choked him into silence.

'You three,' the driver said. 'Pick up your guards. They're only knocked out: they'll recover in half an hour. Drag them to the far side of the wreck . . . and start walking. There's a good café in Löwenthal.'

Van Eyck heard the tramping of many feet. Muttered instructions. The dwindling fury of Peniakov's fulminations. He was unsure of his own place in this unscheduled scenario.

Eventually the engine of the command car was started, and he was lifted out from between the rear wheels and reinstalled in the back, along with half a dozen taciturn men wearing dungarees. The doors slammed shut. The command car swung around in a U-turn and accelerated away in the direction of Storkow.

None of the rescuers spoke. None would reply to Van Eyck's questions. In five minutes, the command car stopped, and the Dutchman was motioned to get out. They were at an intersection on the edge of an anodyne landscape of grey fields and ragged woodland. It had started to rain.

A taxi was waiting by the roadside. According to the plates it was Berlin-registered. 'This will take you back to your hotel,' the man who seemed to be the leader of the hijackers told Van Eyck.

'Yes, but . . . Christ! I mean who . . . ? What the *hell* goes on?' The Dutchman was incoherent. 'I mean thanks, but . . .'

'No questions,' the rescuer said. 'The cab driver knows nothing. He has been instructed to take you back. Period.'

He raised a hand in salute and turned away. Van Eyck heard him say to the driver of the command car:

'We'll junk this heap outside Storkow and regain our own transport, right?'

'OK,' the driver answered. 'Jump in; we're on our way.' If Van Eyck had seen him, he would have recognized him as the insolent youth acting as receptionist at the Siegsdorf inn.

The Dutchman was driven swiftly, efficiently – and in silence – back to the hotel in West Berlin where Riordan had quartered his men. 'But the extraordinary thing,' Van Eyck said to the mercenary leader when he had finished his story, 'is that I heard some of the instructions these characters were given while I was hiding underneath that lorry. And, what do you know, the guy was speaking *in French*!'

Riordan's smile, with one eyebrow quizzically raised, was a little puzzling, the Dutchman thought. Almost, it seemed, as if somehow he had an equally tantalizing disclosure to make himself. But all he said was: 'Surprise, surprise. We'll discuss that later, Piet. But right now' – and suddenly the voice was very serious – 'right now I'm horrified to learn that Peniakov knows we've uncovered his hideaway. Which means he must have known, as you say, about your phone call to me.'

He shook his head. 'That plunges us into a whole new ball game. And even if it's true that they're confident enough not to move the hostages from the island, it means we have to act faster than fast, before they call up an entire bloody army of reinforcements.'

'You're telling me . . . ?'

'I'm telling you,' Riordan said, 'that we've got to get out of here and head hell for leather in the direction of Siegsdorf now. Tonight.'

20

'Harari? Dagmar Harari?' Riordan echoed incredulously when O'Kelly returned to the hotel soon after Van Eyck. 'But that's . . . hell, that's the name of the interpreter girl! The actress who's paid to carry off that charade at the conference centre every night.'

'The same.'

'You hadn't seen her before, of course, but she's lodging at that first hotel we stayed at, the one where someone took a pot-shot at Piet.'

'One wonders,' O'Kelly said, 'just why she happened to choose that particular hotel at that particular time.'

'Yes, but what the devil's she doing at the French Embassy?'

'We're talking here about the SDECE, the Service de Documentaion Étrangère et de Contre-Espionage. Something like Britain's MI6 or the Secret Intelligence Service. It was only formed last year — an amalgam of General Rivet's Military Intelligence Service and the Free French spook group set up in London during the war by De Gaulle. It reports directly to the President and is answerable only to him.'

'Nice work if you can get it,' Riordan said. 'That's what I call a free hand! It figures too: the girl told me her parents once lived in the Lebanon, which explained why she spoke that outlandish dialect — but the language used by all cultivated people in Beirut is French. As it is in Egypt. That accounts for their interest in at least two of our hostages. How do you read their position as a whole, though?'

O'Kelly did not reply directly. 'People tend to dismiss the French,' he said, 'especially in the intelligence field. That is a mistake – probably fostered by the frogs themselves. If folks think they're no good, they won't be taken seriously, which of course makes their job that much easier. But in fact the SDECE are a pretty crafty lot. Rather like the Mossad for the Jews, if there's something they want done they have a remarkable talent for getting it done, even if they don't do it themselves.'

'You think they're actually using us to do their job for them?'

'I think,' O'Kelly said, 'that maybe they were contemplating something along our lines. They knew of course that the kidnap set-up was phoney because the girl, their own agent, was in on it. And then, when your lot came along and she worked out what the score was there, I think our friends simply said: OK. Let's sit back and let them get on with it.'

'And if they *should* help in any way – Please, Miss, it wasn't us! Piece of cake if the only boss you have to answer to is away in Paris. And certainly – rather tactfully and indirectly, now I come to think of it – Mademoiselle Harari steered me in the Siegsdorf direction.' Riordan smiled reminiscently. 'Among other things.'

'Well, it explains Van Eyck's rescue,' O'Kelly said.

Riordan nodded. 'Yeah, that was a smart piece of work. Now we have to do something even smarter ourselves: get those hostages out before dawn. You wouldn't have an eighteen-seater motor boat handy, would you, Captain?'

*　　*　　*

It was as the twelve hostages were being shepherded back to their quarters after a late evening meal that the shuffling file was joined by a thirteenth shadowy figure. Nelson-Harmer materialized from behind a crumbling Romanesque pillar at the moment the leading guard turned the corner of the hut to fling open the door. By the time the guard bringing up the rear of the file crossed the small entrance hall to double-lock the connecting door, the mercenary was out of sight between two of the beds in the dormitory area.

His reappearance caused little surprise among the hostages. Most of them assumed he was just another prisoner taken for one reason or another. The length of time they themselves had been sequestered, cut off from the outside world, had dulled their reactions to the point where apathy was the overriding element.

Glancing quickly from face to face, Nelson-Harmer recognized two French North African politicians, half a dozen men who could have come from any Mediterranean country, a left-wing Australian expatriate, and the three detainees the whole complex rigmarole had been designed to keep out of the way while their countries were 'revolutionized'. Mbotu Ngombi, the West African president; the Egyptian Fayed Nessim; and Prince Said Abd el Hossein, whose family still ruled one of the Gulf states.

Each member of the trio – perhaps because his place in public life placed him constantly in the public eye – looked much as he must have done when he was marched at gunpoint from the final session at the trade conference. Nessim, dapper in a dark-brown suit, looked freshly shaven and his hair shone; Prince Said wore his Arab head-dress. His beard was neatly trimmed and his pale, lightweight suit, although slightly rumpled, retained a crease to the trousers. Ngombi's ceremonial tribal robes were heavily shot with gold thread. The condition of the nine other men varied from the spruce to the dishevelled. Some were unshaven. One or two already displayed nervous tics. All were hollow-eyed, haggard with frustration and fatigue.

Ngombi was the only hostage actually to express astonishment aloud.

'Great Scott!' he cried, the deep voice booming around the iron hut's wooden walls. 'Surely it can't be . . . ? But, my God, it *is*! Teddy Bear! What the devil are you doing here, old son?'

'*Ssssshh*!' Nelson-Harmer murmured. 'Mustn't alert the prefects or they'll call in the beak and we'll *all* be gated.'

'Yes, that's all very well,' Ngombi said in a lower voice. 'But what are you *doing* here, Bear? How did you get in? What's the bally score?'

'I've no time to go into that now,' the mercenary replied. 'Let me just say that there's a rescue team operating, and I'm a member of it. We hope to get you out of this. Soon. Perhaps tomorrow.'

'Fine. Great. About bloody time. But what *is* all this about? Who are these cretins keeping us? What are they on about? What on earth . . . ?'

The President's voice was swamped in a chorus of questions. Most of the other hostages had crowded round once the talking began. Only one man, one of those with a tic, remained sitting with bowed head on his bed at the far end of the room, nervously picking at the sheet.

'Yes, who the devil is holding us?'

'Why are we being kept here? Why does nobody tell us . . . ?'

'What kind of ransom are they demanding, for Heaven's sake?'

'. . . given us no news whatever of the negotiations. Don't we have the right at least to know *something*?'

'Not a word since they brought us here – wherever this

is. The bastards don't even talk: just motion us here or there, or make us shut up.'

'You say rescue. Who the hell are you, and how do you propose . . . ?'

Nelson-Harmer held up his hand. 'Wait! Just a *minute*.'

The questions had been anticipated. 'Naturally,' Riordan had said, 'they'll be crazy to know why they're there, what ransom is being demanded, and how the negotiations are going. The bright ones may even suspect Soviet complicity.'

'So do I say: no, chaps; the Comrades are not in cahoots with the damn terrorists; they *are* the damn terrorists?' Nelson-Harmer had asked.

'I think not,' Riordan had replied. 'We're told not to rock the diplomatic boat. There may be reasons why the Allies would prefer to keep quiet – use it as a lever, a threat to make the Russians behave in some future crisis. Certainly the Soviets themselves won't want a rescue from *them* splashed all over the world – as it would be if the hostages knew. I daresay some tacit, face-saving formula will be agreed with them: specialist undercover units were involved, the hostages were rescued without any casualties, the kidnappers were killed. End of story.'

'It may be difficult, nevertheless, to parry . . .

'Look – we've been hired to get them out. Then vanish. Let the press conference details be decided by the guys paying the bill, OK?'

'Whatever you say, O King. So what *do* I tell them?'

'You stall. Just as the Russians acting as terrorists do. No time to go into that now. Later, man, later. If your minds are cluttered up with questions about who and why and wherefore, you won't be able to concentrate on the vital instructions I'm here to give you.'

'Message received,' Nelson-Harmer had said. 'Over and out.'

Now, in the claustrophobic confines of the prison hut, he did exactly that. He sidestepped every question. And then, before the pressure from the hostages became too acute, he started to talk. Slowly, precisely, and as simply as he could, he outlined the standard instructions given to prisoners in the event of an armed rescue attempt – with a few qualifications of his own added. It was when he was striving to get through to – and allay the fears of – the less bright, that Nelson-Harmer had his own bright idea.

'Look,' he said to his old schoolmate, 'I'm a bit stuck here, to tell the truth. I'm supposed to report back to the CO with all the gen on this place. At the same time, I have to be absolutely sure, spot on, that all the types here understand exactly what they have to do when the baloon goes up. And that's where, so far, I find myself a trifle adrift.'

'And so?'

'So I have to be in two places at once. And it occurs to me, old thing, that the answer is not to try the impossible but turn the problem, as it were, inside out. A case where two into one *will* go.'

'I'm not sure that I understand you,' Ngombi said.

'Why, instead of one chap being in two places, we have two chaps each in one place.'

The African stared at him.

'You take my place and go back with the reports,' Nelson-Harmer said, 'and I'll stay here to make sure these johnnies do the right thing – and lend a hand from inside when the crunch comes, what.'

'You're crazy,' Ngombi said. 'How could I possibly . . . ?'

'Look, old bean, to these oiks one black African looks much like another. We're the same height. I was afraid the perks of office might have made you put on weight, but we're still much the same build. If I were to wear that gorgeous dressing-gown and the little round hat that goes with it, who's to know? Meanwhile, you attire yourself in this black number and hotfoot it back to the boss with the intelligence. Just like the old sixth-form OTC manoeuvres.'

'You're out of your mind. Stone-cold bonkers. How, possibly, could . . . ?'

'Just listen, Zombie. The notes, already shipshape, are in the waterproof pocket of a wetsuit underneath a hawthorn bush beyond the exercise yard. You simply whizz along there, jump into the suit, cross the lake, and hand them over to a bloke who'll be waiting there. Fine chap. A little Italian-American called Aletti.'

'What do you mean, cross the lake? I'm a very poor swimmer.'

'No problem. The bally thing's no more than four feet deep, most of the way. There's only about thirty yards where one has to swim, and I guess even your breast-stroke could cope with that.'

'It's a big lake,' Ngombi said weakly. 'How would I know where to aim for?'

'Give you a tiny torch. While you're upright, you signal: three long and two short, repeated. Aletti will reply with three short and two long.

'We happen to be locked in this fucking prison,' Ngombi said.

'Again, no problem. One of our chaps is a locksmith. He's lent me the necessary. I'll have you out of here in a trice, once your hosts have settled down for a quiet zizz.'

'There's no way of getting out of the exercise yard. That fence is . . .'

'I know the yard. You won't be in it. Once out of here,

you'll be up on a lectern, through a window, and Bob's your uncle. Piece of cake.'

'How the hell will I know where your damn wetsuit is?'

'I'll tell you.'

'Oh, Christ!' the President groaned.

It was the white cat, finally, which tipped Riordan off. There had been just too many for coincidence. Or perhaps one appearing just too many times. This one was sitting washing itself on the rear seat of a streamlined Bugatti sports saloon.

It was very large, with different-coloured eyes – one blue and the other green – and it wore a red collar. Weren't they all?

The Bugatti was parked just around the corner from the hotel. The big cat had uttered a low growl as Riordan approached, then jumped out of the small rear window and run across the road to a traffic island, where it settled beneath a clump of bushes and stared unblinkingly at the car.

Ten minutes later, a tall, athletic-looking young man rounded the corner, opened the offside door, and slid into the driving seat. 'Boanerges?' he called. 'Where have you got to this time, you elusive animal? Come here, Boa-Boa. Come! It's time to go.'

There was no reaction from the cat beneath the bushes. The young man inserted a key into the dashboard and stabbed the starter button. The Bugatti's highly stressed straight-eight engine whined to life. Flipping a lock of hair back from his eyes, the driver turned to the window, looked right and left, then saw the cat across the road. '*There* you are!' he called again. 'Boa-Boa, come *on*. We're in a hurry.'

The white cat remained staring at the Bugatti. It made no move towards the road.

Riordan rose silently from behind the front seats, pressing the cold muzzle of his Browning against the nape of the young man's neck. 'Is that why you have always refused to go back and work in England?' he said softly. 'Because you'd have to put the cat in quarantine?'

Beverley Hills sat very still, his hands resting on the polished wood steering wheel. 'One of the reasons,' he said, staring ahead now through the shallow vee windscreen. 'There are others. Notably, the rotten social system, the inequality, the hypocrisy. How did you find out?'

'Through your cat, actually. But it was all too simple, once it occurred to me that it was always the *same* white cat. I should have cottoned on days ago.'

'Through the cat? Really? He doesn't usually warm to strangers.'

'Not directly. He was just there too often. A white cat outside, the first time I went to see O'Kelly. An Aston-Martin that time, wasn't it? You have a taste for expensive motor cars.'

'I like to play the field,' Hills said.

'A white cat by the old boat-house beside the Havel lake, when we crash-landed. Probably a white cat in the BMW which tried to run down Brod and myself in the old town. Certainly one in the car park at Die Insel, where Peniakov doubtless eavesdropped on my conversation with the interpreter girl. And, for all I know, white cats at the hotel where someone tried to murder Van Eyck, and again at the scene of the fire. When you add that up . . .'

'Not at the fire. He's terrified of flames. He was frightened once by some evil kids lighting a bonfire. That's when I rescued him the first time.'

'What happened to the kids?'

'They're dead.'

There was a short pause in the conversation. Hills

switched off the idling engine. 'Hands back on the wheel, please,' Riordan said. He pressed the gun barrel a little harder against Hills's neck. 'I suppose it should have been obvious. It had to be *somebody* on O'Kelly's staff who had the opportunity to listen in on my briefing, follow me to the post office and booby-trap my car. The same goes for the Hamburg meeting, the details of our flight and the rendezvous by the lake. You would certainly have known about those. You could have hidden in the fish loft, overheard my instructions concerning the hotel, driven there in your smart little BMW, followed Brod to the tavern in the old town and attempted to run us down, all before lunch. Where do you get all these exotic cars, by the way?'

'The Aston's my own,' Hills said. 'As for the others' – he gave an elaborate shrug – 'it's not too hard to liberate stuff in a conquered country.'

Riordan said: 'My biggest mistake, of course, was the call I made to you at the fall-back number here in Berlin. I let on that we knew there were no hostages in the conference centre. I revealed that I planned a diversion. And you stalled. You refused to say whether or not you were in Berlin. You wouldn't tell me where O'Kelly was, and you tried to prevent me contacting him. At the same time you tried to worm out of me my immediate plans, the address of our safe house. It was my turn to stall on those because I was astonished to find you in Berlin – you, the great collector and collator of facts, as O'Kelly says proudly. I guess I should have known then, but I have this ridiculous old-fashioned notion of trusting the people I work with.'

'A great mistake in the modern world,' Hills said.

'The clincher,' Riordan continued, 'was the call Van Eyck made to report that he had located the hostages. You took that message. By the time he'd walked four or five miles back to the inn at Siegsdorf, the cops were waiting – and then Peniakov revealed that he *knew* we knew. That was his mistake: the information could only have come through you. That and the cat.'

'Oh, well. Some you win.'

'I assume you have been reporting back to your Russian masters ever since you learned at the original briefing in Paris that we were coming?'

'Not masters, old boy. It was a matter of choice.'

'Choice? With your background and advantages?'

'Exactly. The guv'nor's a bloody earl. Grouse shooting in Scotland, fishing, point-to-point races, half a dozen sinecure directorships and a couple of hundred thou a year. Fucking disgrace.'

'What made you – er – see the light?' Riordan asked curiously.

'Fellow who visited my college, actually. Talked at a Union debate. Pointed out that ninety-five per cent of the good things in the world were owned by five per cent of the people, and that kind of thing. Frightfully decent type. Chap by the name of Philby.'

'And you really believe that the way our . . . our gallant allies organize their society will make for a better world?'

'My dear fellow! You only have to look at the ants, the bees. *They* know how to *organize* an overcrowded civilization.'

'But then they don't run Bugattis, do they? Hills, do you know what percentage of the population forms the Commissars and KGB men and members of the Politburo holding the reins in your brave new world? Five?'

'Don't ask me. I haven't time to waste on loaded arguments.'

'But you do have time to shoot at people with high-velocity rifles, set fire to their houses, try to shoot down their aeroplanes and run them down in expensive motor cars? Such bourgeois notions of morality as the right to live, the right to have one's own opinions, the right to disagree have been chucked, I suppose, along with the earldom and the grouse?'

'You know what they say: you can't make an omelette without breaking a few eggs.'

'Even good eggs who've been drinking friends and companions in arms? Listen, Hills' – the gun pressed harder again, the edge to Riordan's voice sharpening – 'in just a moment we are going to get out of this car. You will remain with your hands on the wheel while I lean forward and open your door. You will then get out and stand on the sidewalk, remembering that *I* will tip forward the seat before I join you . . . and remembering especially that this gun will never be more than a foot from your back.'

Hills said nothing.

Riordan reached over his shoulder to press down the chromed door handle. The wide door swung open. 'Now get out,' Riordan said.

Very cautiously, Hills clambered out of the Bugatti and stood upright. Riordan eased himself swiftly from the shallow rear seat and stood behind him, the gun steady in his hand. He back-kicked the door shut.

'And now?' Hills asked.

The hotel was in a very quiet district. The side-street was quieter still. Since Hills had got into the Bugatti only two cars had passed and one pedestrian – a woman hurrying by with a bulging shopping bag. There was nobody in sight now. 'It is about twenty yards to the corner,' Riordan said. 'Around the corner, perhaps another fifteen to the hotel entrance. We are now going to walk slowly to that corner and then into the hotel, after which we will discuss with Captain O'Kelly just what we are going to do with you.'

'You can't do anything,' Hills said. 'I don't imagine you will have the guts to shoot me. I haven't broken any laws. It's not illegal to be a Communist, especially in East Germany. It's not a crime to pass on information if it hasn't been obtained by burglary or extortion. As for the other things you see fit to quote – the shooting, the fire, et cetera – there isn't a single shred of evidence to connect me with any of them, and you know it.'

'We shall see,' Riordan said. 'Now walk. I'm just behind.'

Hills shrugged. He began strolling towards the corner.

He was a yard away from it when Riordan sensed a flurry of movement, an almost imperceptible rush of air . . . and then a hissing snarl, a sudden propulsive weight clamped to his right arm, and a searing pain between his thumb and first finger so agonizing that his hand opened involuntarily and the gun dropped to the ground as he cried aloud.

The white cat had streaked across the road and leaped to his gun arm, raking his wrist with razor-sharp claws as it sank its teeth into his hand. By the time he had reached awkwardly across with his left hand to seize the animal by the scruff of the neck and prise it away, his hand was streaming blood and Hills was out of sight around the corner.

Scooping up the Browning, Riordan sprinted after him.

The man was yards past the hotel, running like the wind and evidently heading for a narrow alleyway, an entry on the far side of the street. He dodged out into a line of traffic momentarily held up by a delivery lorry, stepped into the opposite lane, sprang aside to avoid a motorcyclist roaring past on the wrong side of the white line . . . and ran full tilt into a police car which swung fast, siren screaming, out of the alley.

The heavy front bumper, and then the steel radiator grille, caught Hills against the shins and chest, hurling him

244

into the air to crack his head sickeningly against the edge of a galvanized sand bin on the pavement. He dropped to the ground and lay with his head at an impossible angle in the gutter. He was as dead as anyone Riordan had ever seen.

The mercenary leader halted abruptly. A road accident. Nothing to do with him. They happened all the time. The police were already there.

He walked slowly back to the hotel, twisting a handkerchief around his bleeding hand and wrist. The hotel had a small entrance lobby. He walked past a potted plant to a window, drew aside a lace curtain and looked out.

Fifty yards away a crowd was already gathering. Beneath the scarlet smear still trickling down the side of the sand bin, the white cat sat in the road with its front paws planted on the dead man's chest, howling its grief and its fury into the face of a cruel world.

21

'I suppose he'd wheedled every detail of the operation out of you while I was away collecting the gear you'd organized?' Riordan said to O'Kelly.

'Well, of course,' the captain replied. 'He was part of the team, dammit. Very anxious to help out in any way he could. Wanted to do his bit. He even offered to come down to Siegsdorf with you.'

'I'll bet. That would have been a puzzle for the newspapers,' Riordan said bitterly. 'Six foreigners, all shot in the back, found floating in a lake outside Berlin.'

'Thank God you saw the car in time.'

'Yeah.' Riordan shook his head. 'Everyone has his weak link. Odd that his should have been his own cat – and that it was through the cat, and a police car working for his own bosses, that he was finished off.'

Alessandro Aletti was cold. He was also hungry and a little damp. Crouched among the lakeside bulrushes, he wished the wood in which he had concealed the rented Volkswagen was a little nearer; he wished sound didn't carry so clearly across water, so that at least he could have run the engine and used the heater, inefficient though it was; he wished the hip-flask which had contained his schnapps had been larger. Above all, he wished that Teddy Nelson-Harmer would for Christ's sake get a move on and cross this bloody lake. Mist was already rising from the still surface. The faint lights visible from the converted church on the far side had blurred. Before long visibility would be reduced to a point where the torch beam wouldn't penetrate far enough to guide the man to the right point on the shore. They would have to spend the rest of this accursed night walking up and down among these pestilential rushes, hoping to make contact. Aletti swore.

Now even the lowest of the lights from the church, the one off to the left, was appearing to blink . . .

Wait a minute.

Off to the *left*? Blinking?

Yes. Three long and two short, repeated. And again. And again.

Christ, he'd almost missed it! Aletti snatched up his own torch and flashed the reply: three short and two long. Repeated.

The feeble, rhythmic pulses of light brightened, moved to the right, advanced. Finally, as Aletti kept his own signal in operation, they died away. Water swirled. A disturbed night bird flapped away, squawking angrily. Aletti heard the suck and squelch of feet pulling free of mud.

A sudden splashing cascade of water, and the church lights were completely blotted out for a moment as a bulky figure emerged among the rushes.

'Lead, kindly light,' a deep voice intoned.

The beam was canted upwards. Yes, it was Teddy all right – water still sliding from the gleaming rubber suit, white teeth smiling in the dark face.

Wait a minute! The suit was right, the size was right, the colour was right and so was the voice. But the features were different: the lips thicker, the nose a trifle flatter, the eyebrows a completely different shape.

'I should tell you there's a gun in my other hand,' Aletti

said, keeping the torch on the other's face. 'Just who are you, friend?'

'Friend indeed. The name is Ngombi. I've changed places with the Bear, that's all. He kind of insisted.'

'The Bear?'

'Teddy. Nelson-Harmer if you've got the time. He's staying there to marshal the troops, as I understand it, when you attack. All his notes and diagrams are zipped in here.' The black man patted his shining hip.

'OK.' Stalling for time, Aletti improvised. 'What's the password?'

There was a slight pause, and then Ngombi said: 'Swordfish.'

Aletti burst out laughing. 'I should live to see this,' he choked. 'A Marx Brothers fan in the wilds of Eastern Germany! The nightclub scene in *Horse Feathers*, wasn't it?'

'I think so. This is a Marxist country, anyway. The movie, in any case, where Groucho says, 'There'll be no diving after *this* cigar!' as he chucks the stogie out the window.'

'And where the welcoming crowd sing *Hurrah for Captain Spalding!*?'

'No, no. That was *Animal Crackers*. At least I think so. I only saw that one once.'

'Hold on,' Aletti said suddenly. Once again there was a rhythmic pulse discernible. But this time it was audible rather than visible – an intermittent series of sharp, shrill sounds in the distance, a deliberate succession of shorts and longs.

Or dots and dashes.

'My God!' Aletti said. 'The VW!'

'The VW?'

'There's a portable field receiver in there. That's Morse we're ignoring. Don't go away now.' He scrambled up a grassy bank, ran across an unmetalled road, and plunged into the coppice in which the car was hidden.

At the foot of the bank, stripping off the rubber suit to get at the waterproof wallet, Ngombi was able now to make out the different pauses left by the operator between letters and whole words. From the repetitive pattern he finally distinguished, he judged that the message was short.

He was not mistaken. Sliding back down the bank, Aletti blurted out in an excited voice: 'Five words. What do you know. "Stay there: we attack tonight"!'

Aletti was not the only one to be astonished by the change of plan. Well, not exactly change, Riordan himself had said in Berlin; more a bringing forward of what they had always intended to do anyway. With a spot of improvisation thrown in, on account of the lack of time.

And because if they didn't move rather faster than lightning, a certain KGB officer named Peniakov might well have called up half the Soviet Army of Occupation to greet them.

Fortunately for Nelson-Harmer, he had fought with Riordan before. If he hadn't, the tip-off signal might well have passed in his mind as a harmless piece of eccentricity on the part of an overzealous musician. Or maybe a show-off who'd been raising his elbow a little too often.

That was the way it was meant to sound to those not in the know.

The Nigerian had separated the hostages into three groups: Nessim, Abd el Hossein and the Australian, who – being the most precious in terms of release – he was keeping close to himself; and two four-man units which he had privately subdivided into those with guts and the also-rans, the no-hopers. Instructions to this last quartet were simple. Basically they amounted to: keep your heads down and run like hell when told to.

To those with the courage to act and think for themselves, he had suggested certain courses of action, mainly diversionary, which they could employ at their own discretion, according to the way the action developed, without in any way affecting or compromising what he hoped to achieve himself.

This, although he didn't say so, was expressly designed to protect and save the 'important' trio.

'Surprise is the element,' he told the favoured three. 'Whenever the assault comes, it'll be when the guards are at their weakest. At night, I guess, about this sort of time. Maybe even tomorrow, as I said. I reckon that, apart from the sentries outside, the guys in that control room will be reduced to one while the others snatch a few winks, eh? OK, the surprise element we have – which must be used to the maximum before that one guy arouses the others – is that they don't know there's someone in here who can unlock the doors and let you folks out.'

'You mean,' Nessim the Egyptian said, 'that when the fighting starts we slip out of here and take cover wherever you say; that we use the fighting as a cover?'

'I mean that I want you guys, all of you, the hell out of this hut and through the ruined window in the church wall *before* the fighting starts. Before it starts in here, that is.'

'What you're saying, sport,' the Australian put in, 'is that we gotta be clear before the one cove really awake organizes his mates; we gotta move so quick that we're out and through before he knows we're bloody moving, right?'

'Correct. We must act before they *react*.'

'And once outside?' Prince Said enquired.

'It will still be risky. But it's dark, it's misty – and don't ⸺ they may want to kill *us*, but they'll want to preserve *you*. Without you,' Nelson-Harmer said mendaciously, 'they've no bargaining counter, have they?'

'A point,' the Egyptian conceded.

'You'll still be on the islet, but you'll be out of prison. And remember, their initial reaction will be to rush here, to make sure nobody gets you out of this hut you will already have left.'

'If we're fast enough,' the Australian said.

'If we're fast enough, yes.'

'Pity you couldn't have brought us some weapons, sport. As you can see, these bastards are very careful to leave nothing around that could be used against them. They even take the knives and bloody forks away – and they're made of wood!'

'I know,' Nelson-Harmer said. 'But this little twenty-two Beretta was the only thing small enough to fit into the second waterproof pocket of my wetsuit. If only I could have . . .'

He paused, listening. The others had heard it too.

Clear as a bell across the still, dark waters of the lake, the brassy blare of a trumpet sounding the first few bars of a Scottish marching song:

> *The Campbells are coming, Ta-ra, Ta-ra;*
> *The Campbells are coming, Ta-ra.*

'Holy God!' Nelson-Harmer cried aloud. 'We've got to move a hell of a lot faster than we bargained for. That's the colonel's signal: it means the attack starts in thirty minutes!'

22

The vehicle bouncing at forty-five mph towards Aletti and his companion along the woodland track looked like a cross between a thirty-foot motor launch and a military assault landing-craft. It was in fact a Russian BAV-485 – a postwar copy of the American DUKW amphibian which had been used for the transport of supplies from ship to shore as well as overland and across rivers when the bridges had been destroyed.

It was a curious hybrid – basically an armoured, flat-bottomed boat fitted over a watertight six-wheeled lorry chassis powered by a six-cylinder engine developing almost 100hp. An M-36 ring mounting above the shallow cab carried a .50 Browning-type machine-gun.

The craft had been liberated from a Soviet army motor pool on the outskirts of Berlin by Riordan and Brod. Essentially a store for vehicles of all types not actually in current use, the pool was guarded by a sergeant and two men housed in a wooden hut just inside the wood-framed wire entrance gates. They were playing cards in front of an oil stove when the two mercenaries scaled the perimeter fence soon after midnight. They would have severe head-aches when they came to, but they wouldn't remember who or what had hit them, and with luck the amphibian wouldn't be missed until they made a check in daylight.

thing!' Aletti exclaimed when Riordan and Brod

jumped down the eight feet from the steel plates decking the hull. 'You couldn't, I suppose, have commandeered something a little more accommodating? With a roof maybe, and windows? An Armstrong Siddeley Sapphire would suffice, or one of those Daimlers the Queen of England she has to convey her to her horse. I don't ask for central heating, but I am here to say these slinky sheaths, thermal they may be, but they leave the man within fucking *cold*, man.'

Riordan grinned. 'Pull on your Balaclava,' he said. 'At least that'll keep your brain warm. Oh, and – here! – this will heat you further still.' He reached up to the deck of the amphibian and produced a silver trumpet. 'A hot time in the old town tonight,' he said. 'You know our tune. So blow, man, blow.' He handed the trumpet to Aletti.

'Just because I once played at a Yiddisher wedding,' Aletti grumbled. 'You mean like right now?'

'Right now. Teddy will know that means we'll be knocking on the door in precisely thirty minutes. If he's still there, that is. I'd hoped he might be back by now with plans of . . .'

'The plans are here,' Aletti interrupted. 'But Teddy's still there.'

'Say again?'

The Italian-American explained. 'His Excellency is in the Volkswagen,' he concluded. 'You can study the notes and pore over the diagrams in the dashboard light. In any case, he can fill in the gaps and add details I wouldn't know.

Riordan nodded. He crossed the track and went into the wood.

Aletti hauled himself up to join Van Eyck, Brod and Christal aboard the amphibian. He tongued the trumpet mouthpiece, blew through it as he fingered the valves, then raised the instrument to his lips. Very clearly and correctly, he phrased the opening bars of *The Campbells Are Coming*.

He played it a second time, then joined the other three in the cab. 'Even here it's cold,' he complained. 'Couldn't you at least start the motor again?'

Brod shook his head. 'Orders,' he said.

Twelve minutes later, Riordan rejoined them. 'Ngombi offered to help,' he said, 'and in fact I could do with an extra man. But I told him, no way. He's the biggest risk of all: we have to keep him safe at all costs.'

He reached up and switched on a heavily shaded roof light. Outside the cab, the mist, which had thickened considerably, rolled towards the lake as a gust of wind rustled through the trees. No lights showed now on the far side of the water.

Riordan spread Nelson-Harmer's notes and diagrams on a chart table. The mercenaries gathered around, squinting in the diffuse light. 'I want each of you to study all of these,' he said. 'Minutely. Your lives could depend on how well you remember what you see here. I'll give you' – he glanced at his watch – 'exactly eight minutes.'

Riordan paused. Outside in the night an owl hooted shrilly. 'After that,' he said, 'I'll tell you what we're going to do . . .'

For a man normally relaxed and super-cool under the most trying conditions, Nelson-Harmer was unusually tense. Most of the military or paramilitary operations in which he had been involved – organizing a jailbreak, investing a rebel headquarters, storming some stronghold – had been relatively cut-and-dried. You knew exactly what you were up against; you made your plans and you went in; you made it or you didn't. This one was different. There were too many too many factors he wasn't even aware of.

He hadn't the remotest idea, for one thing, of what plan of action Riordan might evolve once he had seen his own notes and diagrams. He didn't know how his companions would approach the islet. By storming the causeway? From across the lake? On rafts? By boat? Or indeed how they would get away. He knew there was mist over the water, but he didn't know if the guardians had searchlights or floods at their disposal.

Most importantly, he had no clue to Soviet thinking with regard to the hostages. Would the Russians be happier to see them dead rather than rescued? Would they attempt to recapture them once they were clear of the church — or would they try and kill them? Again, would the island's defenders be limited to the Caucasian soldiers posing as terrorists, or would Peniakov and his bosses be angry enough to blow the whole charade wide open by calling in units of the regular army of occupation?

Without an insight into the intricacies of Soviet postwar diplomacy, there was no way of answering any of these questions. Or even guessing at the answers. Meanwhile, he was left with an inside job that risked going off at half-cock, since he had hoped for at least another twenty-four hours in which to school his captive team.

Nelson-Harmer sighed. You played the cards as they were dealt.

'We'll go into this one more time,' he told them. 'We have . . . let's see . . . yes, twenty-eight minutes left before we go over the bally top.'

'How do you know?' someone asked. 'Will there be another signal? Suppose we get outside and these so-called rescuers haven't arrived?'

'We already have the signal. They'll be here thirty minutes later. And when Riordan says thirty, he doesn't mean twenty-nine or thirty-one. At that point, anyway, *we're* the signal.'

But, Christ, he thought, whatever Riordan's plan, could they really hope to get away with an operation so full of imponderables in less then ten bloody minutes? 'Once again, please,' he said to the Australian.

'My role, sport? OK. Soon as you open the door, I dodge around to the left, pass between this hut and the cookhouse and stand under some stone projection halfway up to a window in the church wall.'

'An old lectern, yes. But you don't "pass" between – you sprint as if your life depended on it. Which it might.'

The Australian smiled. A crooked grin in a seamed face. 'OK, OK. I run like the hammers. The rest of the guys will be running after me. I give each one a leg-up to this lectern, and he makes it to the embrasure above. You'll be the last one. Then you give me a leg-up, and I lean down and pull you up to my level.'

'Meanwhile?' Nelson-Harmer turned to one of the four men he had classed as reliable.

'We're through the ruined window one by one. You say there are more projections on the outside wall – stone ridges, did you say? Some kind of arcades?'

'Blind arcades. Small arches filled in with recessed brick-work. Two lines of them, one above the other. You . . .' He swung around to one of the also-rans, the man with the tic who had been picking at his sheet. 'How do you find your way down these projections to the ground? In the dark? With a mist lying?'

'How should *I* know?' The man looked as if he was near to tears. 'This is too much for me. I can't *stand* any more. I don't think I want . . .'

'I told you *five times*!' Nelson-Harmer hissed. 'The first man down, our Egyptian friend here, takes my little torch and lights the way for the others. What happens when you're all down?'

Prince Said spoke for the first time. 'We make our way, quietly, in single file, to the beginning of the chain-link fence enclosing the exercise yard. Is one to assume that this, the junction between the fence and the building, is the pick-up point where your colleagues will expect to find us? If all goes well, that is.'

'Correct. Now tell me . . .'

Nelson-Harmer paused. A key was grating in the lock of the outer door.

The hostages froze. The room was lit only by a dim blue bulb inside a wire cage fixed to the wooden ceiling. It was after three o'clock in the morning. Only the second man with the tic was in his bed.

'Don't attempt to pretend you're in bed or asleep,' the mercenary warned in a low voice. 'They'd rumble it at once, and it would make them suspicious. You've every right to be up and talking if you wish. It's not a real prison with rules for inmates . . . and it should hardly surprise them when you've been so many days with nothing to do but sleep.'

Another key turned. The room blazed suddenly with brilliant light. The inner door was flung open. Two of the 'terrorists', each one armed. The one with the sub-machine-gun remained in the doorway; the other, an automatic in one hand, glanced quickly at each captive and then motioned roughly for each to hold out his arms, palm upwards.

Just a routine head count, Nelson-Harmer thought with relief. A check that they were all still there, that no weapons had been smuggled in. It showed nevertheless that the guards had already received orders to double-check. Peniakov wasn't wasting any time.

He bent his head and stared at his own hands as the guard passed by. Beneath the gorgeous robe, the Beretta and Brod's skeleton keys were clamped between his naked thighs.

The man made a cursory search, stripping each bed. He returned to the door, switched out the light. The door was closed and locked. They heard the outer door close. Once more the grating of a key. Footsteps receded, then climbed stairs leading to the control room. A third door, more distant this time, slammed.

'Don't worry,' Nelson-Harmer soothed as a low babble of consternation broke out. 'Just routine. It means there's two guys awake instead of one, that's all. As far as we're concerned – well, we'll just have to move that little bit faster.'

He strode silently towards the entrance, the keys in his hand. In the blue gloom, he unlocked each door but left it closed. He looked at his watch.

Twelve minutes.

'Time now,' he said, 'for our last-minute trick.'

He produced the one other item he had contrived to fit into the waterproof second pocket of his wetsuit. A small, flat box of phosphor-tipped Swan Vestas.

Riordan and his men had in fact arrived at the islet – or at least a few yards offshore – almost ten minutes before the thirty minutes signalled by the trumpet call were due to elapse. This was to allow Christal to wade ashore and climb the decorated bell-tower of the old church, much of whose height was obscured by the mist. Slung across his back, the nimble cat burglar carried the remaining lightweight Czech machine-pistol, rescued from the fire in the old town.

The BAV-485, powered by all six wheels on land, was driven by a single propeller at a modest seven knots when it was afloat, the front wheels and a small rudder serving as directional controls. Fortunately the engine, especially when the craft was used aquatically, was heavily silenced.

'Right,' Riordan whispered when a single shaft of green light penetrated the fog from the third and top stage of the belfry. 'Danny's home and dry. Now it's our turn to advance in the one battle that's never going to be recorded in the history books. You all know what you have to do . . . at first. Alex, you remain at the helm. Piet and Brod and I will fix the sentries. As you know, it's essential that all three pairs are eliminated at the same time. Otherwise, if they're done one after the other, someone's going to notice the gap. In other words, we have seven and a half minutes to get all hell breaking loose, so that, by the time there *is* a gap, their minds will be occupied . . . elsewhere.'

'OK,' Van Eyck said. 'So I wait for a pair to pass and chase after them. Brod turns the other way to meet the next pair . . .'

'And I leg it like crazy towards the causeway to pick up the last two – from where I should be in a good position to cross over to Teddy and the hostages, right?'

'We,' Van Eyck said, 'better can do all we can to draw off the enemy fire once the sentries are done, so that you and Teddy can get the hostages to this amphibian, no?'

'Exactly. One on either side of the church. I'm relying on Danny to discourage any advance along the causeway. Maybe inside the church too, if they get that far. Alex, keep the revs up, but don't set her at the bank until you hear the first shot. Then make for the chain-link fence and pretend you're trying to ram it down. My guess is that they'll expect any escape attempt to go that way. Make sure you have enough room to manoeuvre back into the lake when I call, though.'

'Wilco,' Aletti said.

Riordan looked at his watch. 'Teddy will act in three minutes. By that time, if we're ashore, we should be between sentries.' He smiled, the craggy features splitting into the familiar boyish grin. 'So good luck, guys. Let's go and earn our money.'

Followed by the other two, he dropped from the amphibian's deck into the cold, waist-high water. In a moment they were lost to view among the wisps of white fog wreathing above the water.

Van Eyck turned left along the perimeter path and ran lightly after the footsteps he could hear receding into the obscurity. Brod turned right and waited on the edge of a clump of bulrushes. Riordan was already off on a long, loping run towards the indistinct mass of the church. He carried the only other automatic arm they possessed – a Bergmann MP-38 – and his Browning. Brod and Van Eyck were equipped with Russian Tokarev handguns, which O'Kelly had acquired from some private source, and lead-cored, leather-covered coshes.

The silencing of the sentries was not quite as noiseless as Riordan had planned. Aletti distinctly heard a choked cry from somewhere to his right; it was followed by a single shot, then running footsteps and a shout from the other side of the islet. At the controls of the amphibian, he hesitated. That was definitely a shot – but was it the one Riordan meant? Should he advance now . . . or wait for another?

The decision was taken out of his hands by a sudden volley of shots – guns of different calibres, he thought – which sounded more distant, muffled even, perhaps from inside the church? Ramming the lever into first, he sent the BAV-485 charging through the reeds to career up the shallow bank beyond and across the rough ground on the far side of the perimeter track. Once there, he backed off and drove the machine's blunt bows at the tall fence looming suddenly out of the murk.

The trouble within the church, as Nelson-Harmer had always feared it might, arose from the indecision of one of his also-rans. The sheet-picking one with the tic, who else? Understood if the guy was nervous, not blessed with an abundance of guts. Not his fault. But why drop his mates in the shit?

At exactly the right time, the Nigerian had opened the hut doors and his Australian helper had slipped out, silent as a ghost, quick as a puff of wind, to position himself below the lectern. The Egyptian had followed, and then the Prince. After them the first of the four smart ones. For each, the Australian hollowed his linked hands, making a step from which the escaper could reach the lectern and then climb to the empty window embrasure. In turn, they dropped from view. The control-room lights were low; no guards were visible.

With the fifth hostage, Nelson-Harmer was not so lucky. The tic was very much in evidence. Once the man had put his foot into those linked hands, he appeared to lose confidence and he gripped the Australian frenziedly around the neck. The Australian swore, as did Nelson-Harmer, waiting at his corner.

The Australian heaved the scared man up, so that either he had to grab the lectern or fall. It was then that the single shot rang out.

It was way outside the church, but the man with the tic panicked. Astride the pitched sill, he yelled: 'No! I don't want to go. It's too d-d-dangerous. Leave me alone . . . let me go *back*.'

And it was then that the guards in the control room, rudely aroused, flung open their door and opened fire, shooting blind, with the SMG.

The man on the sill, visible only as a blur against the white mist outside, screamed shrilly, clutched his chest, and pitched out into the night.

At the same time, a shaft of light lanced out from the control room, settled on the lectern, moved downwards as the Australian dodged out of the way behind a pillar. At the corner of the hut, Nelson-Harmer raised his tiny Beretta automatic.

Since he had not at first expected to remain on the islet, he had brought no spare clips with him, and he was hoping to guard all seven shots in the gun's box magazine for emergency use outside the church. But this was an emergency if ever there was one. Sighting carefully, he fired two shots, one aimed just above the flaming muzzle of the guard's sub-machine-gun, the other into the centre of the light beam. He heard a sharp cry, a stumbling fall. The spotlight faded, glowed red and died.

But there would be at least one other man in the control room, probably two. 'Forget the window,' he called urgently to the hostages lined up behind him. 'Now that they're wise, anyone there's a sitting duck.'

Even as he spoke, someone who must have snatched up the fallen man's SMG loosed off a warning burst at the empty embrasure. The 500rpm volley was punctuated by single shots from a heavy-calibre handgun, aimed in the general direction of the corner protecting Nelson-Harmer.

But beyond that now there was light again – a strange, flickering illumination that rose and fell, now scarlet, now orange streaked with black. The joker was being played.

A pile of chairs, shelves, bedclothes and paper, doused with the contents of an oil heater and fired by the Swan Vestas, had blazed up and ignited the wooden walls of the hut . . .

It was no more than a diversion, a device momentarily to

halt the defence in its stride, as it were. Were there hostages still inside? Should they try to extinguish the flames? What were the priorities now?

In the altered circumstances, the stratagem worked very well. The hut occupied almost the whole of the basilica's old nave, leaving on either side only a narrow passage separating it from the original church walls. And now, suddenly, fanned by a draught drawn through the open doors, the fire erupted. A window burst outwards, showering broken glass between the bars, and then another. Flames belched out on either side, trailing streamers of sparks and dense black smoke. The heat was so intense and the oily smoke so choking that guards running in from the entrance were blocked at the beginning of each aisle.

The delay was enough for Nelson-Harmer. After their one casualty, the men in the control room were firing from well inside their refuge. This left a narrow dead area immediately below their wide window. 'Past the block,' he called, 'across the rest of the chancel and into the ambulatory. We're heading for the exercise yard.'

'But there's no way out of the yard . . .' someone complained.

'Shut up and do as I say,' the Nigerian snapped.

He dashed out from the shelter of the hut, skirted one side of the operations block as the guards realized what was happening and directed their fire downwards, and sped between the arches into the semicircular passage feeding the apse and its three chapels. The Australian and the half dozen remaining hostages followed close behind, while the guards blocked by the fire were being ordered to back up, forget the fire, and go round the outside of the building.

Unexpectedly, the door leading to the exercise yard was unlocked. Not so strange really, Nelson-Harmer thought:

the guys who used it were kept under lock and key, and there was no way out anyway. He opened the door.

From his position at the wheel of the amphibian, Aletti saw the rectangle of the doorway, pulsing with crimson light, materialize through the mist. He saw, with aston-ishment, the fugitives swarm out into the wired enclosure. Something must have gone wrong with the original plan – particularly since, so far as he knew, the only weapon between them for defence against eventual pursuers was a single, seven-shot .22 automatic pistol.

Aletti thought quickly. What was the best thing he could do to help?

Although nobody had yet appeared to witness his decoy efforts, he had several times, in a desultory fashion, run the bows of the amphibian up against the chain-link fence. Not that it would do any good: the fence was stretched between iron posts cemented into a low concrete wall, its lower margin itself incorporated in the fabric of that wall.

On the other hand . . . Aletti backed off and spun the craft around as quickly as he could until the squat stern was close to the fence. It could hardly make any difference to Riordan's overall scheme which way the craft was facing. And this way . . . He braked, leaving the motor running, and ran around to the rear end.

Single shots echoed from the sector in which Van Eyck should be operating. Muffled by the fog, he could hear shouting from the causeway. A large body of men seemed to be approaching the islet. The outline of the bell-tower was etched through swirls of mist in sporadic flashes as Christal's machine-pistol hosed a leaden hail down on the new arrivals.

Aletti uncoupled a three-clawed cast-iron hook from the back of the BAV-485. The hook was attached to a steel hawser coiled around a powered winch. It was designed for auto-rescue work if the amphibian ran out of road or became trapped in a ravine or a patch of soft sand. Nevertheless, the winch was programmed to draw anything up to ten thousand pounds. Aletti forced two of the claws between links in the fence and returned to the wheel and engaged first gear.

The stuttering roar of another SMG – Riordan's this time? – rasped out from the right. Aletti could hear his leader yelling orders. He opened the hand throttle wide, floored the accelerator and eased up the clutch pedal.

The amphibian jerked forward. The length of cable Aletti had left linking the winch and the fence twanged taut. The six driving wheels of the craft scrabbled in the marshy ground. The hull shuddered. The wheels spun, churning up gouts of mud. But the fence held.

Aletti backed up and tried again, feeding power to the wheels even more gently, allowing the slack of the hawser – and the following strain – to be taken up gradually. No dice.

For the third try, he aimed the amphibian away from the fence at a slight angle, having paid out more hawser. This time he favoured the brutal approach. Using full power with the clutch fully engaged, he sent the craft hurtling forward. The jolt that brought it up short was shattering, hurling him forward against the wheel. The hawser hummed like the G-string of a cello. The engine stalled; there was a curious, shrill creak from the fence. But it remained upright.

Aletti took a deep breath. He rubbed his bruised chest; at length he stabbed the starter button, shoved the heavy lever into reverse, glanced over his shoulder and backed up towards the chain-link fence.

Riordan had shepherded the escapers – Nessim, Prince Said and one other man – into the shelter of a buttress as near as he could get to the exercise compound. He had no idea why the remainder of the hostages could be seen on the wrong side of the wire. At the moment the defenders were leaving them there. After all, they couldn't get out. Maybe the flames streaming from the church windows had cut them off. But units from the causeway would draw level on the outside at any moment.

The islet had become an inferno. There was shooting all around its eastern end. Riordan left his hostages and ran to the shelter of a buttress nearer the causeway. The straight thirty-two-round magazine of his Bergmann projected too far below the stock for the gun to be used from a prone position. He made himself as small a target as possible by dropping to one knee and firing from the hip

On the other side of the church, Van Eyck was up to his neck in water among the rushes. It was he who had been obliged to fire that disruptive first shot to silence a sentry who had survived his cosh. Now, after he had dropped their leader, he was loosing off single rounds to discourage the rest of a squad advancing on their bellies.

Brod, below the shallow bank in advance of his leader, was holding his fire although bullets from the guards emerging from the church thwacked regularly through the massed dry stalks of the rushes behind him. Twice, the ancient bell of the church had rung sonorously when rounds aimed at Christal had struck it after passing between columns supporting the cupola at the top of the tower. Christal continued to harass men running up the causeway from the lake shore.

It was clear to Riordan that the Soviet authorities had taken a policy decision: no attempt was being made to separate the hostages from their rescuers; there was no pretence that the raid was being resisted solely by those holding them. The order must have gone out. Smash any rescue attempt at all costs – and if the hostages are killed, so much the better. Riordan wondered how the Russian propaganda machine would present the story to the world. The scenario would probably be that the kidnappers, failing to obtain the ransom they demanded, had carried out their threat to execute their victims and fled.

The mercenary leader had a comparable decision to make himself. He already had the three really important hostages, those the whole mission was about: Nessim and Prince Said here with him; Ngombi on the far side of the lake. Should he withdraw with them now, before the pace got too hot, and sacrifice the others? Or was it his duty to get the entire dozen out?

Never mind duty: Nelson-Harmer was in the compound with the others; Christal was still in the bell-tower.

The roaring pulse of the fire within the nave had been partly subdued, but he could see in the roseate glow flooding from the windows that a searchlight was being wheeled around from the basilica porch. He could hear Peniakov's distinctive voice shouting orders. They were directed to a menacing group at the foot of the tower.

Christal had turned inwards, presumably to fire at attackers climbing the stairs inside the tower. Now he turned out again to aim at the searchlight crew. One of the men below stepped forward. He was holding what looked like the hose from a vacuum cleaner, and there was some kind of canister strapped to his back. Peniakov barked a command.

'No!' Riordan shouted involuntarily. 'Danny, *no*!'

He was too late. With a shrill hiss of compressed air, the flame-thrower belched out its hellish incandescent breath. The fiery dragon's tongue licked up the stonework to the belfry, bellowing as it rose.

Christal, leaning out between the bars with his SMG,

had no time to withdraw. He screamed once as his body erupted. Flaming from head to foot, he dropped to the ground. The blazing bundle at the foot of the tower stirred, twitched once, and then lay still. 'Good,' Peniakov approved. 'Now go and get the rest of them.'

Riordan seldom lost his temper. He lost it now. Oblivious of the danger, casting aside for once all thoughts of military expediency, he was already sprinting towards the flame-thrower group, bent low beneath the sheltering bank. Level with the men, he dropped his Bergmann and rose like an avenging angel to the lip with his Browning in his right hand. 'Peniakov, you fucking swine!' he yelled with a shaking voice.

Startled, the KGB officer whirled around, a raised automatic out-thrust. The two shots sounded simultaneous, but Riordan's was a hundredth of a second faster. Peniakov crumpled with a hole between his eyes; his bullet ploughed into the muddy earth of the islet.

Riordan snatched up the Bergmann, slid down the bank, and ran as the stupefied soldiers opened fire.

It was then that Aletti, at the seventh or eighth try, succeeded. This time the amphibian plunged forward . . . but it wasn't brought up short.

The six wheels scrabbled in the marshy ground, the note of the engine screeched up the scale, there was a smell of scorched linings from the clutch . . . but at last something behind the stern was giving way.

The fence itself was not breached, But the iron supporting posts on either side of the hooked section were folding outwards with a groan of tortured metal, canting the flattened chain-link fencing towards the amphibian so that the hostages could swarm up the slope and leap to the deck.

Even then fear took its toll of the captives. Two of them

– the second tic-man and another also-ran – panicking because their escape craft was still stationary, jumped into the lake and began splashing frantically offshore, half wading and half swimming, until they were mercilessly shot down by a sniper firing from beside the searchlight. It was then that the searchlight blazed out to flood the whole of the northern shore of the islet with blinding brilliance: the shadowy soldiers behind the beam, Brod among the rushes, Riordan immobile, back with his two hostages, in the shelter of a buttress.

Nelson-Harmer had been extracting the winch claw from beneath the leaning wall of the chain-link fence. Now, as the firing from the defenders increased in intensity and bullets splatted against the armoured hull of the amphibian, he ran to the far side and clambered aboard. Dodging inside the ring mounting aft of the cab, he swung around the heavy machine-gun and hammered a lethal stream of 1in ammunition up beyond the flank of the church. The searchlight lens exploded and died. In the flickering illumination provided by the fire, men stumbled, fell or rolled aside. The soldier with the flame-thrower pitched over the edge and slid down the bank, expiring across his weapon. A bellowing plume of incandescence boiled momentarily up into the sky.

'Run, Colonel, run!' Nelson-Harmer yelled. 'I'm aiming high.'

Bent double beneath the murderous hail, Riordan and his two charges hared across the seventy yards of marshland separating them from the amphibian. Van Eyck, Brod and Aletti leaned down from the deck and dragged them aboard. Then the Italian-American dropped back into the driving seat and slammed the heel of his hand against the gear lever. The amphibian began to move.

They were into the rushes. Nelson-Harmer, who had

exhausted the machine-gun's belt feed, was threading in a replacement – a lull which allowed the defenders to open fire once more. Against the dark bulk of the basilica, muzzle flashes now twinkled across the whole width of the islet. The armoured hull shook under the impact of hundreds of slugs.

'Christ! For a puny band of hijackers, those guys can sure command a load of firepower!' the Australian said drily.

The bows of the BAV-485 lifted. The hull was afloat. Aletti disengaged the drive from the wheels and the water beneath the stern churned as the screw revolved.

And suddenly it was over. As is so often the case with short, fierce military actions, the hell-fire present, without any apparent transition, is all at once the past. It was . . . and then it wasn't.

White mist rising from the lake veiled and then hid the amphibian from the units on the islet. Soon, there was nothing but the receding beat of the motor to prove that it had ever been there.

'How many miles is it before they can intercept this forest track – if they go round the lake by road?' Riordan asked.

'About six,' Van Eyck replied.

'Then we'd better junk this craft PDQ and take to the getaway fleet,' Riordan said. 'I don't know what transport they have, but it'll certainly be faster in miles per hour than our modest forty-five.'

'I'm doing what I can,' Aletti said from behind the wheel. The amphibian was bouncing frenetically along the track, skidding on the corners, splashing light from its underpowered headlamps on the boles of trees.

'No sweat, Alex,' Riordan said. 'Just keep her going.' He shook his head. 'Thank God we did do it tonight, even if the operation did go off at half-cock. Judging by the clout they're putting into the thing, they'll have choppers and APCs and Christ knows what else on the march once it's daylight.' He looked at his watch. 'How much further?'

'Couple of miles,' Aletti said. 'Is Brod keeping up?'

The Australian safe-breaker was piloting the Volkswagen with the three principal hostages as passengers. He had been instructed to keep his distance as a matter of prudence – in case of ambushes or police checks. Van Eyck looked over his shoulder. 'I can see his lights through the trees,' he said.

'Good. We'll signal him to close up just before we get there.'

The getaway cars – a flimsy Trabant two-stroke and a pre-war Adler saloon – had been chosen because they were both inconspicuous and common in East Germany. They were parked behind an abandoned inn on the fringe of the forest. Half hidden by the trees there was a disused gravel pit in which it was proposed – if possible – to drown the amphibian.

When they arrived at the inn, the car park behind it was empty. In front of the boarded-up building was a huge, black, six-seater Maybach open tourer with the top down. The car had Control Commission diplomatic plates. Seamus McPhee O'Kelly sat behind the wheel, smoking a cigar.

'What the hell goes on?' Riordan cried roughly, running up to the car.

'I have it on the best authority that the cars you left here are hot,' O'Kelly said amiably. 'They have been . . . disposed of. I suggest you do the same with that DUKW, or whatever it is, and let me offer you all a lift.'

The Maybach, a late-1930s model known as a Zeppelin, was powered by a V-12 engine with eight forward gears.

'Roadblocks have already been put out,' O'Kelly said as he threaded the great car through a network of lanes and minor roads webbing the outer suburbs of Berlin. 'But I have been told where they are. This route is circuitous, but safe. And I have diplomatic papers.'

'What about the nine hostages and the five of us cramming this monster and the VW?' Riordan asked.

'You will find that will be ... taken care of ... shortly.'

Less than a mile further on, the captain's words came true.

It was between the high, blank wall of some kind of warehouse and a *Volkspark*, a public garden. Road-works. A heap of sand. A half-completed trench in the macadam. A crew of men in dungarees sitting around a glowing brazier, and a foreman swinging a red lantern. Beyond a trestle barrier, a large ambulance with Soviet markings was parked. Near it was a Mercedes-Benz Berlin taxi.

O'Kelly braked the Maybach to a halt. The foreman – who bore a striking resemblance to Commandant Jean-Jacques Fournier of the French Embassy – walked across. 'We have very little time,' he said. 'The dawn is in less than an hour. By that time the trench must be filled and all traces of this ... masquerade ... removed. Colonel Riordan, I believe?'

Riordan raised one hand as the lantern rose to illuminate his face.

'Just so. Although neither the rescue you have so expertly manipulated nor this meeting will ever officially have taken place, I have to inform you, on the very highest authority, that if you or any of your companions should be seen in any of the three Western zones, you will immediately be arrested.'

'Admittedly,' Riordan said, 'our briefing is to vanish

the moment our mission is completed. But this seems a little steep. How, under these conditions, are we supposed to . . . ?'

'By continuing to use your initiative. Not far from here is the Soviet 16th Air Army base at Johannisthaler. It is used by Shturmovik and Yak pursuit planes, flying from a new extension to the wartime field. But the old aerodrome, now disused because it has a grass surface and no runways, still exists. And around it are parked a number of machines, old but apparently in working order.'

Riordan smiled. 'Message received and understood,' he said. 'And these gentlemen?' He waved an arm at the hostages.

'The ambulance will convey them to the city centre – the Brandenburg Gate, I think, at the junction between East and West Berlin. They will have no precise recollection of how they got there, or of the events preceding that arrival. Suitable explanations, agreed by the occupying powers, will be furnished in due course.' He turned away. 'And now, if you would care to take your places in the taxi . . .'

Riordan turned to O'Kelly. 'Perhaps we could offer you a lift?'

'Kind of you,' the captain said, 'but actually this bus is my own.'

'Good God!'

'Frankly it was a bloody good buy, even if it does only do fourteen miles to the gallon. In any case, I thought I'd drive back to Paris in it once this airlift nonsense is over. After all, there's Boanerges to consider.'

'Boan . . . ? You don't mean the cat? Hills's white devil?'

'Well, yes, as a matter of fact. He's used to good cars, you see.'

'You don't mean . . . ? You're not taking . . . ?'

O'Kelly coughed. 'Er, yes. He knows me, and he's familiar with the house in the Avenue Kléber. I rescued him from that bloody traffic island. Poor old fellow, he was frightfully cut up.'

'He isn't the only one,' Riordan said, massaging his bandaged wrist.

The taxi was driven by Dagmar Harari, very trim and voluptuous in her light-blue uniform. She dropped them at the end of a muddy lane. 'The nearest point on the perimeter fence is half a mile down there,' she said. 'There is no charge.'

Riordan grinned. 'Thanks for the ride,' he said.

Epilogue

The aircraft was a German wartime JU-87 dive-bomber, a Stuka. It was parked on a concrete pan at the south-eastern extremity of the disused airfield. Some of the pans were empty; some were occupied by Messerschmitts, Heinkels, a Dornier 'flying pencil'. In one, an unidentifiable fighter was shrouded by a pegged-down tarpaulin. But the old Stuka was the only one facing a straight-line length of perimeter track which might be long enough for a forced take-off . . . or entry to the unmetalled part of the field which stretched emptily away to a group of hangars perhaps half a mile distant.

Beyond these, spotlights and floods illuminated Russian ground crews busy about Petlyakov light bombers and Shturmovik fighters on the concrete apron of the new aerodrome extension.

Riordan lay in the long grass with Nelson-Harmer and Van Eyck, watching Aletti and Brod approach the Stuka. They had been told that orders from Moscow to the Berlin-based 16th Air Army instructed that all operational aircraft, even captured ex-enemy ones, must be kept at all times in a fit condition to fly. But that could be no more than a rumour: Aletti's task was to check it out, Brod's to get him into the plane.

Eastwards, the darkness was already thinning. A few miles away in the opposite direction a Liberator transport carrying twelve hundred tons of liquid fuel was droning in to land at the American base near Tegel.

Whatever locks there were securing the Junkers' plexiglass canopy and a small door above the wing were clearly child's play to the Austrian. In the pre-dawn half light, they saw him push back the cockpit canopy and open the door. Aletti climbed into the pilot's seat.

The pocket torch showed him an instrument panel with thirteen dials, a floating compass, fifteen toggle switches, an artificial horizon and a collection of warning lights, levers, quadrants and buttons. Most of the instruments were in fact self-explanatory: colour-coded blue for air, yellow for fuel, brown for oil.

A button illuminated all the dials. Aletti studied the fuel gauges. There were 160 litres in the 240-litre inner wing tank. The 150-litre outer tank registered zero. Aletti did some rapid mental arithmetic. He knew the machine's maximum range with the full 390 litres aboard was 600km – roughly 1.5km for every litre. The 160 litres they had should therefore take them some 240km or 133 miles. The distance from Berlin to Hamburg was 250km or 138 miles. Lübeck was fractionally less. Maybe, if he was careful with the throttle, they could just make it.

'In any case,' he said to Brod, 'I don't know any other place to go.' He pushed his toes beneath the straps of the rudder bar and waggled the Stuka's tail. Testing the elevators and ailerons, he moved the control column and twisted the antlers. 'Tell them we'll give it a whirl,' he said. 'The ship's been modified. There was no door originally. And just the navigator behind the pilot. Now there's three seats and they've extended the canopy – though God knows how you're going to squash four into those.'

'Every indiv for himself, and Dev take the hindmo,' Brod said. He went to fetch the others.

Apart from its primrose-yellow engine cowling, Riordan noticed as he leaped up on to the wing step that the Stuka was liveried in North European stipple camouflage. The crosses and swastikas had been removed, but fabric patches along the stressed metal fuselage still charted the effects of flak and cannon fire during the plane's operational life. The only insignia it bore now were the figures six and one, painted in white on the cowling and each wheel spat.

Riordan sat behind Aletti, followed by Van Eyck. Brod was obliged to perch uncomfortably on Nelson-Harmer's knees on the third of the rear seats.

In the grey first light, they could see that the perimeter track was rough, pitted with holes, the tarmac fissured by frost damage. Stretching away for several hundred yards, it finally curved away to the right just before a line of trees. 'You think you can make it?' Riordan asked.

'We should be so lucky,' Aletti said, his hands on the instrument panel.

There was a sudden whine, a rhythmic wheezing as fuel was sucked into the Stuka's 1200hp V-12 Jumbo engine, a rotation of the three-bladed airscrew. The cold motor coughed, choked, spluttered, and rumbled to life. Aletti waited for the oil temperature to register on the gauge, then pushed the yellow throttle knob forward.

The noise of the engine rose to a shattering roar. Fuel and oil pressure gauges quivered alive; the control panel shuddered and the instruments blurred. The whole machine was rocking on its tyres. Aletti flipped off the brakes and slammed the throttle wide open, boosting the tachometer needle to 2800rpm. The plane lurched forwards, gathering speed.

He swung it out of the pan and on to the track. The controls were incredibly heavy, the stick a dead weight under his hands. He crouched over the controls, willing the machine to accelerate more viciously, wrestling with the rudder bar to keep the slewing thirty-five-foot dive-bomber dead centre on the dilapidated roadway streaming past beneath the double wings.

The line of trees was frighteningly close, magnifying with the speed of a zoom lens.

Aletti shook his head. 'No way,' he said, easing off the throttle. 'Not on this surface, not with a ship she may not have been used for two years or more.'

Riordan plucked the intercom handset from a hook projecting from the armoured panel between the two seats. 'And so?'

'We do it the hard way – or perhaps, since it has rained so much, we should say the soft way. We put the old girl out to grass.'

Aletti wheeled the plane off the perimeter track, losing speed now, and they lurched over rough ground towards the empty green space over which Messerschmitt-109 and Focke-Wulf-190 fighters had once scrambled to intercept the Allied air-raiders.

The field was indeed soft. And it was muddy. The Stuka bounced alarmingly as Aletti fed power again to the V-12. Yawing, slewing once more from side to side, staggering over the spongy ground, the machine at last settled into a smoother ride as the speed built up. But for the second time the limits of their take-off area – disused outbuildings thickly clustered around the old hangars – were approaching uncomfortably fast.

'Come on, you old bitch: lift, lift, *lift*!' Aletti growled as he felt the column juddering in his hands, waiting desperately for the moment when the tension would ease, when the air would be streaming fast enough past the aerofoil surfaces to offer buoyancy, when the wheels would stop their accursed jouncing on this *bloody* surface, when they would come unstuck.

And then at last it happened: lovingly he caressed the column back against his midriff. The soggy field and the hangars dropped away and the Stuka soared skyward.

At five hundred feet Aletti banked steeply and saw the new airfield apron – now a scene of frantic activity – slide past beneath his port wing-tip.

'There'll be all hell breaking loose down there,' Riordan's voice said in his ear, 'whether or not they've been alerted by Peniakov's bosses. But there's damn all they can do: it's only a couple of miles to Tempelhof and the Western sector. We'll be well over there before they can get up one of those Shturmos within striking distance. And with things the way they are, they won't dare attack once we're in the zone.'

Aletti straightened up and flew west and north. Through a gap in the clouds – higher and lighter this morning – the low sun silvered the damp streets and squares and spires of the rebuilt city. The Havel lake and the Wannsee shone like hammered pewter away on the left.

'I got the take-off procedures from Gatow off the captain,' Riordan said. 'At four hundred feet, a climbing turn to starboard on to 340 degrees magnetic at 110 knots; proceed to five-five at an increased speed of 135. Then it's Berlin to Rühen, 82 nautical miles, 271 degrees true; Rühen to Lüneburg, 49 miles, 343 degrees true . . .'

'Do me a favour!' the pilot's voice cut in. 'All I'm going to do is tool around the bottom of the sky until I see a Dakota taking off . . . and then follow him home.'

They lost the Dakota somewhere west of Dannenberg and were following the Elbe in the direction of Hamburg when Riordan noticed that the fuel gauge for the Stuka's inner tank registered almost as empty as the outer. 'So what about Novotny and MacTavish?' he asked Aletti.

'Who?'

'Danny's friends. The ones who sold us the Mitchell.'

'Oh. Sure. What about them?'

'They're nearer than Hamburg,' Riordan said. 'Do you think, if we offered in return for their kindness to let them have one slightly used dive-bomber, mileage unknown, one careful totalitarian owner, recently deceased – do you think they might be kind enough to give us all a free lift into the city?'

'It's an idea.'

'Second question. Can you possibly put this crate down without too much loss of life in that God-forsaken forest ride where they hang out?'

Aletti laughed. It was a luxury he rarely permitted himself. 'We can sure as hell try,' he said.

OTHER TITLES IN SERIES FROM 22 BOOKS

Available now at newsagents and booksellers
or use the order form provided

                   continued overleaf . . .

All at £4.99 net

All 22 Books are available at your bookshop, or can be ordered from:

22 Books
Mail Order Department
Little, Brown and Company
Brettenham House
Lancaster Place
London WC2E 7EN

Alternatively, you may fax your order to the above address.
Fax number: 0171 911 8100.

Payments can be made by cheque or postal order, payable to
Little, Brown and Company (UK), or by credit card (Visa/
Access). Do not send cash or currency. UK, BFPO and Eire
customers, please allow 75p per item for postage and packing,
to a maximum of £7.50. Overseas customers, please allow £1
per item.

While every effort is made to keep prices low, it is sometimes
necessary to increase cover prices at short notice. 22 Books
reserves the right to show new retail prices on covers which
may differ from those previously advertised in the books or
elsewhere.

NAME ....

ADDRESS ....

....

....

☐ I enclose my remittance for £_____
☐ I wish to pay by Access/Visa

Card number
☐☐☐☐ ☐☐☐☐ ☐☐☐☐ ☐☐☐☐

Card expiry date
☐☐ ☐☐

Please allow 28 days for delivery. Please tick box if you do not
wish to receive any additional information ☐